LOLA

A Reed Security Romance

GIULIA LAGOMARSINO

Cover Design courtesy of T.E. Black Designs

www.teblackdesigns.com

❀ Created with Vellum

For everyone that hated me after Ryan's book in the series For The Love Of A Good Woman. This is the ending you've been waiting for.

CAST OF CHARACTERS

Reed Security Cast

Sebastian "Cap" Reed- owner

Maggie "Freckles" Reed

Caitlin Reed

Clara Reed

Gunner Reed

Tucker Reed

Lily Reed

Carter Reed

Julia Reed

Team 1:

Derek "Irish" Cortell- team leader and part owner

Claire Cortell
Janie Cortell

Hunter "Pappy" Papacosta
Lucy Papacosta
Rylee Papacosta
Colt Papacosta

Rocco Turner
Brooke
Evelyn Rose Turner

Team 2:

Sam "Cazzo" Galmacci- team leader and part owner
Vanessa Galmacci
Sofia Galmacci
Leo Galmacci
Max Galmacci

Mark "Sinner" Sinn
Cara Sinn
Violet Sinn
Asher Sinn

Blake "Burg" Reasenburg
Emma Reasenburg
Ryker Reasenburg

Beatrix (Bea)

Team 3:

John "Ice" Peters- team leader and part owner
Lindsey Peters
Zoe Peters
Cade Peters
Willow Peters

Julian "Jules" Siegrist
Ivy Siegrist
John Christopher Hudson Siegrist
Katie Siegrist

Chris "Jack" McKay
Alison (Ali) McKay
Axel McKay
Elizabeth (Lizzie) McKay

Team 4:

Chance "Sniper" Hendrix
Morgan James (Shyla)
Payton James

Jackson Lewis
Raegan Cartwright

Annie Lewis
Parents: Susan and Robert Cartwright

Gabe Moore
Isabella (Isa) Moore
Vittoria
Lorenzo (Enzo)
Grayson Moore

Team 5:

Alec Wesley
Florrie Younge
Reid

Craig Devereux
Reese Pearson
Grant Devereux

Training:

Hudson Knight- formerly known as Garrick Knight
Kate Knight
Raven Knight
Griffin Knight
Cade Knight

Lola "Brave" Pruitt

Ryan Jackson
James Jackson (Cassandra Jackson- mother)
Piper Jackson
Ryder Jackson
Paige Jackson

Team 6:

Storm Hart
Jessica Finley

Daniel "Coop" Cooper
Becky Harding
Kayla Cooper (daughter)

Tony "Tacos" Russo
Molly Erickson
Marcello Russo

IT Department:

Robert "Rob" Markum

Chapter One

LOLA

I saw him across the bar looking just as miserable as I was. I had seen him here many times before, but I never talked to him. I didn't know what to say. What could I possibly say to a man that lost his wife just a year after they were married? He had a son and I had no idea how old the kid was, but it had to be difficult. The boy wasn't his biological son, but I had overheard Sebastian talking about how much Ryan loved his son. Based on the way he looked tonight, he was drinking to forget.

As I studied him, I wondered why he chose to drink alone. Why weren't his friends out with him? Couldn't they see how much pain he was in? Maybe it took someone that had already lost everything to know that particular look of pain. I watched as woman after woman walked up to him, rubbing up and down his arm, hoping for him to buy her a drink and take her home. They wanted something he couldn't give though. They wanted more than one night and it was clear from the slump of his shoulders and the look of loneliness on his face that all he would ever have to give was a few hours between the sheets.

I couldn't blame him. All I ever wanted was a night with someone to make me forget. I relied on Hunter for a long time to make me forget, but I felt like I was using him as a crutch and I didn't want it to start interfering with our work relationship. So, when the nights got hard, I pretended like I was fine and I stopped calling him over. He knew that I was still having a rough time, but he respected me enough not to question me about it. Well, I thought he did up until he turned on me at the office.

One job. That was all it took for me to completely lose my credibility with my teammates. All they saw was a broken girl, but I was far from broken. I was psychologically fucked, but I still functioned and was able to do my job. Until a knife was held against my throat. All I could see was that psychopath all those years ago holding that knife to my forehead as he made me watch with a mirror. I remembered sitting in that chair while he drew a line with a marker around my forehead where he was going to scalp me.

It wasn't even the pain so much as the terror of knowing that the man was actually going to do it. Then again, that's what he had wanted. He thrived on knowing that he was going to scare me to death. It was pain like I had never felt before. It ripped through my skull, along with the sound of the knife scraping against my bone. I had passed out at some point and when I woke up, I was in a hospital, but the pain was there. I could still feel that knife and every time I closed my eyes, I could see the evil look on the man's face as he pressed the knife against my skull.

I shook my own depressing thoughts from my head and focused back in on the handsome man sitting at the counter. Except the man was no longer brooding in his drink. His eyes were laser focused on me and there was a hunger there that I knew all too well. He stood from his bar stool and walked over to me. He didn't say anything, he just held out his hand and waited for me to take it.

I knew what he was asking and I gladly took him up on his offer. I wanted the same thing too. To be in the arms of someone who understood, even if it was only for one night. He led me out of the bar and pushed me against the outside wall, his lips latching onto my neck and sucking harshly. His hands coursed over the backs of my thighs and up under my skirt to grab my ass. He pulled back from me, his eyes glinting in the moonlight.

"I don't ever bring anyone back to my place."

"That's fine. We can use mine," I whispered. "Just follow me."

I strutted to my car and slipped inside, watching as he did the same. He followed me home in his pickup truck and inside where I left all the lights off. He didn't need to be shown around or see what my house looked like. He was here to fuck me and then he would leave. I would get some sleep and he could go back to his life with his son.

I took his hand and guided him through the dark rooms, back to my bedroom. I pushed him down on the bed and pulled off the tie that hung loosely around his neck. Spreading his legs, I stepped between them and started unbuttoning his shirt. His hands slid back into place on my ass and pulled me closer. His mouth nipped at my stomach through my dress, down to my pussy that was aching for him to go further.

He stood suddenly, ripping the dress over my head and throwing me on the bed. His stare was predatory and lit my whole body on fire. He was the only one since Hunter that had gotten me this excited, this wet. I could feel my desire soaking my panties and I knew he could smell it too. He undid his belt buckle and shoved down his pants. Spreading my legs, he knelt between them and shoved his hard cock into me, thrusting hard with no foreplay. I didn't care. I didn't need it tonight. I needed it hard and I needed him to take me so high that I forgot my own name.

He knew what I needed instantly. He didn't need a few hours to get to know my body or know what buttons to push. It was like we had done this before, many times before. Every thrust was exactly where I needed and his hands touched me in all the right places. He didn't take his time and make sure that it was flowery or special. He fucked me hard and made sure I came before he went over the edge himself.

We laid on the bed panting afterwards for only a few minutes before he stood and got dressed, leaving without another word. I rolled over and went to sleep, making it most of the night without dreaming of the psycho that took a part of me I would never get back.

I didn't know what to do with myself. I had left Reed Security a while ago, unwilling to bend to Sebastian's demands that I go into counseling over what happened to me. I desperately wanted to kick someone's ass or shoot someone. Call me twisted, but nothing felt better than knowing I had taken someone down. It didn't matter how it happened, but since it was illegal to shoot someone without justification, that left training at Reed Security. It was the only place where I could go and take out my frustrations on someone and there was one person in particular that I wanted to take down at the moment. Hunter.

For all his talk of always being there for me, he abandoned me when I needed him most. He could have stood up for me and told Sebastian that I was doing fine, which I was. Most days. Nights were always hard, but unless I was on a job, it didn't matter how I slept. When I was on the job, I used Hunter as a distraction. Until I didn't anymore. Then he moved on and was now engaged and using him was no longer an option.

When Reed Security came under attack, I was called back

in to help take out the gangs that were coming after all of us. My house had been hit, but since I wasn't home at the time, I had no clue what was going on. I had thought about walking away from it all before I was called back. Even though it was in my blood to be in that line of work, I just didn't know if I could work with people who didn't trust me. Or maybe it was just that I didn't want to admit that maybe Sebastian was right about me needing help.

I had no clue what I would do if I left. I had spent months traveling around the United States, trying to find something that would give me the same passion and fire that holding a weapon did. Everyone thought that I was lying on a beach somewhere, soaking in the sun. Really, I was just hoping that I could find some direction.

I packed a gym bag and headed into Reed Security. Sebastian was still sending daily codes for the building to my phone in case I decided to come in. I hadn't for months, but now it was time. Hiding out from them wouldn't do me any good, and I obviously had been unable to find anything else to drive me forward. What I needed was to feel alive again, like I was in charge. I had that feeling back for a short time when Reed Security was under attack and I wanted to feel it again. I pulled into the parking garage and killed the engine, sitting there for a good five minutes, trying to convince myself to go in. I wanted to, desperately, but then I imagined them all staring at me like I was damaged, the girl that lost it on a job. Suddenly, I wasn't so confident that I could do this. I started my car back up and left, not able to convince myself to go inside.

I did that every day for a week. Every day, I changed my mind and left. Every day, I was angry with myself for being so weak. Today was different though, because when I pulled in, Knight was leaning against the wall in front of the spot I usually parked in. When I shut off the car, he walked over to me and flung open my door, reaching across the seat for my bag.

"Get your ass inside. We have training to do."

"How did you know I would come today?" I asked.

"Because you've been coming for a week and then leaving when you chickened out. You're not doing that today. I'm not waiting around for another week for you to get your ass in gear."

"I don't know that I'm ready," I said as I stepped up beside him. "Everyone thinks that I'm damaged, that I can't handle myself."

His steely, black eyes narrowed in on me. "They know you can handle yourself. They've seen it plenty. Besides, when have you ever given a shit what people think of you? I haven't known you for that long, but I know that you don't take shit from people. If you want to be here, prove to them that you belong here."

"Sebastian wants me to see a therapist," I said hesitantly.

"Yeah, he made me do that too. Go, see the therapist, get cleared, and get back out in the field. What the fuck are you so worried about?"

"That the doctor won't clear me," I said as if he was stupid. "He'll take one look inside my head and determine that I'm so fucked up that I shouldn't be put in similar situations ever again."

"Are you? Fucked up in the head, I mean."

I bit my lip, unsure if I really wanted to answer that question. The truth was, I wasn't sure if I would ever be right in the head again, but that didn't stop me from living my life.

"If you're not sure, then you need to go find out. And if you are, get yourself fixed. It's that simple."

"It's that simple? Just get myself all fixed and go back to work?"

"Yeah. I don't see why you couldn't. You've been working all this time. If you were irrevocably fucked up, you wouldn't have been working all this time, which tells me that you just need to work shit out. So, go work shit out."

"Go work shit out," I repeated.

"Yeah, but not right this minute. I've been waiting a goddamn week to get you back in the ring, so move your ass."

Knight threw me to the ground, but I bounced back to my feet, refusing to let him keep me down. He was fast and a hell of a good fighter, and he had moves that were absolutely magnificent to watch. In fact, a few times, I had been so enamored with what he had done that he got the drop on me because I had been standing around with my mouth hanging open.

He swung with his left and I just barely stepped out of the way, but then he got me twice in the jaw with his right and twisted my arm behind my back before I could get a jab in.

"Is that all you have in you?" he whispered in my ear.

I tried to break his hold, but he had me pressed tight to his body, one leg hooking around my leg, making it impossible to move. A flash of steel glinted in front of my face and I froze.

"Is this what he did to you?"

I started shaking in his arms. Why was he doing this to me? I started to struggle against his strong grip as I saw flashes of that sadistic fucker, Jeffrey Jones, holding a knife in front of me. I saw his twisted smile as he stepped in front of me while I was strapped into that chair.

"Let's begin. Should we introduce Lola to some of our games first?"

My body shook against my will. I was strong and I knew how to take care of myself, but right now, I was powerless to defend myself. This guy's eyes were evil and I knew that once he started in on me, he wouldn't stop until I was dead.

"Please, don't," I heard Alex whisper from across the room where she was tied up. She had tears in her eyes and I could only imagine how terrible it must be to be thrown back into this nightmare. My attention was brought back to the man in front of me when he held up a permanent marker. My heart was thundering in my chest as I tried

to figure out what his game was. I had to hold onto my nerve and take the opportunity to strike back when it came. I could find my way out of this. I had to keep believing that.

"I'll be right back. Just let me grab a visual aide." He walked down the hall toward the bathroom and I glanced back over at Alex. I could see her hands moving and blood dripping down her hand. She had a weapon and was trying to escape. My eyes flew forward, not wanting to draw Jeffrey's attention to Alex. I looked in his hand to see a handheld mirror. He held it up and started laughing.

"Get it. A visual aide. Geez, I crack myself up. Anyway, back to the task at hand."

He knelt down in front of me and started drawing little lines across my forehead. My throat worked overtime to keep the bile from rising and spewing out all over him. It would no doubt anger him and I couldn't afford that right now. So many scenarios ran through my mind, but I already had a pretty good idea of what was about to happen. I tried to draw courage from my training. I tried not to focus on what was about to happen, but it was no use. I was terrified and I couldn't get myself under control. How had I survived all those years in the military, only to be tortured back in the United States?

"This line represents where I'm going to cut you with a knife. When we're done, I'm going to peel back your scalp and then Lexie and I will crack that nut open and see what's inside." He smiled and rapped on my head with his knuckles and that's when I lost it. Tears leaked down my cheeks and a sob ripped free from my chest. I could handle being shot. I could handle knowing that I was walking into danger at every turn, but being held down and having my flesh torn from my body was terrifying.

The marker pressed against my skull again as he continued to draw a line around my head. With every depression of the marker, shivers tore through my body, knowing that soon he would be pressing a knife against my forehead. I squeezed my eyes shut to block out his face, but it didn't help. His breath fanned across my face, the pungent smell on the verge of making me violently ill.

When he finished, he examined my wrists, cutting the tape from my right wrist. This was my chance. But I couldn't do anything. I was frozen in terror, and before I could snap myself out of it, he twisted the tape into a rope and wrapped it around my wrist and back to the chair. I was harnessed to the chair with limited movement. I couldn't reach him. I couldn't defend myself. The panic set in again, causing me to hyperventilate.

"Do be a dear and hold this up for me. I want you to be able to see my handy work," he said, holding the mirror up to me. I shook my head violently as cries ripped free from me. I couldn't do this. I couldn't hold up a mirror and watch him slice into my skull. He punched me hard in the face, his own morphing in anger.

"I told you to do something, Lola. Now, if you don't cooperate, I'll just go slower and make it more painful for you."

I looked one last time at Alex, pleading her to hurry, knowing she may very well be the last person that saw me alive. My body ached with the tension rolling through me. I slowly lifted my shaking hand and gripped the handle of the mirror in my sweaty palm and held the mirror where he wanted. I tried not to look. I didn't want to see, but I couldn't make my eyes leave the dotted lines drawn on my forehead. When the knife pressed to my skin, I tried to hold back. I tried not to scream, but he pressed the knife so deep, the blade scraping against bone and tearing my flesh apart. I squeezed my eyes tight and held my breath to try to stop myself from screaming, but large black spots appeared behind my eyelids as he dug the knife deeper.

I prayed to black out. I prayed for this to end quickly. I prayed that I would never wake up again.

"You're okay, Lola. Come back to me," a distant voice said. I tried to make my way through the darkness to that voice, but the fog was too thick and I couldn't see where to go. The voice seemed to echo around me.

"What the fuck were you thinking?"

"I was thinking that she needed to face her fears. She's not going to get better if you keep babying her."

"She's not going to get better if she keeps reliving that nightmare, you asshole."

The fog cleared just a little and I thought I recognized the voice. It sounded like Hunter, the man that was always there to pull me out of my nightmares and soothe my fears. I wanted to go to him. I wanted him to hold me until it all passed and I didn't see that mirror anymore or feel the blade against my skin. As the fog slowly cleared, I became more aware of my body. I was cocooned in strong arms that were holding me tightly to ward off the tremors. Strong legs were wrapped around mine and holding me still.

When I was finally able to see again, half of Reed Security was standing around me, watching me in concern. I smelled Hunter's scent and instantly knew that he was the one holding me, just like he always did. Knight was standing in front of me with his arms crossed over his chest, looking at me with his unreadable steely gaze. Cap slowly walked toward me and knelt down in front of me.

"You okay, Lola?"

I didn't know how to answer that. I wanted to respond in some way, but the words wouldn't leave my mouth. I felt numb and even though I could see everyone around me, it felt like I was detached from all of them. They were just figures standing around me. I watched as Cap's eyes flicked behind me and I watched as the rest of my teammates stared at me in deep concern. I didn't care. They were seeing me at my worst, but I couldn't bring myself to care at this moment. I didn't seem to be able to give a shit about anything right now.

My head felt heavy and my eyes were gritty. I leaned my head back, feeling the hard chest behind me let out a sigh. I could let go now and forget about what had just happened. It was over and I was free. My eyes slid closed and I felt a jostling as I was lifted and taken away. I felt Hunter murmuring against my ear that I would be okay and he would always take care of me. I let my mind drift off to a place where nothing else existed, but white clouds. I wasn't sure why there were clouds, but they wrapped themselves around me protectively and I never felt anything after that.

I almost got up right away the next morning, thinking that I had a job to do, but I knew I didn't. I had been benched. So, for the first time ever on a work day, I laid in bed and let my body rest. I didn't have to go anywhere or prove anything to anyone. I didn't have to be strong and I didn't have to pretend that I was okay. I stared off at the wall, picking out the little chips that I saw in the paint. My bedroom needed a new coat of paint.

The door opened and Hunter walked in, carrying a tray of breakfast food. "What are you still doing here?" I asked.

"You show up for the first time in months and I see Knight holding a knife to your throat and you wonder why the hell I'm here?"

He set the tray on the nightstand and then sat on the bed, leaning on his knees.

"Shouldn't you be off with Lucy?" I said with as little disdain as I could muster.

Hunter looked at me and I turned away, not wanting him to see the pain in my eyes that he had moved on. "Lola, shit." He ran a hand across his jaw and stared down at the floor. "You always told me we could never be more. I thought..." he sighed and looked over at me.

I rolled my eyes and shoved him. "I don't want you, Hunter. I just...we had something good, in bed. I guess, I thought you would always be there in any way I needed. I thought we were the same like that."

"We were good together, but Lucy and I just happened. You stopped asking for me to help you like that. I just assumed you were dealing with shit in your own way. And then Lucy came around and..." He shook his head. "I'm still trying to figure that one out. I don't know when it happened exactly, but she was under my skin and there was no going back."

"It's fine, Hunter. I don't think you and I would have ever worked."

He smirked at me. "Why's that? I'm too much for you?"

"I think it's the other way around," I smiled. "I was using you as a crutch. That's why I stopped sleeping with you. It's for the best anyway. You have Lucy now and I'll have the next guy that walks in the bar."

"It doesn't have to be like that. You just have to put yourself out there."

"I'm not interested in a relationship. I think I'm too fucked up for that anymore."

"You're not fucked up, Lola. You just haven't dealt with that shit yet."

I got quiet, not wanting to talk about me dealing with that shit. Hunter had turned on me and as much as I wanted to be pissed at him for it, I found myself wanting to wrap my arms around him and sleep for a week. He was the one person that had always brought me comfort and now I couldn't be with him because he had a woman. Women didn't share.

"Lola, you know that I want you with us. Please, I'm begging you to just do what Cap is asking of you. Derek and I want you back on the team."

"You still want me back after I freaked out with Knight?"

"Lola, that fucker held a knife on you. He was trying to make you freak out."

I thought about that and realized he had been. He was taunting me. What if that was what I really needed? I threw the covers up and pulled out some workout gear.

"What are you doing?"

"Getting dressed. I think Knight was on to something. He was trying to help me work through my fears, through my triggers."

"No, Lola. That's not the way. I never want to see that look on your face again."

I pulled on my sports bra and a tank. Hunter had already seen me naked multiple times. I wasn't shy in front of him.

"Then don't be there, Hunter. Look, I get that you've been dealing with me like this for years. I think it's time we put a stop to that. Cap wants me to seek counseling. This is my form of counseling."

"He said therapist," Hunter said forcefully.

"Well, I choose Knight to be my therapist. Either way, I have to know that if I come across someone with a knife that I won't flash back and fall apart."

"Dammit, Lola. You shouldn't be doing this. I won't watch it over and over again."

"Then don't. I'm doing this for me. I need to know that I can be in control. You were right about one thing, I was using you for way too long. It's time I learned to deal with this on my own."

I walked out of my house, not caring if Hunter followed or

not. I felt refreshed, like I could do anything. Even if it took me weeks, I would do this. I would overcome my demons and be able to face my fears without falling apart. I pulled into the Reed Security building and went straight to the training center. Knight was in the middle of training Florrie, Alec, and Craig. When he saw me approach, he stopped and told them to take a break.

"I'm ready to go again."

His eyes narrowed in on me. "After yesterday? You want to go again?"

"Cap says that I need a therapist. I think I need an exorcist. That's you."

He smirked and crossed his arms over his chest. "It won't work."

"Yes, it will."

"No, because if you quit, it'll just make things worse for you. I would want to use methods that would tear you apart. If you can't handle it, you won't ever go out on another job again."

I swallowed hard, knowing he was right. "Let's do it," I said with a firm nod.

He eyed me speculatively, then turned to the others. "You guys are done for the day." He turned back to me and smiled sadistically. "Your ass is mine every day at nine a.m. If you miss even once, I'll tell Cap you're done."

"Sit your ass in the chair," Knight commanded.

I shook my head. I knew exactly what he wanted to do. It was one thing to fight him off when I was standing, but he wanted to tie me down. There was no way I could do that.

"Lola, remember our deal. You know I'm not going to hurt you, so sit your ass down and clear your mind. You can do this."

My whole body was shaking as I prepared for him to tie me to the chair. "You know, this is stupid," I said shakily. "What's the likelihood that I would ever be strapped to a chair again and threatened to be scalped?"

He stood in front of me, his dark eyes burning into me. I was so worked up that he was transforming in front of my eyes. I no longer saw Knight, but Jeffrey. My body went into a complete meltdown as he picked up the roll of duct tape. Tears started dripping down my face and my arms felt numb. I knew that I could fight back. Knight was waiting for it, but I couldn't make myself move. I was paralyzed by fear.

"Come on, Lola. Snap out of it."

It wasn't Knight talking to me though. It was Jeffrey and he was tormenting me with that stupid mirror. He was waiting for me to grab ahold and watch as he sliced me open.

"Hey!" Knight snapped in front of my face. I blinked like I had been drugged and swallowed hard, but it was no good. I couldn't take anymore.

"I don't feel so good," I slurred. I leaned forward just in time to vomit all over the floor and my feet. I was so light-headed that I fell forward, barely being caught by Knight before I fell into my own vomit. My head spun as he lifted me and carried me off. The whole room was spinning around me and I closed my eyes to try to stop the chaos, but it only made it worse. I wanted to shove at his shoulders to put me down, but I couldn't feel anything.

I felt my body being set down on something and when my head lulled to the side, I could make out cabinets against a wall. I blinked hard, trying to focus on what they were. My chest was getting tighter and tighter by the minute and my eyes fluttered shut. Something poked at my arm and then something cold was rushing through my veins. My chest started to loosen slowly until I felt like I could breathe again.

My whole body was slowing down and I started to feel a little sensation again, but it was dulled. Hunter was leaning over me and waving a flashlight in front of my face. I watched as he picked up my wrist and checked my pulse. I let my head fall to the other side so that I didn't have to look at the concern on his face, but I saw Knight pacing on the other side of the room, running his fingers through his hair and he glanced over at me.

I wanted to ask him why he looked so worried, but my thoughts were becoming foggy and I was tired. So, I closed my eyes and let my mind drift into a peaceful oblivion.

The morning rays of sun were shining in through my window. I blinked and rubbed at my eyes. I must have been sleeping a long time, but I still felt groggy, like I could go back to sleep for a few more hours. I sat up and let my legs slide out of the bed against my better judgement. The bathroom was very much a necessity and even the warmth of my bed couldn't convince me to abandon the urge to pee.

After using the bathroom, I went into the kitchen, surprised to see Knight was sitting at my kitchen table. "What are you doing here?" I mumbled as I walked over to the coffee pot and poured a cup. He had made himself at home, obviously.

He didn't say anything, so I took a seat across from him and stared at him until he responded. He sighed and ran a hand across his face. "I pushed too hard yesterday."

I tried to think back to yesterday, but most of it was a blur. I had gone into the gym, I remembered that much. "What happened? I don't really remember anything."

"That's because Hunter had to sedate you. You were having a really bad panic attack and it was because of me."

"What did you do?"

He stared at me with those harsh eyes, like I was the one that had done something wrong. "I made you sit in a chair and I pulled out duct tape. That was as far as I got before you threw up and almost passed out."

I scratched my head and looked down in embarrassment. "I suppose it could have been worse."

"In what way?" he demanded.

I shrugged. "Well, it was worse when it actually happened, so that's something."

"Christ, Lola. I wanted to help you. I wasn't trying to-fuck, I never want to see that again."

"Okay, so we won't do that again."

"We won't be doing it at all," he said fiercely. "I'm done. Pappy was right. This is the wrong approach."

"That's not your call to make."

"How can you be so indifferent about what happened? I sent you into a catatonic state!"

"Well, I don't remember it, so it can't bother me, can it?"

He stood and brought his mug to the sink. "It doesn't matter if you remember or not. I'm done."

"No," I said firmly. "I told you what I wanted. Now we know that yesterday was pushing too hard. So, we stick to what you did the first time. I can work through that. I can fight that."

"When are you going to get it? It's over!" he shouted. "I won't be responsible for damaging you."

"You're not," I shook my head. "I was fucked up long before you came into the picture. You're trying to help me and I appreciate that. Now, stop your whining or I'm going to tell everyone you've gone soft."

"Lola, I can't," he said quietly.

"Yes, you can. When everyone thought you died in that fire, you did what you had to do to get back to Kate. That's all I'm trying to do. I'm trying to get back to me. I know you understand that."

He didn't say anything for a minute, but then he shook his head and his face hardened again. "Fine. But if I think it's going too far, we stop. I barely did anything yesterday and it was way too much."

"And now you know not to do that."

"Hunter's going to kill me," he muttered as he stomped toward the door.

Chapter Two

RYAN

"I don't feel like going in to work today. I think you broke my vagina."

I laughed and walked over to my Cassie girl, stepping between her legs. "I'll stay home with you, but only if you promise to let me do more dirty things to you."

"I'd gladly stay home, but I have a meeting that I can't put off. There's no time to reschedule before we renew our vows."

"Fine. Tease me and leave me."

She pushed me slightly and bit her lip. That damn lip. It drove me absolutely crazy when she did that. I wanted to be her lip in that moment. I wanted to take her and make her mine all over again, but we didn't have time.

"Put your clothes on before I tie you to the bed and force you to be my sex slave."

. . .

I woke with a jolt, sweat running down my body as I panted hard. Every night was the same. I saw Cassandra in my dreams. Some nights, it was pieces of our last day together. Other nights, I dreamt of when I saw her in the morgue, only she came back to life on the table and it turned out it had all been a bad dream. Those were the worst nights because I woke up thinking that had really happened. Then I looked next to me and realized it had all been a dream, a terrible dream that I would relive for the rest of my life.

My room no longer smelled like her and I ran out of her perfume to spray around the room a long time ago. I refused to go buy more, convinced that if I ever did that, my friends would commit me to an insane asylum. There were hardly any traces of her left in the house. Well, there was one and it was the most painful reminder. James. I didn't hold it against him, though. He was what got me through the day. I knew he missed his mom, but he didn't have the nightmares like I did. Sometimes I wondered if he really remembered that much about her anymore.

It had been four and a half years and the first was the worst year of my life. I had shut out all my friends and only talked to Logan because we were business partners. After that first year, when I finally decided that I needed to let my friends back in and start living my life again, I went out to a bar and found the first willing woman and took her to a hotel. I couldn't take her back to my house. That was my special place with Cassie and no woman would ever taint her memory.

Since that night, I allowed myself one night a week, when James was with his grandparents, to go out and let myself feel like a man again. The women were random and I never went back for the same one twice, not that I would ever remember. They were nameless faces that I forgot as soon as I left the hotel. I never spent the night and I never gave out my number. To them, I was just a stranger passing in the night.

I had become what Logan was before he found Cece again. He had been a manwhore and that's what I was now. Before Cassie died, I was a one woman man, always looking for love that would last a lifetime. I found that with Cassandra, but our lifetime ended after only a year. I would never look for that again or want it.

I got out of bed and went through my morning routine of getting dressed. James came running down the stairs, backpack flung over his shoulder. The kid was at least as tall as I was now. He had hit a growth spurt this year. Almost sixteen and learning to drive. If only Cassie could see this. I shook those thoughts from my head and made him some breakfast. If I thought about her too much during the day, I couldn't function.

"Dad, I want to go to a party Saturday. It's at Charlie's house."

"Charlie? No."

Charlie was the most reckless little shit I ever laid eyes on. He got in more trouble than any kid I knew and while at one time I would have wanted to hang with a kid like him, there was no way I was letting James go down that road. He was a good kid and I was going to make sure that he made his mama proud, even if she wasn't here to see it. I would not fail at this whole parenting thing. I would be the father that Cassie always wanted me to be.

"Dad, come on. Charlie's not that bad. Most of what people say about him isn't true."

"His arrest record says differently." I probably wasn't supposed to reveal that, Charlie being a minor and all, but I wanted James to understand exactly what kind of kid Charlie was.

"That's bullshit. Those were trumped up charges. All of his family says so."

"Sean says differently. You've known Sean for years. He would never lie to you."

"This sucks. I just want to have some fun."

"Then why don't you invite some friends over here? You guys can camp in the back yard."

"And you'll get us alcohol?" he asked excitedly.

"Sure."

"And cigarettes?"

"Why not."

"Really?" he asked wide eyed.

"Fuck no."

His face dropped and he grabbed his backpack, slinging it over his shoulder. "This sucks. You suck."

"I know. I'm such a terrible parent. I won't let you smoke or drink when you're not legally allowed to."

"You've let me drink before," he grumbled.

I grabbed my keys and headed for the garage. "That's different. We drink together one time a year with all my friends and your grandparents. We celebrate your mom's life."

"This sucks. All my friends' parents let them drink."

"James, you're a teenager. You don't need to rush into being an adult. You'll get there soon enough, along with all the other joys of adulthood."

"Whatever. Can I have the keys? I have to get to school."

I tossed him the keys and followed him out to my truck. After getting in the passenger seat, I went through all the rules with him. I hated that I had to teach him to drive. What was worse was that it was still winter and there were more things to factor in. More ways for him to get in an accident.

"No phone while you're driving. No music. No other kids in the truck. No-"

"Dad, do we have to do this every morning? I just have my permit. You're sitting right here in the truck with me. It's not like I can do those things anyway with you in here."

"I just want it drilled into your head. I don't want any distractions."

"Mom didn't have any distractions and look at what happened to her," he muttered.

For a moment, my heart stopped beating as I stared at James. That day came crashing back to me, ripping me apart piece by piece. I could feel my throat constricting and the tears welling in my eyes. No matter what I tried, I just couldn't get away from her. She was always there, in every part of my day. But this was different. This was more than just seeing her smile in James. This was a reminder that if James wasn't paying attention when he was driving, I could lose him just like I lost Cassie. I could never let that happen.

I cleared my throat before I completely lost it in front of him. "That's why you have to be very careful. If it could happen to your mom, it could happen to you. You can only control what you're doing. You can't be sure that other drivers are always paying attention."

"You never really told me what happened that day. All you said was that she was in an accident."

"That's really all there is to it."

He turned and looked at me. "I think I'm old enough now to know. I'm about to turn sixteen. I want to see the police report."

"James," I whispered as the tears slipped down my face and I squeezed my eyes closed. "No. I can't do that again. I see it in my dreams every night. I can't..."

I turned away from him and tried to pull myself together. I swiped at my eyes, feeling ridiculous for still crying over this as if it had happened yesterday. It had been almost five years.

"Dad, what do you think it's like for me? Nobody will tell me what happened. I need to know. What if all Sean told you was that she died in an accident. Wouldn't you want to know every last detail?"

"I do know every last detail!" I roared. "I see it in my dreams every night. I saw her in the morgue after she died. I can't get those images out of my head and that's not ever something you need to see."

"She was my mom. She might have been your wife, but you only had her for a year. She was mine my whole life. I deserve to know!"

He was right. As much as I wanted to protect him, I had always treated him like he was a man. He dealt with his mom's death better than I had and still remained the same great kid as before she passed. Maybe it was time.

"I'll talk with Sean. If this is something that you really want, I'll ask him to set up a time to show you the file, but I will be there with you."

"Good," he nodded.

He started the truck and I placed my hand on his arm. "Just remember, once you see your mom like that, you can't unsee it. You won't see her laughing and feel her hugs. You're going to see her as I see her now and it will haunt your dreams."

"I need to know," he whispered.

"Okay."

I walked into Jackson Walker Construction in a piss poor mood. It was bad enough that I just hadn't felt like myself since Cassie died, but every time James did something that reminded me that he was growing up without his mom, it was like a knife to the chest. The only thing that helped was getting laid and forgetting for just a night, but James wouldn't be going to his grandparents again for two more days. That meant two more days of feeling this unbearable pain and two more days of feeling like I was drowning.

"Ryan," Logan said as he walked into my office. "We've got that meeting this afternoon with Rita Prescott." He cringed and shook his head. "Please tell me you'll take this one."

"Why would I take it? She's mostly dealing with your side of the business. I'm only there because I'm a partner."

"I know, but she's got those killer legs and she's always shoving her chest in my face. Cece would kill me if she found out that I had a meeting with a woman like that."

"I doubt Cece would care if she knew it was business. Besides, she'd probably take it out on you in the bedroom. Isn't that kind of your thing?"

"Not lately. With the kids being older, she's always saying that we might wake them up or they might walk in on us."

"So lock the door."

"I tried that. When they start banging on it, she won't tell them to go away. She just pushes me off her and tells me that she needs to take care of our children."

"Yeah, that sucks. You have a wife that takes care of the children," I said, shaking my head.

"It's cutting into our sex life. We have sex maybe once a week now. It's fucking killing me."

"So, be more spontaneous."

"I tried that. I showed up on a lunch break once, thinking

she would be at home. She was over at Drew and Sarah's house helping with the horses."

"Well, why don't you tell her that you want her waiting at home?"

"That's not spontaneous." He shook his head in disgust. "I'm telling you, man. After a while, sex has to be scheduled into your life. We've lost so much of that fire that we had when we first got together."

"That was mostly her taking revenge on your body."

He snapped his fingers at me. "You're right. I need to do something to really piss her off."

"Like ask her to meet you for a business lunch and let her see Rita Prescott drooling all over you?" I said.

"Yeah. That might just work. Either that or she'll make me sleep on the couch."

"It's worth a try. You're not getting any, so what does it matter if you end up on the couch?"

We met Rita Prescott at the Italian restaurant in town, getting a table for four. Logan had called Cece and asked her to join us for lunch. I had a bad feeling about all this, but it was his marriage. I was just the best friend that was there to watch his downfall.

"Rita, it's very nice to see you again," Logan said as he held out his hand. She practically purred as she slid her hand in his. I rolled my eyes and glanced away at her blatant flirting. She knew he was married and she didn't give a fuck. I didn't understand women like that. Why would you want to be second best to someone else?

"Ryan," the she-Devil smiled. "Lovely to see you also."

I nodded, not wanting to touch her hand. I had no idea where it had been recently. I took the seat to the right of Logan, thinking that Rita would take the seat across from him and leave the other for his wife, but she must not have gotten our message because she sat right next to him and even slid her chair a few inches closer.

"I was just thinking that it's been ages since I last saw you."

"It was last Tuesday," I said bluntly. She ignored me and I watched as she slipped her hand under the table on Logan's leg. His eyes widened and he looked over at me in panic. I stifled a laugh as I drank my water. That's what he got for playing with fire.

"Am I interrupting?" Cece asked as she approached the table, her eyes glued to Rita's hand on Logan's leg. He shoved his chair back suddenly, exposing Rita's hand on his crotch. He had to physically remove her hand so that he could stand up. Apparently, Rita didn't care if his wife saw.

"Cece-" He cleared his throat and pulled at the tie around his neck. "This is Rita Prescott. You remember me telling you about her, right?"

"The man-eater? Yes, I do remember you telling me about her. I just didn't realize she was also a home wrecker." Logan barked out a nervous laugh as Cece raised an eyebrow at Rita.

"I do hope you'll forgive my rather harsh appraisal of you, but it seems that the wedding band would be enough to dissuade you from trying to sleep with my husband."

Rita shrugged and took a sip of her water. "Just because he's wearing a ring doesn't mean that he wants to be."

"And just because I'm not carrying a gun doesn't mean that I won't find one and shoot you," Cece said sweetly.

"Ladies," I said as I stood, trying to dissolve the tension before someone picked up a knife and tried to stab someone else. "Why don't we order and talk about the project?"

Rita shrugged and I pulled out my chair for Cece so she could sit next to Logan. I wasn't sure what the hell he had been thinking when he decided this was the way to fix things between the two of them. I took the seat across from Logan and placed my napkin in my lap. Rita started talking to Logan about the project and what she expected when I saw him jerk slightly in his seat. I narrowed my eyes and saw his throat working hard, like he was struggling to stay in control. My eyes flicked to Cece and I noticed one hand under the table and she was leaning slightly toward him.

It was fucking working. That asshole had called it. I wasn't sure why I hadn't thought it would work. Back when they first got together, you couldn't take them anywhere without them groping one another. I heard the distinct sound of a zipper being lowered and I threw my napkin on the table. I didn't need to be here for this.

"Rita, how about we go back to the office and I'll show you some of the plans we've designed for you?"

Logan nodded. "That sounds like a great-"

"No." Cece smiled at Rita and then looked at Logan. "I would love to hear how this all works out. Please stay and...finish."

Logan's eyes rolled back in his head and the silverware on the table clanked when his knee jerked into it. This was so twisted. We all knew what was happening under the table and yet we all sat there and tried to pretend like it wasn't happening.

It reminded me of when I had fucked Cassie up against the window and her parents came home with James early. Her dad hadn't realized that he had rubbed her cum off the window with his thumb. I laughed at the memory and then did my best to fight the pain slicing through my chest, but it was too much. Sometimes a memory of Cassie hit so hard and out of nowhere that I just couldn't control myself. The memories overwhelmed me until I was sweating and felt like I could barely control my breathing. I couldn't sit around this table for the rest of the meeting and pretend to be fine. I needed to get out of here now.

I shoved my chair back, Logan's eyes immediately flying to mine and concern crossing his face. He had witnessed enough of my freak outs to know that I was not okay right now. Cece must have known also, because she immediately pulled back and started talking to Rita. I mumbled out an apology and left the restaurant in a haze. I didn't know where I was going and I didn't care at the moment. I just needed to escape the memories that were assaulting me. Her laugh, her smile, the smell of her hair, her lying on that cold slab.

My body started shaking and I broke out in a cold sweat as I pushed harder down the sidewalk, trying to shake myself of the memories. Tears pricked the corners of my eyes and the pain in my chest intensified. It was so strong that I thought I might actually be having a heart attack. I leaned up against the side of the building and took deep breaths, trying to calm my racing heart. No matter how hard I squeezed my eyes shut or rubbed the heels of my palms against my eyes, I couldn't get the memories to stop replaying in front of me.

A hand brushed down the side of my face and I jerked at the contact. I looked down to see the woman from the other night staring at me. She didn't look concerned or scared. She looked at me with understanding. It was the same look she'd had on her face at the bar. It was how I knew that she was the perfect woman to wrap myself up in and forget. She crushed her lips to mine, shoving her tongue in my mouth as her hands roamed my body. Slowly, the images started to fade and my body hummed to life.

Before I knew it, I was dragging her behind a building and shoving her up against a wall. It all happened so fast that I didn't even realize what was happening until I was panting as I released myself inside her. My mind was suddenly clear and I could breathe again. I felt relaxed. I felt...free. I leaned my forehead against hers and breathed in her strange scent of gun oil and lavender. She didn't say anything else as she cleaned up. She handed me a card and gave me a kiss on the cheek before walking away.

I looked down to see a business card with her name on it. Lola Pruitt. When I looked up, she was gone. I wasn't sure she was even real right now. Everything from the last half hour was so unclear, but one thing I was certain of, whatever that woman did, I needed more of it.

"Keys," James said as he finished up his breakfast.

"No," I said firmly. "I'll drive."

"But, I need to get in my hours."

"I said no," I snapped. "Look, you're just not ready."

"You mean, you're not ready."

"No, I'm not fucking ready!"

"You can't keep me locked up in the house or drive me everywhere for the rest of my life," he yelled.

"Then you can learn how to ride a fucking horse," I yelled back.

"Nobody rides horses anymore."

"Drew has them on his property. I'll take you out there and buy you a fucking horse if it means you won't be getting behind the wheel of a car any time soon."

"If I have to ride a horse, then so do you."

I glared at the kid. "Fine."

"Fine."

He picked up his backpack and headed for the door. I

grabbed the keys and followed. I didn't really have any intention of learning to ride a horse, but it seemed like a good argument at the time. Now, I was just praying he didn't actually want to learn to ride a horse.

When I got to work, I was pacing my office, trying to figure out how the hell to get James to see reason. He wasn't going to be driving. End of story. Except that he would learn eventually and he was right, I couldn't take him everywhere he needed to go.

I picked up the phone and called Sean, requesting that he get Cassie's file out so that James could see it. I would take him after school and he could see first hand what poor decisions when driving could do. It was a cruel lesson, but one that I felt would be effective.

When I picked him up, I drove in the direction of the police station, feeling like this was completely wrong. But he wanted to know. He asked for it. I parked the truck and sat there a minute, just staring at the doors and wondering if I could really go through with it. The thing was, I wasn't sure who I was more worried about; him or me.

"Dad."

"Huh?" I turned to him and saw the question in his eyes. "You wanted to know what happened to your mom. Are you sure you still want that?"

"Yeah," he nodded.

"Then let's do this."

We walked into the police station and when Sean met us, he walked over and led us down a hall to an interrogation room. Cassie's file was sitting closed on the table, just waiting to be opened. I closed my eyes tight and backed up a step. If I couldn't do this, how was James going to.

"I don't think-"

"Dad. I need to do this." James insisted. I nodded and he sat down at the table, staring at the folder. "So, what exactly happened?" James asked Sean.

"Your mom was driving to a meeting. A pickup truck was driving too fast and blew the stop sign." Sean looked at me, wondering if he should continue. I swallowed hard and nodded. "The truck hit the driver's side of your mom's car, smashing in the whole side of her car. The coroner said she was killed on impact. The force of the impact pushed her car into the field."

"What happened to the guy in the truck?" James asked.

"He walked away with a few bumps and bruises."

"Did he go to jail?"

Sean looked at me again, waiting for me to answer. "The guy was in his early twenties," I told James. "Your grandma felt that the guilt was punishment enough."

"For killing my mom?" James asked incredulously.

"I know this is hard for you to understand right now, but at that age, you just don't understand the consequences of your actions."

"What are you talking about?" James asked furiously.

"When you're that young, you don't really get it. You think you're a good driver and that you can text and drive because you assume that nothing bad could ever happen. You drive fast because you think... you assume that you'll never get in an accident. It's not until you see what really happens that it really hits you and makes you slow down and think what happens if you're not being a careful driver. That guy was still too young. He didn't intentionally blow that stop sign. Yeah, he killed your mom and that's something that you and I have to live with the rest of our lives. But that's something that he'll have to live with also. He'll always know that he took another person's life because he wasn't paying attention. Because he assumed that he would always be in control."

"I don't get it," James huffed. "You let a killer walk away. You let him get away with murdering my mom."

It killed me to try and explain this to him, the way his grandparents' viewed Cassie's accident. "James, imagine if it was you. Imagine you're out driving and you're driving a little too fast, but it's the back roads and no one else is around. You don't see the stop sign in front of you and by the time you see the car in front of you, it's too late. Imagine you were him, a cocky twenty-three year old that didn't think he was driving too fast. Suddenly, you've killed a person and not just anyone, but some kid's mother. Your whole life is now destroyed because the guilt will eat away at you the rest of your life. Isn't that punishment enough? Do we really need to send that guy to jail and ruin his life further?"

"What about my life? What about the fact that your wife died? Don't you care about that?"

I hung my head, sad that I didn't really know how to explain this to him. "James, taking someone else's life and destroying it won't bring your mom back. I know that you don't get it right now and maybe you'll never see it the way your grandparents and I do. But your grandma believes very strongly in forgiveness."

"You keep saying grandma. What about you?"

I shook my head. "Sending that guy to prison wouldn't make this right for me. I don't believe that your mother would have wanted me to be so angry at that man. She would have told me that people make mistakes and I should forgive him."

"He's probably out there doing the same thing," James sneered. "He probably hasn't thought about us once since he walked away from that accident."

"Look at the pictures," I yelled, flipping the folder open as tears blurred my vision. "Look at the pictures of the accident. Tell me that that wouldn't haunt you the rest of your life."

James slowly looked down at the folder and picked up one of the pictures of Cassie's car. As tears slipped down my face, I tried to hold it together. It killed me every day that Cassie was gone, but I didn't want James to go through life filled with hate. I wanted him to see what one simple choice could do and how it could completely change everything.

"It was an accident, James," I said quietly. "I hate every day that your mother died and it kills me that I see her in my dreams every night. But you can't go through life carrying that kind of hate around with you for another person. It'll eat away at you until it consumes you. Your grandparents chose forgiveness and I agreed that was the best choice. I'm sorry if you don't like the decision, but it's what we felt was right."

James put the picture down and closed the folder, walking out of the room without saying another word. My heart was breaking for the kid. I didn't know if I had made the right decision bringing him here. If anything, it felt like we were further apart than ever.

Chapter Three

LOLA

I walked into Reed Security feeling stronger than I had in a long time. After what happened the last time I was here, I thought maybe I would be hesitant to come in here and try again, but I kept reminding myself that the only way to truly move on was to push through. Now that Knight knew my limitations, I had no doubt that together, we could get me on the right track. It wasn't that I particularly wanted to keep reliving my worst nightmare, but the idea of it not plaguing me anymore was enough to keep trying.

I went into the locker room and quickly changed into some workout clothes. After loosening up, I headed up to the gym to find Knight. He was working with Pappy in the ring. Not the person I wanted to see right now, but I was a professional. I could deal with it.

"Hey, Lola," Pappy shouted. "You doing okay?"

"Bite me." Okay, maybe I couldn't deal with my anger toward him as well as I thought.

He jumped out of the ring and stalked over to me, grabbing onto my arm and dragging me across the room. If I really wanted, I could break his hold and his neck in a flash. He knew it too. But I was in a better mood today and I wanted to keep that zen feeling going. Whatever the hell zen was.

"When are you going to stop punishing me?" he barked.

"Oh, I don't know. Maybe when you decide that you have my back?"

"I do have your fucking back. Wanting you to get help isn't a betrayal."

"No," I sneered, "but the way you went directly to Cap instead of talking about it with Derek and I first wasn't exactly what I expected of a teammate."

"Look, I'm sorry if I handled it the wrong way, but we need you back on our team. Shit's just not the same without you. Can't you just go to the fucking therapist so that we can move on with our lives?"

That was the crux of everything right there. Deep down, I knew that I needed help; that whatever was going on in my head wouldn't just go away with time. But Hunter seemed to think that me going to a therapist would suddenly make everything better and we would all just move on. I wasn't sure that I would ever be able to just move on.

I got in his face and spoke quietly. "You mean *you* want to move on. You want to pretend like none of this ever happened. I'm sorry that I'm fucked up and can't just drop all this shit going on in my head. I'm sorry that you felt I was too weak to deal with everything. But mostly, I'm sorry that you couldn't be the friend that just stood by me and helped me deal with everything."

I took a step back and watched the anger wash over Hunter's face. If he thought he was angry, he had nothing on me. Anger would work in my favor right now. I had a battle for my sanity to get back to and I didn't have time to deal with his shit.

He shoved his hands in his pockets and steeled the expression on his face. "I'm sorry that I couldn't fuck the demons out of you. I'm still your friend. I just don't know how to help you anymore." He turned around and walked away, leaving me outside the ring with so much anger that I didn't think I would be able to concentrate on anything other than beating someone's ass.

I walked over to the ring and lifted the ropes, stepping inside. Knight quirked his eyebrow at my angry expression and started jumping from foot to foot, keeping his body warm and mobile. I stretched for a few minutes before I went into attack mode. Looked like we were skipping the whole knife incident for today. The one thing I needed right now was to beat the crap out of somebody, and luckily, Knight was always ready for a fight.

"Come on, killer." Knight walked up to me and flung an arm around my shoulder. I looked at him strangely. Knight never touched anyone else unless he had to. Whatever this was, he was freaking me out.

"Uh, what are you doing?"

"We're going for a beer. Some of the guys are meeting us down at The Pub. I need a drink after you almost kicked my ass in the ring."

"Almost? I'm pretty sure when I was standing over you, yanking your arm behind your back and you were tapping out like a little bitch, that was the point that I thoroughly kicked your ass."

"Whatever, Brave."

I grumbled at the nickname. I hated it. The guys all used it on me whenever they wanted to piss me off. My last name, Pruitt, meant brave and the guys thought it was a good nickname. It didn't use to bother me as much, but ever since that night, I didn't feel so brave. I felt like I was always putting on a brave front to appear like I had my shit together, when deep down, I was still trembling in the corner of the room and praying that that ugly fucker's face wasn't the last I saw.

"Do you need another ass kicking?" I asked Knight.

His arm slid from my shoulder and he held them up in surrender. "You won't hear it again out of my mouth. But if the guys ask why my face is so bruised, I'm gonna tell them the truth, that I fought off a four hundred pound crazy woman at Walmart that was going for the last candy bar in the check out lane."

I stopped and took a step back from him. "What's with you?"

"What are you talking about?"

"All this banter bullshit you're doing? This isn't like you at all. You hate chitchat and you hate trying to be someone's friend. You don't go hang out with the guys unless you absolutely have to because you hate being around other people. In fact, the only people you like being around are Kate and Hunter. So, why are you trying to drag me off to a bar with other Reed Security members?"

He looked away and shoved his hands in his pockets. "I'm trying, Lola. Believe me, living on your own gets fucking lonely." He looked back at me and I could see how the years as a lone assassin had knocked him down. "After all the shit we just went through, the way Maggie traded herself for Kate? All those people will have our backs no matter what. I know that now. Before, I thought it was just a bunch of bullshit. I let my views on life cloud my judgement, but all of those people would do anything for any one of us. They may not always have a great way of showing it, but they fucking care."

"My team didn't have my back," I said fiercely.

He nodded in understanding. "I can see how it looked that way, or maybe they just finally woke up and realized that if they really cared about you, they had to make sure you got the help you needed before you got yourself killed. I know that pisses you off, that you feel like they betrayed you, but I've known Pappy my whole fucking adult life. When I needed someone the most, he was there for me. And when you were going out of your fucking mind, who was there for you?"

I lowered my eyes, not wanting to see the truth in his. He was right. Hunter had always been there for me until I pushed him away.

"You have to let people in and let them help. That's what I'm trying to do anyway. So, we're going to go grab a few beers, spend time with other fucking people, and pretend that we're okay with it."

"Fine," I said sharply. "But I'm not singing any fucking karaoke."

Ten minutes later, we were walking into The Pub and I was already itching to leave. Half of Reed Security was there and they all turned and looked at me curiously. I had never had a problem with people staring at me, but ever since that shit went down, I always felt like people were judging me, assessing whether I was going to break.

"Lola, my darling," Maggie said as she came up to me and wrapped me in a big hug. I looked over her shoulder to Sebastian who was just shaking his head. She pulled back and placed air kisses on my cheeks. What the hell was in the water? "Darling, I'm so glad you could join us," she said in a snooty accent as she placed her fingertips delicately against her chest. "It's been ages since we've gathered for drinks."

I looked at Sebastian again and he signaled that she had been drinking quite a lot. Perfect, Maggie was fucking loaded and acting like a snooty middle-aged socialite. I sighed and let

Maggie drag me over to a table where Florrie was currently sitting with a beer in front of her.

"My dearest friends." Maggie placed an arm around each of us and pulled us in close. "Okay, here's the deal," she said quietly. "Sebastian's driving me fucking crazy. I need your help here to get me some action."

"What kind of action?" I asked.

"The kind that sets your panties on fire and makes your heart race," she grinned.

"Ewww," Florrie shoved Maggie's arm off her. "I'm not helping you get laid. That's just....no."

Maggie rolled her eyes and turned to me. "You know what I'm talking about. I want grenades. I want sticky bombs. I want...a machine gun," she wistfully.

I quirked an eyebrow at her and then Florrie. "Why don't you just tell him that's what you need? Use your hand as leverage."

She shook her head. "It doesn't work. Every time he sees my hand, it reminds him of that night and he thinks that I need to be babied. But what I really need is to blow something up. I need some action in my life before the only thing I'm allowed to do is say *Yes, Sebastian.*"

"Is it really that bad?" Florrie asked.

"He takes care of Caitlin one hundred percent of the time. He won't allow me to pick her up because I might 'hurt myself'. Making dinner is off the table and so is driving. Basically, anything that you can think of that would require me to act like a human being is off the table."

"I say take it," Florrie said as she tilted her beer to her lips.

"You don't understand," Maggie said, gripping her arm tightly. "I'm not allowed to shower alone."

"Is there a happy ending?" Florrie asked.

"Every time." Maggie said it as if it was the worst thing in the world.

"I don't understand," I cut in. "You basically have Sebastian at your beck and call. You could use this to your advantage. Imagine all the fun you could have with this."

"I already had my fun," Maggie hung her head sullenly. "It lasted a whole week before it got old. Now, I just want to be able to take a shower without him going in with me and insisting on washing my hair. I want to be able to pee without him standing in the doorway to make sure I don't hurt myself grabbing the toilet paper. I want to be able to brush my own fucking teeth!"

She slapped her hand over her mouth when she realized how loud she'd gotten and spun around with a large grin on her face, holding up a martini glass. "Darling," she shouted to Sebastian. "Would you be a dear and grab me another martini?"

Sebastian nodded and headed straight for the bar. "See? He's basically a robot. No more intense, commanding Sebastian. I'm now stuck with a man that's sole purpose in life is to be my bitch."

She rested her chin in the palm of her hand and sighed.

"Here you are, Freckles. Are you feeling okay? You're not too cold are you?"

She patted his cheek lightly and looked at him lovingly. "Darling, I've never been better. Go play with your friends."

He gave her a chaste kiss and then walked away after she was firmly seated on her bar stool again.

"Ugh, you see what I mean? If I have to put up with this shit for one more day, he's going to have to worry about me taking out Reed Security."

"So, what do you need from me?" I asked.

"You have an in with Knight. I need you to get him to set up a course for us. I want bombs. I want gunfire. But above all, I want to have some goddamn fun!"

"Maggie, are you forgetting that you already have an in with Knight? You saved Kate's life when you took her place. Why would you need me?"

"I figure that I can only use that on him so many times before he starts refusing me. I have to save them up. And since you and he are like apples and bananas right now, I figure you can help me out."

"And why would I do that?"

"Because you want it just as badly as I do. People are walking on eggshells around you and all you want is to kick someone's ass. Come on, ladies," she pleaded. "I need this so bad. Please don't tell me no."

I looked at Florrie and she just shrugged. "You know I'm in. I can always go for blowing something up. But you know what would be even better?" A devilish look crossed her face. "I think you need to set it up that Maggie needs to go through a self-defense course where she's going to be attacked by the men of Reed Security. We could ask them to set it up so that it's like we're leaving a nightclub. They could all start attacking us and we'll all kick their asses."

"How do you know that would work? Eventually they'll catch on," Maggie said.

"Probably not. I can guarantee that Sebastian will threaten their lives if they so much as hurt a hair on Maggie's head. Imagine how much fun this could be."

"Ooh, ooh. I want to do that. That sounds like so much fun!" Maggie bounced up and down.

"I'm all in. You know I love to kick some ass, but I have one favor to ask."

"Anything," Maggie said excitedly.

"Hunter and Derek are mine. You can have the rest of them, but I want free rein on those two."

"Deal."

Maggie and I shook on it and then we ordered another round of beer, drinking the night away with Florrie and the occasional member of Reed Security that walked up. Maggie dropped hints here and there that she wasn't feeling as strong as she used to and wished she could get her confidence back. By the end of the night, everyone at the bar was eating out of Maggie's hand.

"Knight, we have a problem we need to talk about," I said, throwing my gym bag on the floor outside the ring. Knight was wrapping his hands and raised an eyebrow at me.

"You want me to set something up for you and Maggie," he said bluntly.

"How did you-" I huffed out an irritated breath and crossed my arms over my chest.

"Please. Do you think I was born yesterday? The way the three of you were all huddled together at that table and then Maggie kept saying that she didn't feel strong enough anymore. Who did you think you were fooling?"

"Apparently not you."

He smirked and shook his head. "Not even a little. So, what exactly do you want from me?"

"I want you to convince Cap that she needs some self-defense lessons. She wants to set up a scene where the three of us are walking out of a nightclub and we're attacked by the men of Reed Security."

"And you think the three of you are going to take on all of us?"

I smiled sweetly. "See, I think that Sebastian would be awfully upset if he got even the slightest hint that the men were being too rough on her."

"You want me to tell them all to take a fall?"

"No, I want you to convince Sebastian that nobody should be too rough on her. It's not all a lie. She does want to feel empowered again and she can't do that as long as Sebastian is doing everything for her. Nobody lets her do anything on her own."

"And what do you get out of this? You and Maggie aren't exactly chummy."

"I get to kick Hunter and Derek's asses. I've been promised that much."

He shook his head and looked up at the ceiling like he was dealing with a crazy person. "If I do this for you-"

"For Maggie," I interjected.

"No. See, I already know your game. This is a chance for all of you to get to have your fun. You want to play? We play by my rules."

"And what would those be?"

"First, you'll have your own little test that you'll have to overcome during this playtime." I nodded, knowing exactly what he was talking about. "Second, once you kick Hunter and Derek's asses, that's it. This fight is over between the three of you. You let that shit go so that you can finally move on."

I looked away and rolled my eyes in irritation. I wasn't sure which rule I hated more. "Anything else?"

"Yeah. One more thing. You get your ass into counseling so that you can finally put this shit behind you."

"That's stupid. You can't put those stipulations on me. This is for Maggie."

"Is it really? Because I'm sure Maggie could find a way to do this on her own. I think that deep down, you want a crack at everyone at Reed Security."

"Why would I want that?"

"Because, none of them had to suffer like you do and now they treat you like you're damaged goods. You're pissed and you want a shot at them where there are no consequences."

Damn, he was perceptive. Even I didn't realize until this minute how true that was. He was right though. I wanted something close to revenge and this was my shot. I shoved out my hand and shook his.

"Deal."

"Give me a few days to put it together."

"Come on, Lola. Fight it." Knight's voice was breaking through the panic, but only enough so that I didn't go into a complete meltdown. I still couldn't focus on actually breaking his hold on me. Knight released me and I stumbled forward, resting my hands on my knees as I took in deep, cleansing breaths.

"What the hell are you doing?" Hunter boomed as he walked in the door. "Was it not enough when I had to sedate her last time? Now you're fucking doing it again?"

"It's my business and my decision," I said fiercely.

"Knight, come on, man. You saw it last time. You know this is a mistake."

Knight crossed his arms over his chest and glared at Hunter. "I'm doing what she asked. I stop when it goes to far. This is what she wants and you need to deal with that."

"You're a sadistic fuck. I can't believe that you're letting her go through with this," Hunter spat at him. I was pissed at Hunter right now, but one thing I didn't want was for him and Knight to get into it. They were friends and they didn't need to be going at each other's throats over this.

"Look, Hunter. We've got this under control. Don't take out your anger on Knight. He's just doing what I asked."

"Lola-"

"No," I shouted. "You don't get a say in this. This is my life and my sanity I'm fighting for. I get to decide how to deal with this. If it goes sideways, it's not on you."

"I wasn't worried about it being on me," he said sadly. "I was worried about losing my friend."

He walked away, letting the door slam behind him as he left. I wiped the sweat from my forehead and turned back to Knight.

"You ready to go again?"

He quirked an eyebrow at me and shook his head. "He's just looking out for you."

"He's just trying to tell me what's best for me. I don't need a babysitter. What I need is to get better."

"Alright. Come here." I walked over to him and turned my back to him. "You have to find a focal point. When your mind starts going crazy, find something that you can focus on and latch onto it. When you start losing it, take deep breaths to calm yourself."

I nodded and took a deep breath. When he wrapped his arms around me this time, I didn't panic right away, but when the knife flashed in front of me, I was right back in that room. Knight was yelling at me to focus, but it was hard with the spots dancing in front of my eyes. I gasped for air, taking several deep breaths. I could feel my heart pounding in my chest, but with each deep breath I took, I felt it slow down just a little. I was gaining my control back. I stared ahead at a poster on the far wall. The more I focused on that picture, the more I was able to think about the fact that I needed to get away. I bit down on Knight's arm and then pushed the knife away from me. I was too terrified to try and do anything else, but I stumbled away from him and fell to the ground, breathing hard as I fought for control.

"That was good," Knight said proudly. "You wouldn't get away, but it was one hell of a start."

When he held out his hand to me, I could tell by the shaking that I was done for the day. "No more today."

"Tomorrow. We'll try again."

I agreed and stayed on the ground, lying down and looking up at the ceiling until I could feel my body coming back to me.

We put off the 'training' for another two weeks. I talked to Maggie and convinced her that this was something that all the ladies could benefit from. I met with the ladies after work every day and taught them basic self-defense maneuvers that would help them take down any attacker. All the girls were pretty excited to get to do something like this. Maggie, most of all, but I noticed that Alex and Cara also looked especially excited to be getting involved. Hadn't these assholes ever thought before that something like this would help them to feel stronger? Men, they were so stupid. All they wanted to do was protect us, when really, we needed the tools to be able to take care of ourselves.

"Alright, ladies. Let's go over those moves again. When you're doing them against the guys, remember that they are bigger and stronger than most of us. It won't be as easy on them."

Since I already knew all the self-defense moves, I was teaching the class with Florrie. We had twelve women that were involved. Sebastian's friends' wives wanted in on the action too, so they joined our little class as well. All of his friends had agreed to be the 'attackers' when the time came, so there would be plenty of men to take down.

"Don't be afraid to use all your strength, Alex. Remember, you have to treat these guys like they really are your attackers. Don't take it easy on them. They've been in enough fights to know how to take care of themselves."

"I know, but...I won't have to fight Cole, will I?"

"Not if you don't want to."

"I just don't want to associate him with anything that might make me flip out."

"I get it," I reassured Alex. "We'll be sure to put someone else on you."

"Nobody touches Sebastian, but me," Maggie huffed as she took in some deep breaths.

"Are you sure you want to go against him? I think that will piss him off," Florrie said.

"He needs to see that I'm strong enough to take care of myself, and the only way he'll see that is if he feels it himself. Otherwise, he's going to continue to baby me."

"Okay, how about everyone makes a list of who they do or don't want to fight and we'll match it up from there. I can give a list to Sebastian at our meeting. Speaking of which, Florrie and I have to take off in twenty, so let's get those lists put together now."

An hour later, Florrie and I were walking into Reed Security and heading for the conference room where Knight had called us all in for this meeting.

"Now that everyone's here, let's get down to business. This Saturday, we're having a special training session."

A round of groans filled the room and I smirked behind the hand covering my mouth. Knight held up his hand to silence everyone.

"It's not what you think. After everything that's happened, some of the women are feeling powerless to say the least. We've organized a self-defense class for them and some of the wives of Sebastian's friends. Florrie and Lola have been working on basic self-defense maneuvers, but now we're ready to practice those on men that could actually take them down. Now, remember, some of the these women have been terrorized and we don't want to do anything to make them feel frightened."

"That's right. If anyone so much as pulls out one of Maggie's hairs, I'll have your ass running drills with Knight for a month," Sebastian scowled.

Knight rolled his eyes and continued. "We'll meet here at nine am and go for about an hour. If this works out, we might plan a few more. The last thing we want is for our women to feel defenseless."

"I've got a list of people that they are willing to work with. Some of the women didn't want to work with someone in particular because of how it might bring up old feelings."

A lot of the men nodded in understanding. Shmucks. They were all going to be wishing this was over five minutes into the training session.

"I'll pair you all up and let you know who you'll be 'attacking' on Saturday morning. Once again, I can't stress enough how important it is to go easy on these women. We want them to feel empowered, not more frightened."

"Let's get started," Knight shouted above everyone on Saturday morning. I was loose and ready to go, as were the other women in the group. We were all excited to get to show these alpha males what the women had learned. Maybe they would stop treating us all like we were damaged goods.

"Lola, would you like to demonstrate a few times for the ladies?" Knight smirked at me.

"Sure." I stood and walked to the front of the room, motioning for Derek to join me. He walked toward me with an eyebrow raised, but came willingly.

"Ladies, I'm going to demonstrate how you can take out someone that is coming at you from the front. Now, Derek is going to come at me." I motioned him forward and I saw a glint of fear in his eyes. I raised an eyebrow and motioned him forward. He ran toward me full force and I struck out with the heel of my hand, hitting him directly in the nose and sending him backwards. Then I swung my foot as hard as I could into his nuts. He bent forward with a loud groan and collapsed on the floor in a lovely shade of red, breathing like he was in labor.

One of his eyes peeked open and he nodded slightly to me, as if to say that he was giving in. I smiled sweetly and turned back to the girls.

"The heel of your hand is your best bet. Thrust it up hard into his nose. You'll break it, leaving him disoriented with blurry vision. Then, you take him down once more where it hurts most. Make that kick count. You don't want him recovering too fast."

Claire raised her hand high in the air.

"Yes?"

"How long is *too fast?*"

"He'll definitely be down long enough for you to get away."

"But, I mean, when will his functions recover? You know, his manly bits. Because I had this scenario I wanted to try later tonight and I want to know if I have to change my plans."

"Change your plans," Derek grunted. He stood slightly and shuffled off to the wall where he sank down in a tight ball.

"One more example before you all begin. Hunter? Would you care to join me?"

He narrowed his eyes at me and slowly shook his head.

"Hunter, don't be such a baby," Lucy shouted. "Come on. This is to help us out."

Hunter shot a death look at his fiancée, but stepped forward.

"Okay, Hunter is going to come at me from behind and wrap his arms around me in a bear hug."

"No," he said firmly.

"What's wrong, Hunter? Are you scared of a woman?"

"Yes," he said immediately.

The women snickered and jeered until he finally relented and walked up behind me. When he wrapped his arms tightly around me, I dropped my weight down, planting my feet firmly apart and swung back as hard as I could, chopping at his dick with my open hand. His breath huffed out against my neck and his arms loosened enough for me to break free. I swung an elbow back, slamming it into his solar plexes and then finished him off by slamming his face down onto my knee. He dropped immediately to the ground and I grimaced when I saw that I had knocked him out.

"Oops. Well, maybe I took it too far, but that was a great example of how to take a man down. Are you all ready to try?"

The men all stepped back as the women jumped up eagerly.

"Feel better?" Knight asked as he stepped up next to me as Hunter groaned on the ground. I looked down and took a deep cleansing breath.

"Much. Let's get this shit started."

Maggie stepped up first to Sebastian. "You ready, Cap?"

"Maggie, I don't think this is a good idea. You could injure your hand. Those stitches-"

"I don't have any stitches and my hand has been healed for a while now. It'll be fine."

Cap looked at her warily and then to me.

"Cap, you have to go at her full force if she's going to try this on you. Don't hold back," I said sternly.

Cap ran up behind Maggie, grabbing at her right wrist, jerking her back against him. Maggie went with the motion and swung her left elbow back, clipping him in the jaw, but he saw it coming and moved just in time to avoid the full impact.

"Gotta move faster than that, Freckles. An attacker won't go easy on you," Sebastian poked at her. He swept her leg out from under her and she fell to her back, but just as he was bending over to attack her, she thrust her foot into the side of his knee. Sebastian wobbled and Maggie thrust her other foot into his groin. When he collapsed to one knee, she gave one final kick to his face, sending him backwards onto the floor.

Maggie stood over him smirking as he held his nuts and

face. "Did you mean something like that, Cap? Or were you going easy on me?" She walked away confidently and the other women started to join in, getting their hits in where they could. Before long, all the members of Reed Security were on the ground, holding onto some part of their body. Mostly their groins. That seemed to be the favorite strike zone of the day.

Arms wrapped around me tightly and I had sensed them coming. What I didn't anticipate was the knife that was thrust right in front of my face.

"Let's begin. Should we introduce Lola to some of our games first?"

My breaths came faster and harder as that night flashed in my mind. I could feel the sharp, cool blade being pressed against my forehead. It was practically burning the scar that was already there. I felt vomit rise in my throat as I fought off the waves of panic.

"This line represents where I'm going to cut you with a knife."

I shook my head violently. I knew this wasn't real, but the panic was taking over until I couldn't think straight. I could vaguely see Hunter standing in front of me, yelling something. There was some kind of fight going on in front of me and I tried to focus on that.

I took a deep breath, trying to figure out what to do. This wasn't real. It was all in my head. I just had to break this hold. I would be okay. Just keep breathing.

"When we're done, I'm going to peel back your scalp and then Lexie and I will crack that nut open and see what's inside."

I screamed as I felt the first cut digging into my scalp. Oh,

God. This was really happening all over again. Why wasn't anyone helping me? Maggie came into my line of vision and I saw her hand with only three fingers. I focused on that. Survival. That's what it represented. I needed to find a way to survive. I fought against the darkness that was taking over my vision and tried to focus on where the hands around me were. There was one hand clamped across my chest, holding my arms and body to his. The other hand held the knife against my forehead. Think. Think.

I took a deep breath and slowly lifted my arms in front of me. I latched onto his wrist and forearm with both hands, lifting my right shoulder to hold his arm in place as I twisted underneath his arm. I wrenched his arm behind his back and kicked him in the face, then shoved him to the ground.

In my mind, I still saw that crazy fucker holding the knife against me, but I somehow knew that it was Knight on the ground and quickly dropped the knife, taking a step back before I grabbed it again and stabbed him in the back. I was breathing hard, my chest heaving with every breath I took. I could faintly hear cheers all around me, but my mind was still trying to process what had just happened. I had worked my way out of the attack. I hadn't had a complete breakdown.

A wobbly smile filled my face as Knight struggled to his feet. He had blood dripping from his nose and when he smiled at me, I could see that his teeth were also outlined in blood. I gave a shaky smile back and almost screamed when I was swept off my feet a few seconds later in a big bear hug.

"That's my girl," Hunter grumbled in my ear. I squeezed

him tight, relishing the feel of his arms around me for the first time in a long time. I had been so busy pushing him away because of my hatred for what he had done that I didn't even consider how much I had missed my teammates.

When he set me down, I looked at him with tear filled eyes and nodded. "I'm sorry," I whispered.

"Does that mean that you're not going to attack me anymore?"

"Not unless you do something to piss me off," I answered.

"So, we're good?"

I nodded and took a step back, letting Derek wrap me in a similar hug.

"Good to have you back," he said in my ear.

"I think a few more times of that and you won't even hesitate," Knight said.

I wasn't looking forward to going through that again, but now that I knew I could do it, I knew I would get stronger every time.

"That was so awesome," Claire said as she ran up to me. "But we're gonna have to talk about what you did to my husband. I had big plans for tonight."

"Sorry about that. It was payback."

"Well, as long as it's out of your system and I don't have to worry about you going all crouching tiger on his ass again. Ooh," she gasped. "Maybe I should have you show me some moves. That could be kind of fun, you know, me being the badass warrior instead of him." She winked and turned around to go help Derek limp off to the side of the training center.

Honestly, it was a little ridiculous how far these men were taking their injuries. They were all walking around like they had just been shot. *I guess a shot to the nuts counts.*

I quickly said my goodbyes, not wanting to stick around for anything more. I was shaken more than I would like to admit and I needed to get out of there. I went home and took a shower, washing away the feel of the psycho's hands on me. Realistically, I knew that he was dead, but whenever something like that happened and I was thrown back to that night, my mind just couldn't erase those feelings that came along with it.

I tried to relax the rest of the day. I worked out in my home gym, trying to wear myself out. It didn't work and I took another shower. Watching my favorite TV shows didn't help and neither did going to the gun range for target practice. There was no way I would be able to sleep tonight. I was too wound up. I grabbed my keys and headed to The Pub, hoping that Ryan was there and available. I drove on autopilot and quickly parked my truck, not even realizing that I had already made it when I swung the door open to the bar.

Chapter Four

RYAN

I walked into The Pub, looking around for Lola. She wasn't there, but the night was still young. When she slipped that card into my hands the other week, I knew I would be using it. I didn't want to just outright call her though. It felt wrong. At least if I picked her up at the bar, it felt like we were choosing to go home together. If I called her, it would feel too much like I was using her as a prostitute.

Seeing Logan, Jack, and Cole at a table, I headed over to them and raised my hand, signaling the waitress.

"Hey, man. How's it going?" Logan asked.

"Not bad."

"So, Cassie's parents took James for another night?"

Just her name brought an ache to my chest that had me pressing hard against it to ease the pain. "Yeah. Her dad wanted to take him to some robotics convention this weekend. They're out of town until tomorrow night."

"The whole weekend free," Jack grinned. "Taking anyone home tonight?"

I shook my head with a slight smile. I hated that this had become my life. I was once the only man of our group that actually wanted a monogamous relationship. Now, I was the current man-whore. All my friends were happily married and I was the widower that slept around when my kid was at his grandparents' house.

The guys liked to give me shit now, probably because they didn't know how else to address the fact that I took a different woman home every weekend. It had been almost five years and I was still acting like she had just died a year ago. No matter how I tried, I just couldn't get her out of my head.

"Not seeing anyone yet," I responded. The waitress brought over my beer and I quickly drank it to force images and thoughts of Cassie from my mind. The one thing I didn't want to think about tonight was her. I wanted to find Lola and sink myself deep inside her so that I could forget.

Jack hitched up his leg on a bar stool and grimaced. "What's wrong?" I jerked my chin at him.

"Sebastian had this self-defense thing at Reed Security this morning."

Cole snickered next to me and Logan groaned.

"Yeah? And?"

"And the women all took turns beating up on us. After what happened with Reed Security, Sebastian thought it would be a good idea for all the women to know how to defend themselves. Someone invited along all of our wives and we got our asses handed to us. If you thought Harper had a mean streak before, you should have seen her today. She literally tried to take out my balls."

"Yeah, you're lucky. I'm pretty sure Cece cracked a few of my ribs." Logan lifted his shirts, showing bruises all down his side.

"You're right. I'd much rather have a swift kick to the balls than some bruised ribs," Jack shook his head sarcastically.

"What'd Alex do to you?" I asked Cole.

"Nothing. She didn't want to fight me. She said if she freaked out, she didn't want me to be associated with that."

"So, who kicked your ass?"

"I got lucky. No one fought me," Cole smirked. "But the most impressive one there was that chick that works for Sebastian."

That perked up my ears. "Who?"

"Lola. Remember, she was one of the ones on Alex's guard duty all those years ago?" I nodded. "That Jones guy really fucked with her head. I guess she's been having a rough time all these years, but she's been pretty good at hiding it. Knight has been working with her and today she was able to work past some of it."

"What did he do?" I was almost a little pissed by this, but I wasn't sure why. I didn't know much about Lola, but suddenly, I was feeling very protective of her.

"He held a knife on her just like the night she was

attacked. I guess she goes into some kind of trance when shit like that happens. This time, she was able to get herself out of it. Honestly, it was fucking brutal to watch. It was like when Alex would have those flashbacks and I couldn't break through to her. I don't think I ever want to see someone like that again."

"Then why the fuck did you allow it to happen?" I snapped.

Cole jerked back in surprise and I shook my head at my outburst. "Sorry. Shit just gets to me sometimes," I mumbled, though I wasn't sure this had anything to do with Cassie. The idea that Lola suffered through that shit really grated on me.

"Did you guys see what Maggie did to Sebastian?" Logan laughed. "Dude, you should have seen her take him down. It was fucking hilarious. He was thinking that he needed to be all gentle with her, but you know Maggie. She handed him his ass."

I felt her before I saw her. I looked up to see a panicked looking Lola storm into the bar, chest heaving and her eyes looking wild. I instantly knew that whatever was going on in her head was more than she could handle. I didn't even think about Jack, Logan, and Cole as I walked away from the table and over to her, grabbing her hand as I pulled her out the door. I could hear her ragged breathing as I pulled her over to my truck. Her hand was clenched tight around mine. After shoving her in the passenger side, I quickly got in the driver's side and threw the truck into drive.

She was shaking slightly as I drove away from the bar. She

squeezed her eyes closed and her hands were clenched tight into fists.

"Just hang in there, Lola."

"I'm okay. I just need some space to breathe," she said shakily. If space was what she needed, I could definitely give her that. I drove out of town toward my house and the peace of the country. It wasn't until I was pulling into my driveway that I even thought about the fact that she was the first woman since Cassie that had been to my house. I shoved that thought aside because Lola needed me and I could help her. When I parked, I pulled her out of the truck and led her over to the patio. She took one of the chairs and stared up at the stars, her breath puffing out in a fog in the cold night air.

I grabbed a few beers out of the house and sat down beside her, waiting for her to say something. We sat there for a good hour before she opened her mouth.

"Thank you for that."

"All I did was take you out of there."

She laughed lightly. "You saw that I was freaking out and you took care of me."

"Yeah, well, you did the same for me. Do you want to tell me what happened?"

"Bad memories. I just couldn't shake them this time."

"Cole told me what happened today. Why would you put yourself through that?"

"Because I need to get past it. I've been hiding from the memories for so long, but I can't keep doing that." She took a sip of her beer and then looked over at me with sad eyes. "I was on a job a few months ago and a guy pulled a knife on me. I went into a complete meltdown. I don't even remember what happened. I just know that I was back in the safe house the night that psycho tried to scalp me. My team leader went to Cap and told him that I needed help. He said that I had been avoiding it for too long." She huffed out a laugh as she pulled at the label on her beer. "The truth is, I thought I was handling it pretty well until then. I mean, I had nightmares almost every night, but I was fine when I was working for the most part."

"So, what happened?"

"I don't know. I think my mind just had enough. I've been taken off my team until I get counseling."

"That was years ago, Lola. Why haven't you gone yet?"

"I guess I didn't want someone telling me how fucked up I am. I thought I could handle it myself. Knight had this idea that if he could force me into a similar situation and I learned to work through my fears, that I could finally get past it."

"How's that working so far?"

"The first time, I completely freaked out. I was out of it for at least a day afterwards. I had some rough ones after that, but I'm getting better. Today? I was able to fight my way through, but now I'm just messed up. I don't know what's different about this time, but it's like I'm still fighting what happened. I just need to clear my head."

She looked up at me and I knew exactly what she needed, what she was asking for. I stood and held out my hand to her. When she took it, I pulled her beside me into my house. I stopped inside, not sure that I was really ready for this, but what she was saying resonated with me.

"Are you sure you want to do this? I mean, here?" she asked.

"Like you said, how can you move past it if you don't try? The only thing I know for sure is that I'm stuck in the past with Cassie and I can't move forward." I looked toward my bedroom and sighed. "I don't want to be this shell of a man anymore. I don't know that I'm ready to move on, but I want to at least try."

I pulled her into my room and looked around, seeing Cassie everywhere. I really didn't know if I could do this. It felt like a betrayal. The only woman I had ever truly loved lived with me and made love to me in this very room and now I was going to sleep with another woman and erase all those beautiful memories.

Lola stepped in front of me, her lithe body swaying so temptingly in front of me. She cupped my cheeks with her hands and placed a soft kiss on my lips. "Let's help each other forget," she whispered.

I closed my eyes and took what she offered. When she kissed me harder, I walked her backwards until I was pushing her down on the bed and climbing on top of her. I opened my eyes and saw her beautiful eyes staring back at me with the same lust I felt for her. Sliding down her body, I unbuckled the belt on her jeans and slid the zipper down as I flicked the button open. All hesitation was lost as I pulled her pants off her beautiful, toned legs. God, she was fucking gorgeous.

Her legs spread wide for me as I kissed and licked my way up her legs. I could smell the desire wafting off her and I wanted a taste more than anything in my life. When my tongue flicked across her soaking pussy, I groaned at the sweet taste of her juices. She was fucking edible. I lapped and sucked at her until she was writhing on the bed and coming apart underneath me.

Her legs wrapped around my neck and then she was twisting me beneath her, straddling my face. She tried to move away, but I wasn't through tasting her yet. My hands wrapped around her ass and I held her to my face as my tongue darted in and out of her sweet cunt. She started grinding against my face and my cock hardened at how much she wanted my mouth on her. I slid my hand up her smooth skin until I latched onto her tight bud and pinched. Her pussy clenched around my tongue and her cream flooded my mouth.

I licked her clean as her orgasm shuttered through her. When her body finally relaxed, she stood on shaky legs and yanked at my pants, completely forgetting the zipper. I groaned as the pants caught on my strained erection and she chuckled, like I wasn't in excruciating pain. But it felt fucking amazing to know that she was that impatient for me.

Somewhere between trying to calm down my dick and watching her pull my pants off, she straddled my hips and sank down on me. I almost exploded inside her the minute I was fully seated in her tight pussy. Damn, it was fucking amazing. I had taken her before, but this felt different somehow. Like this was the first time I was really paying attention to the sway of her hips as she rocked against me or the way her hair fell down from her ponytail and tickled my nose.

I sucked a nipple in my mouth, memorizing every shudder of her body and the way she tightened around me when I flicked my tongue a certain way. There was so much of her that I wanted to taste and every lick of her neck had my hips jerking against her. She cradled my head in her arms as she pulled me in closer. Her breath fanned against my face as she rode my cock, pulling me deeper and deeper into my lust-filled haze. Her body was perfect, the smell of her hair was intoxicating, and the way she felt in my arms was more than I could have ever hoped for.

When she collapsed against my sweaty body, I pulled her tighter against me and fell back to the bed, keeping her tight in my arms. Our breaths mingled in the blissful silence of the room until it slowly evened out and she drifted off to sleep. As I started to slip off, two thoughts floated through my brain. I really liked her wrapped in my arms and in my bed. And second, I didn't know how I was going to keep this casual knowing now what this could be like for us.

I woke to fingernails digging into my skin, and not in a pleasant way. Lola's head was resting on my chest and her fingers were scratching against my chest like she was trying to fight me off. I gripped onto her hand only to have her twist mine back painfully until I was writhing in pain. Damn, this girl was a hellcat.

"Lola!" I shouted, not getting through to her. "Lola, sweetheart, wake up. Hey!"

Her eyes flew open and she was panting wildly as she looked around the room. "Sorry," she mumbled as she stumbled from the bed and over to the bathroom. She slammed the door behind her and returned several minutes later, sliding into bed like nothing had happened. I pulled her into my arms and stared at the ceiling in confusion. What the hell was I supposed to do? I didn't particularly want to relive anything that happened when I dreamed of Cassie, but maybe she needed to talk about it.

"You want to tell me what that was?" I asked.

"Nope," she said swiftly. "Good night."

She rolled over, effectively cutting me out of her life and I realized that I didn't like that. I didn't want to be cut off from her. Whatever this was between us, we had something and it was good, even if it wasn't meant to last. She helped me and I knew that I was doing the same for her. I pulled her back against me and nuzzled her neck.

"When I close my eyes at night, I still see Cassandra's body in the morgue. I wake up most mornings in a panic, like it just fucking happened, even though it's been almost five years. On nights that I don't dream of her dead body, I dream of the accident, like I was there or something. I can see her getting killed and I see her suffering. Then there are other times that I just dream of her and the short time that we had together. Any one of those dreams is fucking painful, so much so that I hate sleeping at night. If I could make it without sleep, I'd do it just so that I don't have to see her in my dreams."

She was quiet and didn't say anything for a minute, but then I felt her chest rise, like she was taking a deep breath. "I dream of the night I wasn't strong enough to get away. I think I hate that more than anything else. I'm trained and I should have found a way to get away, but I was terrified and I let that control me. I hate that my teammates suffered when I could have prevented that. If I had just turned around a second sooner, he wouldn't have gotten that knife around my throat. And even then," she laughed, "I knew how to break someone's hold when that happens. I should have gotten away."

She went quiet and I ran my hand up and down her arm, trying to soothe her anger at herself. "Most of the time, I dream about that knife slicing into my skin, the pain and the fear of knowing what he was going to do to me. He actually brought out a mirror and had me hold it up so that I could watch what he was doing. I keep wondering if I had had my shit together if I could have found a way to escape. And I hate that I have to live with these nightmares because I didn't use my training."

Neither of us said anything as we laid there in the dark. When morning came, I saw a beautiful, strong woman beside me that I craved more than anything in a long time. I slid between her thighs as she wrapped her arms around my back, pulling her in close to me. Every thrust, every moan drove me closer and closer to the realization that this woman would not be someone I could shake off so easily. She was quickly becoming ingrained in my soul and healing my shattered heart.

I rested my head against her chest as my breathing slowed to an even beat. I slid off her and laid next to her stomach, trailing my fingers over her toned abs. "Everything about you is so fucking gorgeous," I murmured as my hand slid down her hip. It wasn't sexual. I just wanted to touch her everywhere, feel her smooth skin under my fingertips.

"Even with the scar that I wear like a crown?" she asked sarcastically.

"Well, that's fucking hideous," I laughed and she shoved at my shoulder. I cringed and held onto my shoulder like I had been deeply wounded. "Why do you even care? It's hardly noticeable anymore."

"Because people stare. It's not something I can hide unless I get bangs and trust me, that's not a good look on me."

"Fuck people. Who cares what they think? They don't know what happened and they don't really care. People want to pretend like they know what's going on in someone else's world, like they understand what everyone else is going through. Most people don't have a fucking clue."

"Do your friends?" she asked as her fingers slid through my hair.

"I don't know," I said softly. "I think they mean well. They're always there for me, but there are times that I just want to yell at them for being so fucking insensitive about something. And then there are other times that I want to strangle them for walking on eggshells around me. It's a fucking crapshoot. I never know what's going to set me off and when it'll happen."

"So, what you're saying is that you're really like a woman and you can't make up your mind what you feel."

I looked up at her and grinned at her ability to break the tension in the room. "Are you calling me a girl? Was what I did to you last night and this morning not manly enough? Because I can give it the old college try if you need more proof."

She squealed as I dove between her legs and threw them over my shoulder, sucking at her clit like my life depended on it. The sound of car doors slamming had me jerking upright in bed and tripping over the sheets to get to the window.

"Fuck, my son's home."

"Oh, God. I didn't even think about him. Where was he?"

"His grandparents had him for the weekend. They weren't supposed to be back until tonight. Why don't they ever fucking call ahead?" I muttered to myself, thinking of when they had come home early when I had been fucking Cassie up against the window. I shook that thought from my head as I pulled on a pair of pants and a shirt. When I looked over, Lola was already dressed and was fixing her hair. Damn, I loved a woman that didn't take forever to get ready.

"Do you want me to hide or something?"

"No," I said, not even sure why it slipped out of my mouth so easily. "They know I'm not a fucking saint."

"But your son..."

Fuck, I didn't even think about how this would affect him. I should have thought about this before I brought her back here. I was such a fucking asshole.

"No," I didn't want her to think that she was someone I had to hide. Especially since she was already insecure about her appearance. "It'll be fine. It's not like we're in the middle of sex right now."

I grabbed her hand and pulled her out into the foyer just as the door opened. James stepped inside and looked at me and then Lola, calculating what was going on. His grandparents were stopped behind him, staring at me like I was an aberration. I cleared my throat and they're eyes snapped from my hand firmly clasped around Lola's to my face.

"Hey, little man. How was the weekend?"

"Dad, I'm almost sixteen. When are you gonna stop the *little man* shit?"

"When you're thirty or forty."

"Who's your friend?" he jerked his chin at Lola, his eyes wandering down to where my hand was connected to hers.

"This is Lola. Lola, this is my son, James, and his grandparents, Calvin and Jane Crawford. Cassie's parents."

I looked over to see Lola rubbing at the scar on her forehead before she pasted on a fake smile. "It's nice to meet you."

I leaned over and whispered in her ear, "Stop touching it. You're fucking beautiful."

Her face blushed bright red and she bit her lip. I wanted

to suck that lip into my mouth right now, but that would be inappropriate in front of my dead wife's parents.

"So, are you in the army or something?" James asked as he took in her camo pants and black t-shirt.

"I used to be. Now I work for Reed Security."

"With Sebastian?" His eyes went wide and flicked to mine. "That's so cool. Do you think I could go with you sometime and practice at the gun range?"

"James," I scolded.

"That depends," Lola stepped in, completely ignoring me. She crossed her arms over her chest and raised an eyebrow. "Do you know how to shoot a weapon?"

"Dad's been taking me paintballing for the last six years."

"Is that so?" She looked over at me like she didn't know what to say.

"It's true. The kid took out Sebastian and his whole team the first time we played together. He's pretty good. Stealthy."

James grinned at my praise, but his eyes remained on Lola. "So?"

"I think we could work something out. But in order to use the range, you have to pass the training course first. My rules."

"As long as Dad has to do it with me. I don't mind going up against him and whipping his ass."

"James," Jane scolded.

"Do you want to see my paintball gun collection?"

"Sure, kid."

He ignored the kid comment and led her downstairs to

where we stored all the paintball gear. I looked up at Jane and Calvin, not sure what they would think or say.

"She seems nice," Calvin said after a minute.

"Is this serious?" Jane asked suddenly.

I rubbed the back of my neck as I blew out a breath. "Look, I don't know what this is exactly. I didn't mean for you two to meet her already. I just didn't realize that you would be back so early."

"Yeah, sorry about that," Calvin said sheepishly. "It seems we have great timing when it comes to you and your sexual encounters."

Jane smacked his arm and I winced, not really wanting to talk about sexual encounters with him.

"Look, I know this is probably...strange."

"You with a woman?" Cal said. "Yeah, that's pretty strange."

I hung my head and sighed. I felt so terrible, but I didn't know how to describe this to them. Hell, I didn't even know what it was.

"It's okay, Ryan," Jane said gently. She placed her hand on my forearm and I looked up into her tear-filled eyes. "We didn't expect you to stay single forever. It's been almost five years."

"Cassie wouldn't like knowing that you've been sleeping around anyway," Cal muttered. "That's not who you were with her."

I blinked back the tears that were threatening to spill down my face and rubbed at the ever present ache in my chest. "I just miss her so much. It's hard to breathe sometimes."

"We know," Jane said. "But you can't put your life on hold for someone who's not coming back. Besides, what kind of example does that set for James? He needs to see you happy."

"When's it going to get easier?"

"Give it time," Cal said.

I laughed as I shook my head. "Time. I've given it five fucking years and this morning was the first morning that I didn't wake up in a cold sweat thinking about Cassie. What am I supposed to do? Kidnap Lola and keep her locked in my room?"

"It's an idea," Jane said lightly. "But I don't think she'd go for that. She doesn't strike me as the type to let a man take control."

"Uh...Jane, that's a little too much."

"What? I'm a woman. Maybe you need a woman's perspective."

"Not from my mother-in-law."

"I think we've definitely shared enough over the years that me saying something like that shouldn't faze you at all," she grinned.

"Whatever you decide, son, we're behind you. We just want you and our grandson to be happy. Just make sure you break it to James the right way."

"I don't want him to think I'm replacing his mother."

"He won't think that," Jane said. "Just explain it to him like you have everything else in his life. You have a way with him. That kid has always taken everything you've said like it was straight out of the Bible. There's one other thing though."

"What's that?"

She looked at Cal and nodded. "You're supposed to be teaching that kid to drive. He's got his permit and you haven't been taking him out, so I did it."

"He doesn't need to drive," I snapped. "You shouldn't have done that."

"Were you planning on never letting him drive?" Cal asked. "Do you really think that'll keep him safe? He'll just end up getting a ride from some asshole kid that drives like a lunatic and he'll get himself killed. Is that what you want?"

"Of course not," I said angrily.

"You can't protect him from everything. Cassie didn't die because she didn't know how to drive. She died because of someone else's mistake." Cal gripped onto my shoulder and gave me a slight shake. "Teach him what he needs to know so that he's not a fucking idiot when he gets behind the wheel. And then pray like hell that what you've taught him is enough."

I knew he was right, but I didn't want to teach him to drive. I wanted him to go back to being the little kid that I first met six years ago. I was never prepared to be a single father. I was never prepared to be a father to a kid that wasn't biologically mine. I wouldn't trade it for the world, but I was so fucking scared that I was going to screw him up and Cassie would be shaking her head at me from heaven.

"Dad, Lola said that we can go to her work next weekend and run the course."

I grinned and nodded at Lola. Every time I looked at that kid, I still saw the ten year old boy and not the man he was becoming. Cal was right, I needed to get my head out of my ass and prepare him for life. He already experienced more than any kid should have to at his age.

James said goodbye to his grandparents and then we all stood in this uncomfortable silence in the foyer. "So, I'm going to take Lola home. Why don't you finish up any schoolwork you have?"

"So, are you two like together?" James asked, totally ignoring what I said.

"Uh..."

"We're..."

Lola and I both fumbled for something to tell the kid, but we hadn't even had a chance to talk things over yet.

James nodded and jerked his thumb for the stairs. "I'm gonna do my homework. See you next weekend, Lola." He ran up the stairs and I quickly grabbed my keys, wanting to get the hell out of there. Lola followed me out and as we pulled out of the driveway, I blew out a harsh breath and glanced over at her.

"So, what are we doing?"

"I don't know, Ryan. What are we doing?"

"That's not an answer," I pointed out.

"Well, I like you. I feel good when I'm with you."

"Wow, a winning endorsement if I ever heard one," I said sarcastically.

"Well, it's not as if there's a rule book for how to handle this. I'm sure this is awkward for you, especially with your in-laws showing up right when we were about to have sex."

"Yeah, they have a way of doing that," I laughed.

"So, this has happened with other women you've brought home?"

"I've never brought another woman home. Nobody except Cassie," I said quietly.

"You know, you can talk about her to me. It's not weird. She was a part of your life and I don't expect you to just stop thinking or talking about her. Okay, that's a lie. I would really appreciate it if you didn't think about her when we have sex."

"I can guarantee that when I'm inside you, you're all I'm thinking about," I smirked.

"Then there's no problem."

"So, what do you want to do then?"

"Why don't we just take it one day at a time?" she said. "I don't know if this will go anywhere and I know we have to be careful with James in the picture. I'm not even sure that you're ready to move on."

"I'm not sure either," I admitted. "I can tell you that last night was probably the best night I've had since she died."

"Then I'll see you when I see you," she said as we pulled into the parking lot of the bar. She moved for the door, but I grabbed onto her arm and pulled her back to me, smashing my mouth against hers. Just the taste of her lips against mine soothed me in a way that I never expected. When she pulled back, I almost grabbed her and asked her to stay with me, but we both needed space right now. I had a son to think about and I couldn't just thrust another woman into his life without talking to him first.

Chapter Five

RYAN

When I got home, I decided to talk to James, but when I went upstairs, he was busy with homework, so I pushed it off until after dinner. I ordered pizza and we sat down in front of the TV. I had no clue what he was watching. It could have been porn for all I knew, but I was so focused on the right way to approach Lola with him.

I could be a straight shooter with him. It had always worked in the past for me. How would that sound exactly? *Son, I've been sleeping with this woman to forget your mom and she takes away the pain. I'm going to continue fucking her.*

Maybe a little too straight forward.

James, there's a point in every man's life where he just wants to get laid.

Who was I kidding? He was probably already at that point and just wasn't telling me.

Lola and I are screwing. It's really none of your business, but I wanted you to know.

No, I needed to be sensitive to his feelings. This had to do with his mother more than anything. And Lola was more to me than any other woman I had taken home. I didn't want him to think that I was only using her for sex.

I've been seeing Lola for a few weeks now and I really like her. I'm going to continue seeing her, with your permission. I don't want you to think that I'm replacing your mother, but it's been five years and it's time for me to move on.

Not bad. Technically, I wasn't seeing Lola, but I wanted to. And asking his permission might be going a little far. Still-

"So, Dad, how did you know you were ready to have sex again after Mom died?" James asked around a piece of pizza. I was currently taking a sip of beer and spit it out all over the place.

"What?"

He rolled his eyes at me. "Come on, Dad. I'm not stupid. I know you've been sleeping with other women and I know Lola spent the night last night. I'm just wondering how you knew it was time."

"Uh..." I blinked several times, trying to get my brain to work around the fact that not only did he know that I was sleeping around, but he was looking to me for advice on timing.

"Because, there's this girl I really like and I wouldn't mind dating her and everything, but I think I'm ready for more. Is there a standard waiting time or something?"

"Wait, like, you're ready for sex? To sleep with her and stuff?" I stuttered, unable to form a coherent thought to save my life. This was worse than when he asked me about why I had a woody in the morning.

"Well, yeah, Dad. I mean, I'm almost sixteen and I want to know what it's like, other than with my hand."

"Oh, shit." I covered my ears and tried to wipe that image from my brain.

"What? You were my age once. You know what it's like."

"James, I always had monogamous relationships. I didn't like sleeping around."

"Well, you do now," he snorted.

"That's a different situation. If your mom hadn't...If she were still here, I would have been happy with her for the rest of my life."

"But she's not and you need a release," he urged me on.

I pulled at my button-down shirt, feeling like it was strangling me all of a sudden. "James, don't you think it's a little odd to talk about your mom like that?"

"I'm not talking about the two of you having sex. I'm talking about you, man to man. I don't want to have sex for the first time and not know what I'm doing."

"Hold that thought." I stood and went into the kitchen, flushing water on my face. This was all too much. I couldn't handle this. I picked up my phone and sent an SOS to all the guys, hoping at least one of them would come over and help me out. As luck would have it, every single one of them showed up within ten minutes after I promised beer.

We all stood around my kitchen as I nervously wiped my hands on my pants, glancing into the other room to make sure James was still watching TV.

"What are we doing here?" Logan asked. "You said it was urgent."

"James wants to know about sex," I said bluntly.

"So, tell him," Jack shrugged. "It can't have been that long since you've gotten some. You still know how it works."

"He started talking about using his hand and knowing that I was screwing other women because I needed a release. Then he said he didn't want to have sex for the first time and not know what he was doing."

"And what did you tell him?" Cole asked.

"I fled the room." I shook my head and started pacing. "I'm not prepared for this shit. My dad didn't have the talk with me. I fumbled through it and found my way. I don't know the first thing about sex talks."

"What would Cassie say?" Sean asked.

"Are you fucking kidding me? She'd yell at me and tell me not to tell him more than he needs to know."

"Well, you can't just send the kid out into the wild, sticking his dick wherever he wants. The boy has to know how to use it," Sean huffed. "Come on. His uncles will set him straight."

They all walked into the living room like this was the easiest thing in the world. I brought the beer. I knew better.

"James," Sebastian jerked his chin at him. James shut off the TV and leaned forward, resting his elbows on his knees.

"Listen, your old man is being awkward about this whole thing. Sex is natural. Ask anything you want and we'll tell you."

"Cool," James nodded. "Okay, so when I want to have sex with a girl, what's the best way to tell her?"

Sean snorted. "Well, you don't just go up to her and tell her you want to stick your dick in her. You date her for a while and if you feel a connection, then you start moving on the bases."

"Which bases?" James asked.

"Christ, Ryan. Didn't you tell this kid anything?" Jack crossed his arms and leaned against the wall. "Bases, like in baseball. First is kissing. Second, is touching her boobs, and third is touching her pussy. I think you can guess what a home run is."

"No, that's not the way it works," Logan said. "First is french kissing. Second is groping. Third is oral sex. A home run is the full monty."

"Really?" Sean quirked an eyebrow. "That's not what I went by."

"Of course you didn't, jackass," Drew shoved him.

"Listen, it's really easy. First is kissing and light petting. Second is oral. Third is intercourse. A home run is when you stick it in her ass," Sean said.

"Whoa!" I held up my hands and shook my head. What the fuck was wrong with these guys? "You can't say shit like that to my kid."

"Girls really let you do that?" James asked in wonder.

"Kid, if you get that, it's like going on a fucking world tour," Jack said.

I dropped my head in my hands and sighed. This was not what I had in mind when I called them over. Advice? Sure. This? This was my worst fucking nightmare.

"You know, I was thinking maybe we could stick to the basics and stay away from ass fucking for now," I glared at all of them.

"Alright," Cole sat down by James. "Basics. You have to know how to please a girl. You can't just ram it in there and hope for the best. You have to take care of her first. I'd suggest watching some porn."

"Porn? Really?" I snapped.

"You could read one of Harper's books. She's very descriptive," Jack grinned. "It'll give you a good idea of what women like."

"It's not stuff that the two of you do, is it?" James's nose scrunched in disgust.

"Maybe. It's not like I'm going to tell you what, though. You won't know the difference."

"Okay, but you still haven't told me how I know when it's time. How will I know she's ready?"

"She'll be wet," Logan said.

"But how will I know? I can't just go grab a girl and test her moistness," James said.

"Well..." Sean scratched his jaw as he thought about it. "You just know."

"Shouldn't you be advising against sex, Mr. Lawman." I glared at Sean, but he just shrugged.

"What? I was a kid once. I had sex before I was eighteen. Just don't get a girl pregnant. Then you're fucked."

"What about speed and all that stuff. How do I know what to do?"

"If you really want to know what to do, find an older woman that wants to teach you. That's your best source of information," Logan said, taking another sip of his beer.

"How old?"

"The older the better. I'm not talking fifties, but late twenties, early thirties is ideal," Logan said.

"Please tell me you did not just tell my kid to go fuck an older lady."

"What? They know what they want and they're willing to teach," he shrugged.

"You know what? This was a really bad idea. I shouldn't have asked you guys to come over."

"What? We just answered his questions," Jack shrugged.

"So far, you've talked to him about fucking girls in the ass, told him to watch porn, and told him to go fuck an old lady."

"Hey, I advised him not to get a girl pregnant," Sean pointed out.

"Right. So helpful."

"So, back to ass fucking. What's that like?" James asked.

"It's the holy grail," Drew said quietly.

"I don't know. I love head," Sebastian said.

"You know, when Caitlin is fourteen, I'm going to have a sex talk with her. See how you like it," I glared at Sebastian.

He snorted. "You can't even talk to your son. What makes you think you could talk to my kid?"

"It's different when it's your own kid," I growled.

"Okay, back to my questions," James interrupted. "So, this girl, she's really awesome and totally hot. How do I get her to go out with me?"

"Just ask her if she'd like to go out to dinner with you," I said.

"Yeah, only if you want to get turned down," Logan snorted. "Listen, kid. Women want to be finessed. You have to tell her how gorgeous she is. Let her know that you want her and only her. Whisper in her ear all the things you want to do to her body."

"Dude, the kid's fifteen. He's not picking up a chick in a bar." Drew punched Logan in the arm and Logan feigned injury.

"What did you do when you picked up Lola?" James asked me.

"Lola?" Sebastian's eyes went wide and he stalked toward me.

"What? She's a grown woman."

"She's my fucking employee. Why her? She's going through some shit right now and she doesn't need you using her as a fuck toy."

"My kid is sitting right here. Watch your mouth," I snapped.

"Yeah, now he needs to watch his mouth," Jack grumbled.

"She's an adult. She doesn't need your permission to have a good time."

"She's messed up," Sebastian growled.

"Yeah? And how do you think she's getting through that?"

"So, what? You two are using each other to forget?" he snapped.

"You want to forget Mom?" James asked.

I glared at Sebastian before turning to James. "This has nothing to do with forgetting your mom. Lola and I enjoy each other's company. We're just trying to see where this is going."

"Whoa," Logan shook his head. "Are you fucking serious? You think you're ready?"

"I don't know, man. I'm just trying to be happy again, and Lola does something to me-"

"Gives him orgasms," Logan muttered.

"It's not just that. We just fit. We're just taking it a day at a time."

Sebastian assessed me before giving me a chin lift and finishing his beer. "Well, this has been fun, but I've gotta get home to Maggie."

"Sure, give my kid the worst advice imaginable and then hit the road."

"I figure we've done enough damage for one night," Jack agreed.

"Did we help, James?" Cole asked.

"Not at all, but maybe I'll check out some porn for some tips."

"See? This was good practice for us," Sean said. "Now we all know what not to say to our own kids."

They all walked out, leaving me alone with my kid in an uncomfortable silence that felt like it was strangling me.

"So...you want to watch some porn?" James asked.

I shook my head and stood. "First, you don't watch porn with other dudes. Second, if you really want to see that, I'll get you your own TV for your room. I can guarantee that I don't want to see what you do when you watch it."

If Cassie had heard that conversation, she would be so fucking disappointed in me right now. Ass fuckings and porn. Just what she wanted her kid to know. I was failing miserably at this single parenting thing.

"Thanks for doing this," I said to Lola as James and I walked into the Reed Security training center.

"No problem. I love running the course."

"Are you ready for me to kick your ass?" James grinned at me.

The thing was, I was pretty sure that James *could* kick my ass. He had a ton of energy and while I worked out, I just wasn't in the same shape that I was ten years ago. And I hated running.

"You know, you're gonna eat those words, little man."

James grinned and walked over to the course, checking it all out.

"So, just how difficult is this course?" I asked Lola.

"Well, let's put it this way, we use this course to decide if people qualify to work here. If you don't pass the course, you don't stand a chance at working here."

"Perfect," I grumbled. "That kid really is going to kick my ass."

"What's wrong, Ryan?" Lola smirked. "Not in top shape anymore? You look like you can hold your own."

"I can definitely hold my own, but there's a difference between working out and doing a training course that the military would use."

"Well, it should at least be entertaining. Would it make you feel better if I did the course with you?"

"I'm pretty sure that would make me feel a whole lot worse."

"Come on. I'm sure you're not as bad as you think."

Twenty minutes later, I was panting and gripping my side like I was in extreme pain. Lola was laughing at me and James was telling Sebastian how he had just kicked my ass on the course.

"Your kid beat you?" Sebastian asked.

"As surprising as this may be to you, I'm not the badass that you are."

"Yeah, but you look pretty strong and you're fast."

"Apparently not fast enough," I panted.

"You want a job, kid?" Sebastian asked James.

"Hey, back off," I growled.

"What?" Sebastian grinned. "Did you expect me to offer you a job?"

"He's just a kid. Don't go putting ideas in his head."

"He's just a kid that beat your ass and was damn close to my slowest guy's record. A few more years and this kid will be working for me, kicking ass and taking names." Sebastian rubbed his hands together greedily.

"You try that and I'll make sure you never walk again."

"You'd have to catch me first." Sebastian winked at Lola and walked out of the training center. Lola came over and gave me a pat on the shoulder.

"Don't let him get to you. Just because your kid is faster, stronger, and smarter than you doesn't make you less of a man," she grinned.

"I'm sorry, were you hoping to have sex again with me anytime soon?"

"Yep, just giving you some motivation." She threw me a sly grin and then went over to help James with something on the training course. I shook my head in disbelief. Damn, that woman was going to be the death of me.

"Alright, before you even think about pulling out onto the road, you check your mirrors. Make sure your seat is adjusted properly and that your feet reach the pedals perfectly."

James rolled his eyes next to me. "Dad, we've already gone

over this in Driver's Ed. I'm just supposed to get in my hours with you."

"And when you're driving with me, I'm going to be making sure that you follow the instructions to a T. Now, check your mirrors."

He sighed and went through the process of checking all his mirrors and adjusting his seat. He put on his seat belt and stored his phone in the console where he couldn't be bothered by it. He pulled on his sunglasses and then checked that he was all in the clear to back out of the driveway. I held my breath as he moved the gear shift into reverse. He backed out more swiftly than I would have liked, but overall, he had done a good job.

Then he threw it into drive and my heart started racing in panic. Shit. He was going to be out on the road alone soon. I wasn't one of those dads that couldn't wait for my kid to get his license so that he could drive himself places. I was the parent that freaked the fuck out because my kid was going to be driving on the streets with all the other crazy assholes.

He pulled out onto the country road and drove around for a while with me slamming my foot on the imaginary emergency brake that was on my side. He passed a car that was going five miles under the speed limit and drove way too fast to get back in his lane. We were coming up on an intersection and I saw the truck up ahead and totally flipped out.

"Pull over the fucking truck right now!"

"What?"

"Just do what I say," I shouted.

James maneuvered the truck over to the side of the road as the truck that was on the crossroad came to a complete stop before crossing the intersection. Shit. I felt sick to my stomach. I shoved the door open and climbed out on shaky limbs as I coughed and heaved at the bile churning in my stomach.

"Dad, what the fuck is going on?" James asked as he walked around the side of the truck. I knew he was irritated with me. He seemed to have moved on over the past five years while I was still stuck with every fucking memory. Of course, I had been dealing with the images of Cassie's death for a lot longer. They had time to simmer and fester in my brain, eating away at my sanity day by day.

The road we were just driving down was the same one Cassandra was on the day she died. The intersection up ahead was the one that the truck had blown and smashed into her car, killing her instantly. Now, I had to teach my son how to drive and he would probably cross this intersection weekly. Maybe I could ban him from ever taking this route.

"Dad."

"Just give me a minute." I sank down on the ground against the side of my truck and held my head with shaky hands. This was fucking crazy. I couldn't do this. Images of Cassie tortured my mind as I sat on the cold ground, trying to pull myself together.

"Love you, Mrs. Jackson."

"Love you too, Mr. Jackson."

A tortured sound burst from my mouth as pain shot

through my chest. It was like she had just fucking died. My face was wet and my body was racked with sobs. The pain was so intense and I just couldn't fucking take it. I squeezed my eyes tighter, but the image of her lying on the cold slab in the morgue assaulted me over and over no matter how hard I tried to forget. I could feel her cold skin under my fingers and see the blue tinge to her lips. I could still remember the hope that filled my chest as I placed my fingers against her neck, hoping to feel her pulse fluttering underneath. The shattering feeling of knowing she was never coming back to me consumed me.

"Ryan." I could hear the voice in the distance, but my mind wouldn't leave the hell I was in. "Ryan." A smack to my face finally brought me out of that day and back to the present. Though the tears and pain, I could make out Logan squatting in front of me, his eyes crinkled in concern.

I dropped my head into the crook of my elbow, ashamed that I had broken down on the side of the road with my kid watching. I hadn't had a meltdown like this in years. I felt a hard squeeze on my shoulder and heard the shuffling of feet and some low voices murmuring near me. I didn't want to look. I didn't want to know who else was here to witness this.

When my breathing finally returned to a somewhat normal rhythm, I swiped at the stray tears on my face and lifted my head, resting it back against the door of my truck. Logan sat down next to me and rested his arms on his knees.

"You never told James this was the road, did you?" I shook my head and he sighed. "He didn't know why you were freaking the fuck out. He called me in a panic, said you were having some kind of heart attack on the side of the road." He chuckled and ran his hand over his jaw. "You're lucky I only called Sean. He was already in the area and saw you. He knew what was happening and blocked the road so that you didn't get hit by another vehicle."

"Where's James?" I asked, my voice hoarse from all my fucking crying.

"Sebastian came, picked him up and took him to Reed Security. He figured he could keep him entertained for a while."

"I was taking him out for a driving lesson. It was that fucking intersection. All the sudden, I just couldn't fucking breathe. How the hell am I going to teach him to drive? I can't stand the thought of being in the truck with him right now. I'm so fucking scared that he'll end up like his mother."

"We'll take care of it," Logan said, patting me on the shoulder. "We'll make sure he gets in his hours. When you're ready, you can take him out with you again. Hell, we could have Sebastian give him a defensive driving class. If anyone can teach him the shit he would need to know, it's his guys."

"I appreciate that," I mumbled, staring off across the corn field. I felt wrung out now and I didn't know what the hell to do. I felt like I could crawl into bed and sleep for a year. "Can you do me a favor?"

"Anything."

"Keep James for the night for me. I just need some space to get my head on straight."

"Are you sure that's a good idea?"

"I'll call James and explain."

"Alright, man. Anything you need. Let me drive you home."

"I got it."

He stood and brushed off his pants. "Yeah, I'm sure you do, but it would make me feel better if you let me do this for you."

I nodded and followed him to his truck, waving at Sean as we passed. When we got back to my place, Logan shifted into park and held out his hand.

"Give me your keys. I'll bring your truck back here."

I gave them to him and shuffled inside, feeling like my whole body was dragging on the ground. I collapsed into bed and stared at the wall, hating that I was fucking feeling sorry for myself.

Chapter Six

LOLA

"Lola." I turned to see Cap walking up to me, a weird expression on his face. He stopped in front of me and rubbed the back of his neck.

"What's going on?"

"Shit. I don't know how to say this."

"What? Are you firing me?"

"No," he jerked back in surprise. "I need a favor."

"Sure. What do you need?" I was relieved that he needed a favor and wasn't here to tear me to shreds over fuck knows what.

"Ryan had a bit of a breakdown on the side of the road while giving James a driving lesson. He's pretty fucked up right now. James let it slip the other night that you two were..."

"Fucking?"

"Yeah." He cleared his throat and looked away from me like he was embarrassed. "I think he needs someone right now and he said that you make him happy. I was wondering if you could just go check on him?"

I blinked in surprise. "Cap, are you asking me to go fuck your friend?"

His face turned bright red and he shook his head quickly. "No. No, I would never ask you to prostitute yourself out or do anything that-"

"Cap, shut up. I'm fucking with you. I'll head over there now."

"Thanks," he murmured as he walked away.

Well, that was only slightly awkward. I gathered my shit and headed for my truck. I wasn't sure what had happened with Ryan, but I knew that after the way he helped me the other night, there was no way I would walk away when he needed someone.

When I pulled up to his house, I realized that I hadn't bothered to call first and let him know I was coming over. I knocked on the door, but no one answered. I twisted the knob and walked in when I found it unlocked.

"Hello? Ryan?"

He didn't answer, so I started wandering around. He had a nice house. I hadn't really taken it in the other night. I was too wrapped up in my own shit and then the awkwardness of meeting Cassie's parents. When I found his bedroom, I saw him asleep on the bed. Walking over, I kicked off my shoes and gently climbed onto the bed, not wanting to wake him up. He still had on his shoes and his clothes, like he had just walked in and plopped down on the bed. I started to pull off his shoes and stopped when he jerked away from me.

"Lola? What are you doing here?" he asked, sitting up groggily. I pulled his feet back to me and finished taking off his shoes.

"Sebastian told me what happened. I wanted to come check on you."

"Fuck." He ground the heels of his hands into his eyes. "I'm not a fucking charity case."

"I didn't think you were. Was I when you pulled me out of the bar the other night?"

"You know you weren't."

I climbed over to him and slipped beneath the covers, pulling his arm behind me and snuggling into his chest. "So, what happened?"

He blew out a breath and shifted on the bed to get more comfortable. "I was taking James driving. He's in driver's ed and I've been putting off taking him out. Cal told me the other day to get my head out of my ass and take him out. It was fine. I mean, I was scared shitless with him driving, but he was doing okay. I guess I didn't realize what road we were on until we were coming up on the intersection. I just flipped out. I started yelling at him to pull the truck over. It was all downhill from there."

"Where's James now?"

"Sebastian took him. I was so lost in my head that James

called Logan. He was worried I was having a heart attack." He let out a self-deprecating laugh as he shook his head.

"You know, it hits me like that sometimes too. You can't prevent when that happens."

"I just hate that it happened in front of my kid. I haven't lost it like that in years."

"Tell me about her," I whispered. I wanted to know what she was like. He obviously loved this woman very much if he was still so broken up over her all these years later.

"I chased her for two years. She was just this amazing woman and from the moment I met her, I knew that she was the one. I didn't even know she had a kid until two years after I'd been taking her out. We never dated in all that time, but I could get her to come out with me every now and again."

"Why didn't she tell you about James?"

"She really didn't think I would be interested when I found out she had a kid. I came around one day and she was freaking out. His biological dad was back and wanting custody. I had the brilliant idea that we run off and get married."

I shifted so that I could see his face. He had a big grin that was lighting up the room. "Did she agree?"

"Reluctantly. I wanted to help her out and I saw that as my chance to keep her." He laughed again and ran a hand over his face. "Shit, when I realized what I had done, I was a mess. I was like *holy shit. I just married someone and now I have a kid.* It was a total mind fuck and it took awhile for us to find our rhythm."

"But you did."

"Yeah. And James, man, I hit it off with him almost right away. We had a little trouble in the beginning. I kept calling him the wrong name because I couldn't believe what I had just done. We started reading together one night and it's been our thing ever since."

"Was it hard? Going from being single to having a family?"

"At first, but I instantly fell in love with both of them. I think I had already been in love with Cassie. There was something about James, though. That kid instantly won me over. He didn't take any shit from me and I just kind of realized that I was responsible for him. I didn't want to let him down."

"How did he deal with his mom's death?"

"A hell of a lot better than me," he said grimly. I almost regretted going down that road when he had just been so light, but I wanted to know. I wanted him to tell me what he went through. "He was just a kid and the most important thing to him was knowing that I would still be there for him. I was just a wreck. I insisted on going to see her in the morgue. I had to see her for myself. It was probably a fucking stupid thing to do because that's what haunts me most nights, the image of her there on that table. But I just knew that I would always question if she was really dead if I didn't see her for myself. How fucking stupid is that?"

"Not at all. I get it. It's not real until you see it."

His fingers started running up and down my arm, almost like he was trying to soothe me. I was the one that was supposed to be comforting him, though.

"The hard part about it, the thing that just fucking killed me, was how sudden it was. You always think you're going to have a chance to say goodbye to someone. That you'll get to tell them one last time how much they mean to you. That morning was just like any other. You know, she almost stayed home that day. We were supposed to renew our vows in another two weeks and we were fucking like crazy. We just couldn't get enough of each other. She had a meeting that she couldn't reschedule before the wedding. So, I got James and took him to school. I remember she told me she loved me before she left for work, and that was the last time I saw her. I went to work and it was just before lunch when Sean came in and told me that she had been killed."

His voice choked and I rested my hand on his chest, hoping that it brought him some comfort.

"She was just gone," he whispered. "Everything we had planned, it was gone just like that. We only had a year together."

"At least you got that time with her. You were meant to be with her, even if it was only for a little while. You have James and he's a great kid."

"I know." He was quiet for a moment, staring up at the ceiling as his hand moved up and down my arm. "Have you ever met Drew?"

"I think at Sebastian's wedding. Big guy, right?"

"Yeah. His wife died of cancer years ago. I sometimes stop and wonder what would be worse. I feel lost because I didn't get a chance to say goodbye, but Drew watched his wife slowly deteriorate until she passed away. Maybe this was a blessing. The coroner said that she was probably dead before she even knew what happened, but I always wonder what her final thoughts were. Did she see the truck coming? Did she know that she was about to die? Were her last thoughts of James and me? I think most of all, I just want to know for sure that she wasn't alive for minutes after the wreck before she died. I can't stand the thought that she knew she was going to die and she was all alone."

"I know those questions bother you, but you'll never get your answers, Ryan. Torturing yourself isn't going to change the fact that she's gone."

"I know. I just can't seem to stop thinking about those things. I don't know how to let her go. You know, it took a year for me to finally pack up her stuff, and I couldn't even do it. I had my friends' wives come take care of it."

"Did it help to have her stuff gone?"

"Not really. I used to spray her perfume in here just so that I felt like she was still here. The book she was reading is still sitting on the table by her favorite chair."

"That's not a bad thing. James knows that you still think about her. Maybe that's what helps him."

"I don't know. He's just so much more adjusted than I am."

"He's just a kid. I'm sure he misses his mom, but he has you."

We laid there in silence for what felt like hours until the sun finally set in the sky. I got up and made us some dinner and we ate in the living room before heading back to his bedroom. He didn't try to have sex with me that night and I didn't expect it. He was too strung out over what had happened. I slept snuggled up to him all night, just holding him and hoping that I was doing something to help him.

Seeing Ryan all broken up yesterday was enough to spur me into action. I needed to deal with my own shit so that I wasn't still fighting my demons in another ten years. Sebastian gave me the number for the psychiatrist that he kept on speed dial for the company. He was able to fit me in right away today and I took the appointment, ready to finally move on.

"Sebastian sent over your file," Dr. Penwarden said. "Why don't you tell me why you're here today?"

"You read about the incident. I'm here to work past that finally."

"Is that what you like to think of it as? The incident?"

"I'm not sure what else I would call it," I said, trying not to let my emotions take over.

His eyebrows lifted and he nodded slightly. "I would think it would be more significant to you than that."

"What I call it doesn't change what happened. Why does it matter if I refer to it as the incident?"

"You're downplaying what happened so that you don't have to deal with it. *The incident* sounds a lot less terrifying than almost being scalped."

"That's not what the problem is," I said hastily.

"Then why don't you tell me what the problem is?"

I hesitated, not really wanting to go into this anymore. Why had I agreed to therapy? I didn't need it. I was working through my issues.

"If you're not willing to talk about it, you're not going to move past it. Keeping it all inside isn't going to help."

I knew he was right. This was why I was here. "I don't like to think about it if I don't have to. I don't want to feel anything about that day. I hate that I walk around with a scar on my forehead, but at the same time, it's a reminder to me."

"A reminder of what?"

"To not make the same mistakes. To be stronger than I was."

"Do you blame yourself for what happened?" he asked.

"In a way, yes. I was trained and I didn't have the strength of mind to beat him."

"But you weren't the only one injured on your team, right?"

"No, but it was different. Derek was shot trying to defend our client. You can't stop a bullet. And Hunter was smashed in the head with a rock. He didn't even see it coming."

Dr. Penwarden nodded. "I see. So, you think that Derek never thought that if he had been faster, he wouldn't have been shot and could have saved your client? Or Hunter didn't beat himself up for not hearing the man sneak up on him?"

I didn't know what to say. I was sure that they had thought that many times.

"It's sometimes easier to blame ourselves than to look at a situation and say *there's nothing I could have done."*

"But there was something I could have done. I was trained and I froze. I could have fought back a half a dozen times and I was so...terrified."

Dr. Penwarden set down his paper and pen on the table and leaned forward. "Did you ever know anyone during your military days that froze when they were in battle?"

"Yes."

"Why do you think that happened to them?"

"It was war," I said dumbly.

"It was, but yours was just a different kind of war. Extreme circumstances can make the best of any warriors freeze up. Your teammates had already been taken out. A woman's life was at stake and you were her last remaining hope. That's a lot of pressure for anyone, and sometimes our brains can't work through all that under all the stress."

"But, then how can I be sure that it won't happen again?"

"You can't. Life doesn't work like that. All you can do is your best under the circumstances."

"That's not very reassuring for my teammates."

"Nothing in life ever works out the way we want."

"What about the nightmares? How do I stop those?"

"Ask yourself, what is it that wakes you up at night?"

"Reliving that moment. Every time I dream, it's about that night and what happened."

"And what is the overwhelming feeling that comes with that dream?"

"Fear," I said, confused by the question. "Isn't that what a nightmare usually is?"

"Think back to your dreams, what are you afraid of in the dream?"

"I'm afraid of what's happening to me. I'm so paralyzed by fear that I can't move. It's like it's happening to me all over again."

"So, take back that control that you lost."

"Dr. Penwarden, can we just cut to the chase here? I'm not very good at reading other people's minds about psychobabble. Just lay it out for me."

He smiled and sat back in his chair. "What you fear is fear itself. Let me ask you this, have you made any mistakes on the job since that night?"

"One," I said, looking down at my hands. "Someone pulled a knife on me and I was suddenly back there in the cabin that night."

"So, you've had no problem doing your job except the one time that you were faced with something that was very similar to what happened that night."

"Okay?"

"Sure, you're having nightmares because what happened was horrible, but the root cause of your dreams is the fear that you won't be able to defend yourself again in a similar situation."

"My teammate has been working with me, attacking me with a knife," I said hesitantly.

"And, how did that go?"

"The first time I completely lost it. Then, we took it too far and I had a breakdown or something. We stay away from that trigger and stick with the knife. Since then, I've been getting better at breaking the trance I fall into. But I'm still a mess afterwards."

"That's good," he smiled. "Keep working on that. You need to work through your control issues. You need to work through the fact that you may be put in similar situations that are difficult to control. Once you feel like you've gained back your confidence, you'll start to heal."

"That's it?" I asked suspiciously.

"Well, it's a lot of work and it's definitely a kind of therapy, but it's doable. You just have to believe in yourself again. And if you feel that you need to come talk through something, my door is always open."

"Come on, Lola. You can do this," Knight shouted at me.

Sweat was pouring down my face and my heart was racing out of control. I could do this. I could get past this. I gripped onto his wrist holding the knife and shoved his arm away as I twisted out from under his arm, wrenching the knife away from him in the process.

I was panting hard and my whole body was shaking, but I had done it again. I had fought my demons and come out on the other side. Hunter raced over to me and swooped me up in his arms, wrapping me in a tight bear hug. For the first time, I truly let myself feel what had happened. Not the fear and the pain, but the relief that I was going to get past this. I was going to come out on top. My breath seized in my chest as I broke down in Hunter's arms. I was crying uncontrollably and I could feel Hunter stiffen and pull away.

"Hey, you did it. Why are you crying?"

"I did it," I cried. "I..." My cries interrupted my thoughts and Hunter pulled me tight to him again.

"It's okay, Lola. We all knew you could do it," he whispered. I stayed in the comfort of Hunter's arms for another few minutes as my body came down from the rush. When I pulled back, everyone was in the room, the entire Reed Security company at my back, looking at me like I had just overcome some incredible feat. And I had. Today, I didn't freeze. Today, I won against my demons.

"So, are you ready to get back in the field?" Cap asked.

I nodded, still feeling the lump in my throat.

"Good. I have a job for the three of you. The rest of the teams want a break. That is, unless you want to continue with security installs?"

"Hell no!" Hunter shouted. "She's ready. We're ready. Give us the job and we'll be there by the end of the day."

Cap chuckled and nodded for the door. "Conference room, thirty minutes."

I walked over to Knight, who was preparing for his next training session and cleared my throat. "Thanks, for helping me."

He shrugged like it was no big deal. "I knew you could do it."

"But I didn't. I really thought that this would haunt me forever and because of you believing in me and trying your less than orthodox practices on me..." He raised an eyebrow in challenge. "I finally feel like I can work past my issues and move forward."

He nodded, not saying anything else and I walked away. Knight wasn't exactly the touchy feely type and I hadn't really expected him to say anything, so I was shocked when he grabbed onto my arm and pulled me back into him, giving me a tight squeeze before pushing me away and glaring at me.

I quickly showered and headed up to the conference room. The rush of the fight was still thrumming through my body, but I felt more confident than I had in a long time and nothing would stop me now.

After getting our assignment, we loaded up the Reed Security SUV and headed out for our three hour drive to our protection detail. It was at least a week long trip, so we swung by our houses and packed our bags. Derek was driving and I was sitting up front. Hunter leaned over the back seat and tapped me on the shoulder.

"So, this thing with Ryan, is it serious?"

"What?"

"Cap told us about you going to help him out the other day."

"He did, huh?"

I didn't picture Cap just going and running his mouth about someone else. It just wasn't his style.

"Yeah, well, I kind of tricked him into telling me what was going on. You know, when you rushed out of the building, it just had me wondering. So, I pestered him until he told me what was going on."

I nodded. That sounded a whole lot more like what had really happened.

"So? Are you going to tell me?"

"Tell you what?"

Hunter growled in frustration and pushed back in his seat. "Fine, don't tell me."

"Why do you even care? You're engaged to Lucy."

"Because, if this is just some casual thing, then it's none of my business. But if this is more serious, then I need to go have a talk with that fucker."

I turned around in my seat and glared at him. "Okay, first of all, this is none of your business no matter what. Second of all, Ryan is one of the most decent men I've ever known and he sure as hell isn't a manwhore like you."

"That's not what I've heard," he grumbled.

"His wife died. I think he's allowed to do whatever the hell he wants if it makes him feel better."

"Not with you," Hunter said firmly.

I turned to Derek. "Are you this concerned about my relationship with Ryan?"

"Not really," he shrugged. I turned back to Hunter.

"I think this has more to do with the fact that we slept

together than anything. You know that you don't have to protect me like some big brother, right?"

He just stared at me for a moment. "I'm pretty sure that no big brother would do the things that I have to you. I know that you're a big girl and you can take care of yourself, but I still care about you and I want to make sure that he doesn't fuck you over."

I grinned. "Believe me, he fucks me over good."

After a week away on the job, I was ready to see Ryan again. I was torn because I was so happy to be back to work, but whatever this was with Ryan was the first positive relationship I'd had in years. Even his son seemed pretty cool, and while I wasn't the least bit interested in being a parental figure, it was still early enough that I could see where this went. Besides, the kid was almost sixteen. At the pace Ryan and I were moving, the kid would be off at college before we really took things too seriously.

We had unloaded the SUVs and were ready to head home, but it wasn't unusual for us to stand around bullshitting for a few minutes before we hit the road.

"Oh, damn." Derek was looking at his phone and grinning.

"What?" Hunter asked.

"It's just Claire. She's been missing me."

Hunter groaned and grimaced as he caught sight of the

photo on Derek's phone. "Dude, you two are so fucking weird. Why do you keep showing me that shit?"

"I didn't show you anything. This is just what we'll be doing later tonight."

"What will you be doing?" I was suddenly very curious about this. I had heard a little about Derek and Claire's extracurricular activities, but I hadn't heard first hand.

"We're going to a cabin in the mountains for the weekend."

"Well, that sounds...not at all like you."

Derek grinned. "It's all Claire. She wants a mountain man to come rescue her."

"Wait, what happened to the whole bad boy thing she wanted to try?" Hunter asked.

"Well, after what happened with the Night Kings, it kind of ruined the fantasy a little for her."

"So, where did she get mountain men from?"

"A book she was reading. Ideally, there would be a blizzard and we would be stranded up there together, but since it's not snowing, we'll just have to improvise."

"Do you guys ever think of having, you know, normal sex?" I asked.

"We do occasionally, but this is fun. Besides, you should have heard the last thing she wanted to try. Voyeurism."

"What the hell is that?" I asked.

"It's when you get off watching other people get off."

"And she wanted to watch?" Hunter asked incredulously.

"You know, I'm not sure if she wanted to watch or have

others watch us. Either way, that's just not something I'm into."

"Well, sorry to be boring, but I'm just going home and fucking Lucy the old fashioned way. Hard and fast."

"What about you, Lola? Do you have plans with Ryan tonight?"

I shrugged, trying to play it cool. I didn't want them to know how much I liked spending time with Ryan. Then they would start ragging on me all the time. "I don't know. It's not like we make plans a whole lot."

"So, this *is* a booty call situation," Hunter said reproachfully.

"Hey, what I do with Ryan is none of your business. We've already talked about this."

"Yeah, yeah," he grumbled. "Alright, I'm heading home. Have fun with whatever you're doing."

He turned and headed for his truck and I barely heard Derek talking to me and wishing me a good weekend. My mind was firmly set on Ryan and getting to him as fast as possible. I thought about heading right out to his house, but I wasn't sure we were really at the stage in our relationship where drop ins were okay. Instead, I went home and showered, taking my time on calling him. I didn't want to seem too eager.

This was ridiculous. Why was I acting this way? I was an adult. I could call him and let him know I was back from my trip. If he wanted to see me, he would say so. Brushing off my girly idiocy that was so unlike me, I dialed his number and waited for him to pick up.

"Hey, Lola. How's it going?"

"Good. I just got in a few hours ago."

"Everything went well?"

"Yeah, it was a pretty simple job. What are you doing tonight?"

"Um, James is going to his grandparent's house for the weekend. Do you want to come over in maybe an hour?"

"Yeah, that sounds great. Should I bring anything?"

"You mean like lingerie?" Ryan asked in a husky voice.

"I meant like food. I don't do the whole girly shit lingerie crap. What you see is what you get."

"Hey, I'm not complaining."

"So, food," I said, grinning into the phone.

"Food, sorry. I'm just not really thinking of food at the moment."

"Okay, well, I'm going to let you go and I'll see you soon."

I needed to get off the phone before I started to talk dirty to him. His son was still there.

"I've got dinner covered. See you in an hour." He hung up and I bit my lip, trying to stop the smile that was quickly becoming a permanent fixture on my face when I talked to Ryan.

"Stop it," I scolded myself. "Don't be such a girl."

I shook it off and wandered around my house, trying to do anything to distract myself from thoughts of Ryan until it was time to leave. This was ridiculous. I was not this girl. I was not going to start swooning over a man.

Still, when it was close to time to leave, I couldn't grab my keys fast enough and head for the door. It took me all of ten minutes to get to his house and before I knew it, he was swinging the door open and pulling me into his arms. My clothes were torn from my body as he shoved me back toward his bedroom. We were barely inside when he was lifting me up and shoving me down on his hard cock. I was so wet for him and there was absolutely no foreplay. I didn't need it with him for some reason.

It was quick and dirty and completely satisfying. I didn't like to go slow all the time and drag out sex. Sometimes I just needed to be fucked good and hard. Tonight was one of those nights. And when he shoved me down on the bed and took me from behind, I was ramming my ass back into his hips so that I could get every last centimeter of his cock inside me.

When we finished, I collapsed on the bed, barely able to breathe. He only let me have a short reprieve before he was crawling over me again, fucking me harder than he had the time before.

We ate leftovers from his fridge after hours of having sex. I was standing in just his t-shirt and he had on some low hanging pants that had me licking my lips at his sexy V. I knew where that led and I wanted more.

"I see that look in your eyes, Lola, but it's not gonna happen. My dick needs a break."

I raised an eyebrow at him. "Having trouble getting it up?"

"Not at all, but we've already fucked three times and I need food."

"Fine," I pouted.

"So, how's work going?"

"Work?"

He shrugged. "It's not the least bit sexual."

"I don't know," I said, walking around the counter. "I work with a lot of big guns."

He grinned and shook his head. "That's only sexual for women. Seriously, how's it going?"

"Good. I'm out in the field again and that's a relief. I hated being stuck behind a desk. I don't know what I would have done if Sebastian had kept me from getting back out there."

"Do you think that could have happened?"

"Possibly. If he thought I was a liability to the team then he would probably offer me something at the office, but I don't think I could do that. I need some action. I can't stand the boredom of working in an office all day. No offense."

"None taken. But I don't work in an office all day. I'm constantly going and checking up on job sites. Even though I run the business, I still have to make sure that the quality of our work is as it should be." He started shoving his food around his plate with his fork, frowning like he was thinking about something.

"What?" I asked when he didn't say anything.

"Nothing. I was just thinking...are your jobs dangerous?"

"Not usually. I mean, there's always the chance that something will go wrong, but most of our jobs are pretty tame."

"It just seems like the past few years have been intense. I mean, Sebastian doesn't really talk about what kind of shit happens at Reed Security, but with what happened with Maggie, it just seems a little crazy."

"Well, that was a special circumstance. That wasn't so much about Reed Security as Chris's ex-girlfriend coming back into the picture."

"Yeah, but didn't someone get shot a few years back?"

I could see where this was going and I didn't want to sugar coat it for him. "Well, we've had a few cases that have gotten pretty intense, but they were mostly connected in one big tangled web. It was pretty insane, but when you look at how often something like that happens compared to the number of boring jobs, it's really not that frequent that something happens."

He didn't say anything for a minute and I got worried that he was starting to freak out about the dangers of my job. I knew that it could be difficult for him considering that his wife had died, but since I wasn't sure what was really happening between us, I hadn't really thought about it too much.

He picked up his plate and shoved it in the dishwasher. Grabbing my hand, he dragged me back to the bedroom, tossing me down on the bed and stripping me of my t-shirt. The time for talking was over.

Chapter Seven

RYAN

"Hey, big guy." Logan strolled into my office with a little too much cheer in his voice.

"Big guy? Do I look that bad?"

"No," he scoffed. "You look great. Like a million bucks."

I scratched my forehead as I leaned back in my seat. "Out with it."

"What do you mean?" He took a seat across from me, his eyes running discreetly over my body, like he was expecting slash marks or something.

"I mean, you're acting like you need to handle me with kid gloves."

"Psh. Nah. I don't know what you're talking about."

"Logan, cut the shit and tell me what's on your mind."

"Look, I'm just worried about you. I haven't seen you that

bad in a long time and I just want to make sure you're not going off the deep end."

"Well, I was really thinking of going and crashing my truck and leaving my kid all alone. You could take him."

"What? Dude, no. I think after our talk with him about sex, it's pretty clear I'm not ready for a teenage kid."

"You don't have too many more years. How old is Archer again?"

"Eight."

"Yeah, you know, James was asking questions about his dick when he was ten and I considered him a late bloomer. Face it, you have maybe two more years before you start having to deal with this shit."

"Whatever. You're getting me off track here." Damn, I thought I had evaded him. "Are you okay after what happened?"

"I'm fine." I sat up and pulled some papers out that I had to go over.

"Because if you need some time off-"

"Logan. I'm fine. I had a moment and that moment passed."

"I just want to make sure that shit's okay. You know, you never talk to me about that and you can."

"You're right. We should grab a bottle of wine and some chocolate. We can light a fire and I'll tell you my feelings."

His face turned hard and he leaned forward in his seat, staring me down. "You don't have to be an asshole. I'm serious here. You hold all that shit inside and you don't have to."

I threw the papers down on my desk and sighed. "Okay, you want to know what's going on? I took Lola home. We've fucked a few times and it's fucking fantastic. But then she had a little meltdown of her own and she needed some space. So, I took her to my place since James was out of town. She stayed the night and I thought, damn, I could actually move on finally. Then Cassie's parents showed up and it was a little uncomfortable, but they were all for it. Then, I took James out driving and I came upon the intersection where she was killed and I fucking flipped out. I had a panic attack or something and I lost my shit. It was like I was seeing her in the morgue all over again and it fucking tore my heart out. So, now my head's a little fucked up because I really want to be able to move on with Lola, but I'm still torn up over Cassie and I don't know where the hell to go from here. On top of all that, Lola's back in the field and after all the shit that went down with all of them not too long ago, I'm wondering if I can deal with her job or if it's going to freak me out."

Logan stared at me a minute, just nodding and taking it all in. "Is that it?"

I laughed at his humor. Logan always had a way of making me laugh when I needed it most. He was a pain in the ass, but the best friend a guy could ask for.

"You know, it doesn't have to be one way or the other. You don't have to stop thinking of Cassie in order to move on with Lola."

"That's the thing, Lola told me that I could talk about

Cassie with her. You know, she came over after Sebastian told her what happened and she stayed the night with me."

"You were able to get it up after that?"

"No sex," I said. "She just sat there with me. I told her about Cassie and I, and it was so great to talk about her again. I've been avoiding it because it always kills me, but with her... I don't know. She didn't know Cassie. She couldn't tell me any stories or remind me of times that something happened. And she gets the pain. She lives with things that torment her. I don't feel like I'm talking to a wall."

"Is that how you feel with us?" he asked, almost offended.

"No. I'm just saying that it's different with her. You all knew Cassie. You watched me fall in love with her. This thing with Lola is the one thing in my life that doesn't have anything to do with Cassie. Even James, it kills me to be with him day in and day out because he's hers. Not that I don't want to be his dad. He's what holds me together most days, but he's also what makes it so difficult."

"That makes sense. I mean, he's a constant reminder of her. You know, you could have told us all this shit a long time ago. You pushed us all away for a year and even when you let us back in, you only really let us in on the anniversary of her death. You're gonna end up like Drew, talking to imaginary people, if you don't start to work this shit out."

"So, what do you suggest I do?"

"Bring her out with us. We'll get to know her," he grinned.

"You know she could kick your ass, right? I mean, total beat down, leaving you a bloody mess. She's a trained killer."

"I know. It's hot. Maybe she can give Cece some lessons. She's not quite the hellcat she used to be."

"You're kind of sick, you know that, Logan?"

"Hey, blame Cece. That woman just does it for me. I like her brand of crazy and I want more of it again."

"I'll see what I can do," I said, rolling my eyes, but already coming up with a plan.

"Are you sure this is a good idea?" Lola asked as we walked toward the woods behind my house where everyone was waiting.

"Trust me. This is the best idea I've ever had."

"Why? Because you think you'll kick our asses?"

"Nope. Because I know you guys are going to win."

She stopped me with a hand on my arm, glancing at everyone waiting for us. "What makes you so confident?"

"Well, first of all. I know that you're a badass. Second, these women are very creative. There's not a single time that we've gone paint balling with them that they've lost."

"Do they know how to shoot?"

"Not at all. Well, Maggie does, but everyone else is just very determined," I grinned.

"What do you get out of it?"

"Sebastian, Cole, and Sean pride themselves on being the best shots and therefore, always think they're going to win. I love to watch them get knocked down a peg by these women."

"You're not going to go easy on us, are you?"

"Definitely not. But I can't change what I know is going to happen. Just make sure when Sebastian starts bragging about winning, you make the stakes high."

She grinned at me and we continued walking to the rest of the group. Everyone was decked out in camo and had on their game faces.

"No kid today?" Sean asked. "Were you afraid he was going to tip the scales in our favor?"

James was a natural at paintball. He was fucking awesome actually. "No, just wanted to keep this a friendly game," I grinned.

"This will be over in less than an hour. Just watch," Sebastian said.

"Why are you so confident?" Lola asked. "I'm a great shot."

"Sure, *you* are, but come on. We have three trained fighters on our side."

"I have a bunch of women that want to kick your asses."

I looked over at the women. Lillian, I could very clearly pick out. She was looking at the ground in disgust. Tromping through the mud wasn't her idea of a good time. Cece looked bored and kept checking her hair in the compact that she kept in her pocket. Maggie was fumbling with the large gun. It was obviously still awkward for her to hold a gun with two missing fingers. But she looked determined. Alex was holding her gun like it was diseased, and Harper was doing jumping jacks to prepare. Sarah, she just looked completely lost.

"Yeah," Sebastian smirked. "I can't wait."

"Want to make a friendly wager?" Lola asked, stepping into Sebastian's space.

"Anytime."

"If we win, you and your boys sing karaoke. Our song choice, our choreography."

"And if we win?"

"Same thing."

"Private show or public?" Sebastian asked.

"I think we both know a private show would be best."

"Deal."

They shook on it and walked back to their teams. Sebastian pulled out a map and spread it out on a table I had positioned back there for occasions like this. "Alright, ladies. We're going back to this location here," Sebastian pointed at the map. "Everyone have your emergency kits and radios on?"

"Yes," the women responded dully.

"Good. If you get lost...just call us for help."

"Not likely," Maggie muttered.

We broke apart, going our separate ways. There were two different paths we had cut through the woods so that we could play paintball back here on my property. I had a lot of acreage, so it was a perfect haven for us. We trekked through the woods, keeping a strong pace so that we could pull ahead of the ladies and get there before them and set up.

"I'm getting too old for this shit," Jack grumbled as we hiked to our location.

"Since when?" I asked.

"Since I hit forty. I'm running a garage and restoration shop, I have three kids, and I work out every fucking day. This was supposed to be my day off."

"If you work out so much, why is this so hard?" Sebastian chuckled.

"Let's just say my workouts aren't quite what they used to be."

"I'm with Jack," Sean said. "When I hurt my knee last year, it never really healed right. By the end of today, I'm gonna be hobbling around the woods, praying to God that I make it out of here."

"You should try a hot soak when you get home," Logan suggested. "Cece does this lavender shit and it really helps you relax. They also make shit to put in baths for inflammation. It's supposed to be really good."

"You know what else works pretty good? Meditation," Drew said. "I'm serious. When you start focusing on pushing that negative energy out of your body and just let yourself relax, it really helps a lot."

"Or, you can put an onion in your sock at night when you sleep," Cole suggested. "The onion is supposed to draw out illness in your body, but when I've used it, it also lessens pain."

"You just stick an onion in your sock?" Logan asked.

"Well, you have to have the sock on your foot, dumbass," Cole jabbed at him.

"Jesus Christ! What's with you guys? Are we men going to play paintball or should we head for the spa for a detox day?" Sebastian snapped.

"I could actually go for a spa day," Jack said. Sebastian glared at him. "What? They give great massages."

"I could go for that too," Drew sighed. "I'm not as young as I used to be and construction is kicking my ass."

"Man, you could have told us," I said, a little shocked that we hadn't known that.

"It's no big deal. It's more that I have fucking two sets of twins at home and they drive me fucking batshit crazy on a good day. I come home from work and the last thing I want is the chaos of what's waiting at home."

"You need to think about Sarah. Do you have any idea what that's like for her all day?" Logan asked. "I mean, think about it. You get a fucking break from them. She's at home all day with them, plus doing the cooking and taking care of the house. That sounds fucking brutal to me."

"Yeah, man. You have to be considerate of her feelings," Sean said. "Lillian goes to work, but with my hours being so crazy, she's the one that's always responsible for the kids. She never gets a break because it's always on her to make sure that the kids are taken care of."

"It's true. I'm the same way with Harper. I was just expecting that she would take care of the kids always because she works from home. I walk in the door and just assume that she has it all under control. I shower when I want, I go grab a beer when I want, and it never really occurred to me that I have the liberty to do all that shit because she's always the one making sure the kids are showered, have eaten, have done their homework. All that shit that I just take for granted because I've never had to worry about it."

"They truly are the ones that hold our lives together," Logan agreed.

Sebastian spun around, hands on his hips with his gun slung over his shoulder. "Okay, can we all get our heads in the game? I feel like I'm watching a fucking Oprah episode here and I don't even have any beer. You want to be men and go kick our wives' asses or do you want to go to the fucking spa?"

We all looked at each other and Jack shrugged. "I kinda want to go to the spa."

Sebastian shook his head and walked away, leaving the rest of us laughing. The guy really needed to take it easy.

Chapter Eight

LOLA

"Okay, ladies. If we're going to take these guys down, we need a solid plan." I looked around at the group around me and seriously wondered how they had managed to beat these guys every time they went against them. "How has this worked in the past? What did you guys do? What was your strategy?"

"Strategy?" Lillian asked. "I've actually never played before. I just want to be clear that this is my first time."

"Me too," Sarah said.

I nodded, feeling a little less hopeful. "Okay, not a problem. What about you, Harper? What did you do?"

"Um, well, I ran like crazy and shot at anything that moved while I screamed my head off. But that was before I had kids and I was in better shape. Disclaimer here: I wasn't actually in shape at the time, so I'm probably a little worse off now."

Fuck. Why was Ryan so sure we were going to win? "What about the rest of you? Cece?" I looked at her hopefully. She looked like the type of girl that didn't take any shit.

"Well, I was with Vira-"

A pain-filled groan escaped from Lillian's mouth, but Cece cut her a sharp look.

"As I said, I was with Vira and our strategy was to strip down to our underwear and distract them while the other ladies took them out."

"Of course that was her plan," Lillian grumbled. "Ladies of the evening are always willing to strip naked for someone else."

"Hey, I did it too," Cece said defensively. "No matter what she did to you, she's still my friend, so how about we cut the crap for just a few minutes?"

"Can we focus? I'm not sure that stripping down is the key here."

"Well, it probably wouldn't work anyway. It's not like I have the same body I did then," Cece groused.

"You're being too hard on yourself," Sarah said sympathetically. "You know Logan wants you no matter how you look. In fact, I think he wants more of the old Cece back. He's not getting any younger. You think these men aren't chasing their youth too?"

"You know, she has a point," I said.

"I'm not stripping," Cece said firmly.

"No, but maybe we need to give them a little reminder of

who you were when you first met. It'll definitely distract them."

"It's true," Lillian agreed. "You know, when Sean and I were dating, we did all this fun stuff together that was so out of my element. I'm not sure if I still have it in me, but I definitely want to bring some of that back."

"What about you, Alex?"

"Umm...I'm not sure that I have anything to offer. I'm actually pretty terrified of the woods, but I wanted to try this for Cole."

"I think we can use that. As long as you don't totally lose it, Cole won't kill me when this is all done."

"So, what exactly is the plan?" Harper asked.

"Distract, evade, and conquer," I said fiercely. I don't know what I was expecting, but it wasn't the blank faces that were staring back at me. I guess I had hoped for a warrior cry or something. Sighing, I pulled out the map that Ryan had given me, marking where we would be playing.

"Okay, ladies. Here's where we're headed. Now, we're going to have to split up if we're going to make this work. We're going to get into position and then Alex, you'll be up first. You're going to call out for Cole, scream like you're fucking terrified."

"That shouldn't be too hard." She bit her lip, but I watched as she steeled her spine. This girl was ready to do shit.

"Cole will go running to you and that'll take him out. I'll be positioned here," I pointed to the map. "I'll be up in a tree, taking them out as you ladies draw them out to me. With any luck, we'll get someone running to you with Cole."

"Next, Cece. Find your most seductive song and get that body shaking. You need to distract Logan as much as possible. No matter what happens, if you're hit, you don't go down. You shake that ass until he comes out."

"Got it."

"Sarah, since you don't know jack shit about playing this game, you're going to be stumbling through the woods, calling out for us. Just act like you don't know where the hell everyone is and you're lost. Meanwhile, Maggie, you'll be making your way around the guys." I pointed at the map. "See this trail? Cut across here. Follow the trail, but stay in the woods so they don't see you coming. You need to move fast, but quietly."

"I can do that. Do we have any paintball grenades?"

"Uh....yeah. Why?"

"Grenades are sort of my thing. Give me a few of those and I'll take out as many as I can," Maggie grinned.

"Good. Alright, Harper and Lillian, I'm counting on you to run through the woods, screaming like banshees. Do your thing."

"What would our thing be exactly?" Lillian asked uncertainly.

"Whatever worked last time," I said.

"Well, see I don't really have anything that works. I just kind of wing it and hope for the best," Harper said.

"Fine. Wing it."

"But what if we don't actually draw them out with this?" Lillian asked. "I mean, they'll know what we're trying to do."

"That's the point. They'll be distracted by everyone and I'll be doing my thing. It's not a perfect plan, but it's the best I have right now. Normally, I would have tactical maneuvers and shit, but this will have to do."

"Thanks for the vote of confidence," Maggie grumbled. I looked at her pointedly and she shrugged. "Yeah, okay."

It took us longer than I would have liked to reach the battleground and I was sure that the guys had been set up for a while, scoping out the place and getting into position. They definitely had an advantage over us.

"Alright, ladies. This is where we split up. Make sure you're on channel 3. Let's move!"

I crept off to the left, slipping through the trees until I found one that worked for me. I hadn't seen any movement yet and I prayed that the girls didn't all get shot up before I had a chance to take anyone out.

Chapter Nine

RYAN

"Goddamn, it's cold out here. How much longer are they going to take to get here?" Drew grumbled.

"They probably stopped to get their nails done," Jack replied.

"This coming from the man that wanted to go to the spa," Sebastian grinned. "Just relax. This is the thrill of the hunt."

"What's wrong with just hanging out with a beer around a fire?" Logan asked.

"Hey, you were the one that suggested we all hang out to get to know each other," I replied.

"Yeah, but I meant grabbing a beer at the bar or meeting at your house and having them all make us food. This requires an actual effort on my part. I didn't sign up for this shit," Logan grumbled.

"Yeah, well, this is something Lola likes to do and at one time, you did too."

Logan sighed and rested his elbow on his knee. "Yeah, at one time I did. Maybe it would be more fun if it was just the guys, but we've been sitting here for a fucking hour and we'll probably take them down in like, five minutes."

"Cole!"

I looked over at Cole with a *what the fuck* expression. "Is that Alex?"

"Help me, Cole. I'm so terrified," she shouted.

I choked back a laugh and so did he. "Is she trying to draw us out by trying to sound scared?"

Cole nodded. "Sounds like it. You would think she could do a better job."

A piercing scream filled the air and we all looked at each other, knowing that one wasn't fake. Cole was up in an instant running through the trees and shouting for Alex.

"Should we go out there?" I asked.

"And give up our position?" Sebastian scoffed. "Let's find out if that was even real first."

He was watching through binoculars and started shaking his head. "She got him. Damn, that was pretty good."

"Let me see." I grabbed the binoculars from his hand and looked. Sure enough, Cole was covered in paint and helping Alex out of a hole. "Crap. She definitely got him."

"What the hell is that?" Logan asked. We were all quiet for a minute as we strained to hear what the sound was. "Is that...*Hot Stuff?*"

Jack started laughing. "They're going to have to do better than that."

Cece strutted out from behind a tree and Logan put a hand on Sebastian's gun, stopping him from shooting her. "Wait. Let's watch the show first."

Cece started dancing and swaying her hips, adding in some gyrating.

"Damn. She's still fucking sexy," Logan murmured.

Her hands were in her hair as she lifted the long strands off her neck and then she went stiff, screaming as she started running through the trees. Harper and Lillian ran out from the side, holding their guns like they were about to shoot someone until they saw Cece doing some kind of weird dance that had us all shaking our heads.

"Where are they?" Harper shouted.

"I don't know! There was a huge spider on me!"

Lillian pointed at the ground and they all shrieked. "Snake!"

The three of them took off running, tripping over one another to get away as fast as they could.

"Isn't there a river down that hill?" Drew asked nonchalantly.

"Yep," I nodded. "Wait for it." Three screams filled the air as we heard what sounded like rolling and then splashing. "And they found the water."

"Let's go get a better look," Logan nudged me. Logan, Sean, Jack, and I made our way over to the edge of the hill where the steep embankment could be seen. All three women were standing in the water, squealing and ripping their clothes off as they all splashed each other. At least, that was the way I saw it. Judging from the looks on my friends' faces, they were seeing something completely different.

I could picture it exactly as they were seeing. Everything was in slow motion while Barry White's *Can't Get Enough of Your Love Baby* played in the background. The tiniest little droplets of water could be seen as the girls slowly ripped their shirts over their heads and swung them around their heads while shaking their hips. The shirts went flying and then the girls were reaching out and touching each other, like they were at a nightclub and were dirty dancing with each other. When the pants started to come off, I shook my head, not really wanting to see my friends' wives completely naked.

"Get it off! Get it off!" Cece yelled. The other girls were tearing at her clothes, trying to find the spider that had crawled into her clothing. Then Lillian yelled and started ripping off her own clothes.

"Snake! Oh, golly. Oh, gosh. Oh, darn!"

"Uh, you guys gonna step in here any time soon or are you just gonna let them strip each other bare?" I asked.

"Strip each other bare," they all answered.

"You know that there could be chiggers in the water, right? I'd hate to have that near your junk if they bring those home with them."

That got them all moving. They were up and running to the edge of the embankment in seconds.

"How does this work?" Sarah yelled at the girls. Our heads

all turned to the left to see Sarah walking toward us, gun pointed at us, but her head looking at the gun. "Is it this thing?"

Before we could move, she pulled the trigger, the force sending her tiny frame spinning. Paint balls whipped by all of us as she tried to get control of her gun. Bullet after bullet struck each of us in a machine gun rhythm. When she finally ran out, we looked at each other, seeing every one of us had been caught by her randomly firing her weapon.

"No real guns for you," Sean pointed at her. Then he stormed down the embankment and into the water, grabbing Lillian around the waist. "What the hell are you doing? You don't get naked for anyone but me," he scolded.

Logan walked into the water, hauling Cece off into the woods, most likely to have his way with her. Jack stormed up to Harper, anger all over his face.

"What the hell? Are you trying to get killed? You don't go running through the woods when you don't know the terrain. You could have broken your fucking neck!"

"As you can see, I'm fine and I don't need you running to the rescue to save the day!"

"I came here because you're fucking naked and my friends can all see you."

"I'm not naked. I have a bra and panties on. And boots!" she pointed to her feet.

"Yeah, I'm sure those boots are doing a great job of hiding your SEXY FUCKING TOES!"

"Don't yell at me."

"Don't strut around naked!"

He grabbed her head and pulled Harper toward him, kissing her and lifting her under the ass. He stumbled up the embankment until he shoved her against a tree.

"Yeah, I don't need to see that."

I walked over to Sarah and took the gun from her.

"There are no bullets left, you know."

"Let's just say that it's for the best if you never come paintballing with us again," I smirked.

Two loud explosions behind me had me turning around and running for our hideout. Sebastian and Drew were covered in paint and Maggie was standing behind them examining her nails.

"Who gave her grenades?" Sebastian yelled.

"Looks like we won," Maggie said as if she didn't have a care in the world. "What do you think of that? Seven men beaten by a few clumsy women, two that have never handled a paintball gun, and one woman who doesn't even have all her fingers." Maggie smirked and walked over to Sebastian. "I think I'll go discuss what song you'll be singing with the ladies." She kissed him sweetly on the lips and walked away.

I felt a paintball hit me in the back and I turned around, raising an eyebrow at Lola. "You know I'm already out, right?"

She shrugged. "I didn't get to shoot anyone."

"So, was that all part of your plan?" I asked, waving to the mess of women that were scattered around us.

"Not at all. I see now what you meant by 'they always

seem to win'. I don't know how the hell that happened, but it was only loosely based on my plan."

"Okay, where is everyone?" Maggie asked as she walked back over.

"I think Logan is showing Cece his snake," I grinned.

"Whatever. I've talked with Sarah and Alex and we've all agreed on the song we want you to sing."

"What's that?" Sebastian asked.

"Don't I get a say in this?" Lola asked.

"Trust me. You'll be happy with our choice," Maggie smiled.

"Well, don't leave us in suspense," Sebastian quipped.

"You're going to perform *You Can Leave Your Hat On.*"

"Wait, isn't that the song from that movie?" I asked, snapping my fingers.

"Yep," Sarah popped her p and laughed.

"No," I said firmly.

"Yes, and we'll be expecting *The Full Monty*," Alex beamed.

Chapter Ten

RYAN

"So, what's this song we're supposed to sing?" Drew asked as he sat down on my couch with a beer. All the guys were over and we were going to watch the dance from *The Full Monty* so that we knew what we had to do.

"*You Can Leave Your Hat On*," I said.

We watched the guys all walk out on stage and then start to do hip thrusts. "This doesn't look too bad," Cole said, taking a seat on the couch.

Sean sat next to him and leaned back, getting comfortable with a beer. "I'm pretty sure that we'll look better than these guys when we do it."

"Now, see, that move right there, we have to change," Drew said. "I don't like the idea of walking down the stage with one of you. It's creepy."

"These guys are terrible dancers," Sebastian said. "That's not sexual at all."

"Have you ever seen the movie?" I asked. Sebastian shook his head. "The whole point of the movie is that these guys are all down on their luck and trying to do something to survive."

"So, they strip?" Jack asked.

I grinned. "Just wait for it."

"Oh! That dude right there. That's me." Logan pointed to the screen where a guy just jumped over another guy and landed on his knees, slowing ripping open his shirt.

"Do chicks really go for guys that look like that?" Sean asked. "I mean, stripping and looking like that. There's only one good looking guy out of all of them."

"Which one are you talking about?" I asked, just giving him shit because I wanted him to say it.

"What do you mean? You can see which one."

"I don't know. There are a couple of guys that don't look too bad," I shrugged.

"Are you looking at the same group of men that I am?" Sean asked with a baffled expression. I leaned forward and looked him dead in the eyes.

"Why don't you just tell me which guy you think looks good?"

"Fuck off," he turned back to the TV and I chuckled.

"No!" All the guys started to shout when the guys ripped off their pants, revealing they were wearing red thongs.

"No. No fucking way," Sebastian shook his head.

"I'm with him," Cole agreed. "There's no fucking way I'm wearing a thong."

"I'm afraid we don't have a choice," Logan said. "A bet is a bet."

"Just wait for it," I said again, laughing inside that they hadn't seen how it ended yet.

"What are they doing?" Jack said in shock. "No. No, no, no. Shit!"

The guys pulled off their thongs and raised them over their heads, swinging them and covering their junk with their hats.

"Holy shit," Sebastian whispered. "They're not going to..."

The guys spun around and shook their naked ass to the crowd and then spun back around, tossing their hats into the audience.

"Oh!" The guys shouted.

"We're supposed to do that on a fucking stage?" Drew spat. "With each other?"

"That's what Alex said, the full monty."

I paused the TV on the image of the guys standing bare ass naked in front of the crowd of women. The guys all looked shell shocked, except for Logan, who looked surprisingly fine with the whole thing.

"So, are we gonna do this as policemen?" Logan asked.

Sebastian glared at him. "That's what you have to say about this?"

"What?" Logan shrugged. "It's not like we haven't seen each other's dicks before in the locker room."

"That was showering. This is fucking dancing on a stage in front of each other's wives," Drew yelled, pointing at the TV.

"Yeah," Logan grinned. "Imagine how amazing the sex is going to be after that?" He waggled his eyebrows and Jack punched him in the shoulder. "What? You guys are taking this way too seriously."

"Ryan?" Cole jerked his head at me. "You aren't saying much."

"I guess I don't really care," I shrugged. "When Maggie suggested it, I'd already seen the movie. I've had time to adjust."

"Okay, so if we're going to do this, we need to decide on a theme." Logan pulled out his phone and started taking notes. "I say we do firemen. It's so much sexier than a policemen."

"Hey," Sean said.

"Sorry, but they make more calendars about firefighters than policemen. I'll work on finding costumes. And we're definitely going to have to find some better choreography than that," he pointed to the screen. "Maybe even a better song."

"You know, I think you're having a little too much fun with this," Sebastian said.

"Embrace it, man. Jack, don't tell me you wouldn't mind spicing things up with Harper a little."

"The last time we spiced things up, we ended up with another kid."

"Ouch, has it been that long?" I asked.

"No, douchebag. That's the last time we did something crazy. We fuck just fine, thank you very much."

"Okay, what about Lillian?" Logan asked Sean.

"You've met her. Do you really think this is something she'd like?"

"Just shout out a couple of misplaced modifiers and you'll have her creaming in her seat," Logan joked.

"Real funny, asshole."

"Seriously, you guys just need to roll with this. You know that if we had won, we would have made them do something equally sexy," Logan pointed out.

"Well, if we don't want to look like a bunch of dickheads, we need to put together a practice schedule," Drew suggested.

"You're not serious," Sebastian glared at him.

"Well, fuck. You're the one that got us into this mess with your damn bet, and I'm sure as hell not doing that," he pointed at the TV.

"You know, he's right," Cole said. "And since he was the one that suggested it, he can be up front at the end."

I laughed until Cole looked at me. "And since your girlfriend agreed to this, you get to be right behind him."

"And since your wife suggested the full monty," Sean grinned, "you get to stand right next to him."

"So, where is this all going to take place?" Logan asked. "And more importantly, where are we going to practice?"

"You're way too fucking excited about this," I said.

"Do you think we should all match?" Logan asked, completely ignoring me as he looked off in thought.

"That's kind of the point, isn't it?" I asked.

"No, I mean, should we all match...down there?" he pointed at his crotch.

"Our underwear?" Cole asked.

"No," Logan stressed. "Our...maintenance."

Sebastian shook his head. "What is it with guys now? I walked in on some of the guys at work checking out each other's maintenance. Why do we have to all look alike?"

"Well, we might look..." Logan cleared his throat uncomfortably. "Different if say one of us is trimmed and another is waxed."

"Yeah, who gives a shit?" Drew asked.

"Well, I wax," Logan put out there. "And I'm just saying that waxing makes you look...larger." He held up his hands in apology. "I just wouldn't want to show any of you up."

"So, what? We're all supposed to go get waxed?" Sean asked. "I'm not a girl. I don't do that shit."

"You know, he might have a point though. Let's face it, the girls are going to see *all* of us. I want to look my best," Jack said.

"I'm kind of with Logan," Cole admitted. "I'm not normally one to do that kind of shit, but I'm really hairy. I keep it clean, but I would look like a hairy beast next to someone that waxes. I vote we all go for the same look."

"Okay, so we take a vote," I suggested. "All those in favor of waxing, raise your hands."

Logan, Cole, Jack, and I all raised our hands. Sebastian, Sean, and Drew all glared at us.

"Okay, so are we all going to make an appointment and do this together?" Logan asked. Sean smacked him upside the head and that was the end of that.

"I hope you don't mind, but there's a Harry Potter marathon on today. James and I watch all the movies whenever there's a marathon on." I hoped to God that Lola was okay with this. She said she was fine with hanging out all day, but it was different when there was a kid involved. I really didn't know if she would be okay with just lounging all day.

"I'll pick up snacks. You can't have a movie marathon without a full day's supply of munchies."

"Alright. It starts in an hour, so don't be late. You can't miss the first one."

"I wouldn't dream of it."

I hung up and grinned down at my phone, relieved that this wasn't an issue. I was really enjoying Lola's company and James seemed to also. I didn't want to look too far beyond that yet. We were having a good time and I was fine with just seeing where things went from here, but it was really important that she got along with James. If she didn't, it would be a no go. James was my first priority and always would be.

"So, is she coming?"

"Yeah, she's stopping for snacks on her way."

"Cool," James said as he took a seat. He had all his Harry Potter books with him. We always fact checked along the way with the movies, even though we knew all the aspects of every book. "You don't think she's going to be bored, do you? I mean, the movies might be kind of..." He shrugged and looked down at his books.

"What?"

"Childish?"

"I like the books and I like watching the movies with you. If she doesn't like them, she'll just leave early."

I hoped like hell that didn't happen. I didn't want James to think that his interests were childish in any way. This was more of a ritual than anything for us. It was what originally brought us together. I never wanted him to think it was stupid.

"Maybe we should choose something else," he said uncomfortably.

I shook my head. "She sounded excited about it. Besides, you can't go through life not doing what you like because of what others might think."

"So, you don't care if she thinks you're a dork?"

"Hey, I already have on my Gryffindor shirt. If she doesn't run away as soon as she sees me, I think we'll be fine."

Forty-five minutes later, Lola was pulling up and James was already at the door, rushing out to help her carry in her goodies. She had a trunk full of groceries with her and best of all, she was wearing Harry Potter sweats and a Gryffindor t-shirt. It looked almost exactly like mine.

"Nice shirt," I said as I took some bags from her.

"Well, I wanted to be prepared. I saw this at Target and I knew I had to get it."

I wrapped my arms around her and pulled her in close. "You're amazing," I whispered before I kissed her. "So, what did you bring?"

"Well, I figured that this was going to be an all day and possibly all night event. Am I right?"

I nodded and smiled.

"So, I got frozen pizzas, ribs that we can do in the crock pot, fries, cornbread, coleslaw, beans, and a chicken. I figure we can do the pizza for lunch. I'll put the ribs in now and they'll be ready for dinner. We can roast the chicken for a few hours in the oven. And..." She smiled big and pulled out another bag. "I got muffins and orange juice for now. I'm assuming you have coffee."

"You would be correct. I can't believe you did all this," I said in amazement.

"Well, this is my first movie marathon, so I wanted to do it right. I tried to get-"

I cut her off with another kiss, pulling her tight against me. I knew she had done all this for my son and I loved her for that. I pulled back at that thought and cleared my throat uncomfortably, afraid that I had said that out loud.

"Everything okay?" she asked. She had a funny look on her face that said she knew I was freaking out over something.

"Good. Everything's fine."

"Right. Well, I'm going to get the ribs started. Save me a seat."

I followed her into the kitchen and pulled out the crock pot for her and got down a couple of cups for coffee. After pouring them, I brought them into the living room just as the first movie was beginning. She followed me in with cups of orange juice and the muffins.

"Should I have brought something more healthy?"

"This is fine. Some days you just have to eat stuff that's not good for you."

Throughout the movie, Lola laughed as James and I pointed out little things that were different in the movie from the book. There weren't that many. This movie was pretty close to the original. Lola gave the movie her full attention and even seemed to be enjoying it. After the first movie ended, the second was on in minutes. We all quickly got up to run to the bathroom before the movie began and Lola even pulled a blanket on to get comfortable.

I liked the idea of her lounging around the house today with us. I couldn't stop looking over at her to see if she was having fun or if she was bored out of her mind. By the third movie, I had her laying down with her head in my lap just so I could touch her. I saw James smirk at me when he saw me pull her toward me, but then his focus was back on the movie.

We took a break to get the chicken started and then we started watching again. Lola seemed just as content as James and I. It wasn't uncomfortable or awkward at any time the whole day, and by the time night came, we were all pigging out on the food Lola had made while we watched the movie. Seeing as how I hated a mess in the kitchen, I quickly went and started cleaning up and was surprised when Lola joined me.

"You don't have to do that. I just hate the mess."

"It's fine. If I help, it'll get done faster." She smiled sweetly at me and got to work putting stuff away. I was finding that there was a lot more to Lola than I originally thought. I had always pictured her as this badass warrior. I had met her several times through Sebastian, but I had never really bothered to learn her name or anything about her. Of course, at the time, I had been grieving over Cassie and any other women weren't even a blip on my radar.

We finished up quickly and sat back down on the couch to finish up the movie. By the time we were on the last movie, it was late and Lola was dozing in my lap. Her warm breath fanned out across my leg and I smiled as I thought of how comfortable this was. My fingers started sliding through her silky strands, gently massaging her scalp each time I started to rake my fingers through.

It was so strange to feel this level of comfort with her after such a short time. I knew that I had to be careful though. I couldn't let myself get too far ahead. I didn't know if I could actually handle another relationship at this point and I wasn't sure that Lola wanted one either. But for the rest of the night, I enjoyed having her in my house and in my life. No matter how long it lasted.

Chapter Eleven

LOLA

Do you want to come hang out with us?" Ryan asked over the phone.

"That depends. Will there be food?"

"Pizza."

"Action, comedy, romance?"

"Sorry if you like romance, but we don't watch those."

"Neither do I."

"Great, then get your ass over here."

"I'm on my way."

I hung up, grinning like an idiot and it hit me that all the times that I had slept with Hunter, I had never felt this way. He was a great friend and I loved spending time with him, and I really liked fucking him. But I was never excited to get to see him. I had been seeing Ryan now for a few months and every time we got together, it felt like it was growing into something stronger.

By the time I got to Ryan's house, I couldn't wipe the smile off my face to save my life. And when he answered the door and pulled me into his arms, giving me the most spine tingling kiss of my life, I knew that I was in over my head. I liked him way more than I ever thought I would like someone.

"Hey, beautiful."

"Hi," I smiled. I was staring at him like it was the first time I was seeing him and after a few moments, pulled my eyes away to stop from acting like some love-crazy fangirl. That wasn't me. "So, did James decide what movie we're watching?"

"He wanted to wait for you to choose."

"Wow, I get to choose the movie? I feel special."

"Well, I just got back with the pizza, so why don't you go choose a movie while I get some plates?"

"Alright."

I walked into the living room and sat down on the couch where James had a slew of movies set out. "So, what are my choices?"

"Well, I was trying to pick movies that I thought you might like. We have the new *Jurassic World* movie. There are the classics, *Die Hard* and *Lethal Weapon.*"

"What about this one?" I picked up *The Lord of the Rings* and waved it in front of his face.

"I wasn't sure if you liked that kind of movie."

"Are you kidding? It has some great battle scenes."

He grinned at me with a smile that made me feel like I had just handed the kid a bag of gold. He got up and quickly put in the movie, grabbing a chair off to the side. Ryan winked at me as he came to sit down and handed out plates, napkins, and cans of pop.

"Have you ever read these books?" James asked excitedly.

"Yeah, the books are definitely better."

"They usually are. I can't think of a single movie that was better than the book. Like *Harry Potter*? Dad and I read the series together and the first two or three movies were pretty good, but by the fourth, they changed so much and I just didn't like them as much."

"I've never read the books, but from what I could tell, the movies weren't bad. Maybe I'll have to read them so I can compare them."

James grinned and started turning on the movie. Ryan grasped my hand in his and gave a firm squeeze. "Do you really like this movie?"

"Of course. But I did choose it because I thought James would like it best. I figured you two had read the books together."

"We did."

The look on his face was somewhat like wonder and something else I didn't want to name, but that couldn't be. Things were still too new with us. We were just hanging out. He leaned in and gave me a soft kiss on the lips, his fingertips running along the length of my jaw. "Thank you," he whispered.

The movie started and we dug into the pizza, devouring the whole thing in less than ten minutes. "Damn, I didn't realize that you could eat like a guy. I should have gotten more pizza," Ryan smiled. "Where do you put it?"

"Hey, food is fuel and I'm very active. I need to keep up my energy."

"So, was this fueling your body for later tonight?" he whispered, nipping at my ear. Shivers ran down my spine and I glanced at James, just to make sure he wasn't paying attention. "Are you staying with me tonight?"

"Is that okay? I don't know what the protocol is for sleepovers when a kid is involved."

"He won't be attending this sleepover."

I shoved at his chest and smiled. "You know what I mean. Are you okay with me being here when he's in the house?"

Ryan pulled back and ran a hand through his hair. "Shit, I don't know."

"I just don't want to make him uncomfortable. I've never had a kid, so I don't know what you want to do."

"Maybe we should just wait. Do you want to come over tomorrow night?"

"Yeah. Honestly, I'm not sure I'm comfortable with doing...you know, when he's here."

"You guys know that I can hear you over the movie, right? You're not being as quiet as you think," James said, still watching the movie.

My eyes went wide and I slapped a hand over my mouth. Shit, this was really bad.

"She can stay, you know. I know that you have sex. Just don't be too loud."

I covered my face, completely embarrassed that James was talking about sex with us. It was just weird.

"Well, I guess that answers our question," Ryan muttered.

We stayed up for the rest of the first movie, but by the time it ended, James was half asleep in his chair. He mumbled something about going to sleep and headed upstairs. Even though he had basically given us permission to have sex with him here, it was still weird and I didn't know if I should leave.

"Um, so, should I head out?" I asked Ryan.

"Stay," he said quietly.

"Are you sure?"

He nodded and stood, holding his hand out for me. I placed my hand in his and followed him to his bedroom. It was different tonight than the other times I stayed over. This was more intimate. Every time I had come over before, we were always rushing to get each other's clothes off. This time, he led me into the bedroom and pushed me slowly onto the bed. My eyes trailed over his body as he removed his shirt, pulling the tails out from the waistband of his pants and unbuttoning from the top to the bottom.

He wasn't built like the guys at Reed Security. He had muscles and he took care of his body, but he wasn't built like he was ready for war and I really liked that. He had a softness about him that the men I worked with tended to hide from.

Working with those men was great, but sometimes I needed to feel like a regular woman that was wanted by a regular man. I didn't want to always be seen as the badass woman that could take out someone with my bare hands. I wanted to be a woman that was treated gently and cherished. I couldn't have that persona around my teammates, but around Ryan, I could finally let down my guard and just be a girl needing something special.

When he pulled off his pants, I couldn't help but stare at his cock pushing against the fabric of his boxers. He climbed over me and kissed me, trailing his tongue over my body as he undressed me. Soon, I was bare under him and feeling him rocking inside my body. There wasn't a nerve ending inside me that wasn't on fire. Every part of me craved his touch and hardness of his body pressed against mine.

I felt a connection with him that I had never felt with any other man. It was electric and intense. It was a bonding of two broken souls that were slowing piecing each other back together. It was something like love.

As we laid together in the darkness of the room, his fingers slowly trailed up and down my back. His heart was beating a steady rhythm that slowly lulled me into a sleepy state. The soft press of his lips against my head brought a faint smile to my lips right before I drifted into dreamless slumber.

"Hey, beautiful." Ryan's soft voice broke through the fog of sleep and I groaned, not wanting to get up. I could feel the warm rays of the sun pouring across the bed and warming my skin.

"I don't want to get up yet."

"You don't have to. James is going to be up soon. I'm gonna start breakfast. His grandparents are picking him up in a few hours."

"Mmm-Hmm," I responded. I heard him chuckle slightly and then he kissed my cheek.

"I liked you staying with me last night. We'll have to do that more often. Go back to sleep."

I heard the soft snick of the door and then silence. I went back to sleep and when I woke again, I felt more refreshed than I had in years. I sat up, pulling the sheet with me and looked out the window at the beautiful view of the trees. Ryan really did have a touch of paradise here. Since I didn't have anything to do today and Ryan had made it clear that I could stay in bed, I sank back down into the comfort of his bed, staring out the window and wondering if I could have more of this someday.

When the door opened, I smiled at Ryan standing there looking at me with a sexy grin. He was dressed in jeans and a t-shirt and his hair was tousled in a sexy, just fucked look. "Are you going to get up any time today?"

"Maybe. I was just enjoying the comfort of your bed. I haven't slept that good in years."

"Me too."

"What time is it?"

"Ten."

"Oh, wow. What time are Cassie's parents coming?"

"They'll be here in an hour. I made some breakfast, but I'm pretty sure it's cold now since you've slept the morning away."

"I couldn't help it. With the sun coming in and the beautiful scenery, I didn't want to leave the room."

He walked over to me and knelt down on the bed beside me. "I can't blame you there. Come on, get up and eat some breakfast. I'll grab some coffee for you."

"You know, if James wasn't still here, I would try to lure you back to bed."

"If that door was closed, I would let you."

"If I didn't have such good hearing, I wouldn't be on the verge of throwing up right now," James shouted from the hallway.

I covered my face and shook my head. "I'm definitely not used to a kid being around."

"Does it bother you?" Ryan asked. I could see the worry in his eyes. We had had a great night and things were starting to go somewhere between us. He was worried that I wouldn't be able to deal with the whole package.

"No. And even if it did, I would just have to deal with it. He's a great kid. I just have to get used to watching what I say."

He leaned forward and kissed me, his fingers gliding along my cheek in a gentle caress. His tongue flicked across my lips as he pulled back. "Breakfast," he said in a low, gravelly voice. He got up and left, shutting the door behind him. I wanted to stay in bed longer, but James was a part of Ryan's life and if I was going to be here, I couldn't hide from his son. I got up and took a quick shower, throwing on my jeans from yesterday and one of Ryan's t-shirts. At least it would appear that I wasn't wearing the same outfit.

When I walked into the kitchen, Ryan had a plate of waffles warmed up for me on a plate with a mug of coffee beside it.

"Mmm. This looks delicious."

"Well, it was two hours ago. I don't know how it will taste right now."

I shrugged. "Ever had an MRE?"

"Can't say that I have."

"Eat one of those and you'll never complain about food again."

I took a bite of the waffles and sighed in delight. I didn't cook very often and most of my meals were take out or freezer meals. I ate in just a few minutes and then picked up my mug of coffee to enjoy.

"If you want, there's a nice view off the deck," Ryan suggested. I followed him out there and sat down in a beautiful adirondack chair. It was still chilly this morning since it was only early spring, but Ryan had brought out a blanket and wrapped it around me. I snuggled into the chair with my coffee and relaxed.

"Wow. These are really nice."

"James and I built them with his grandfather for Cassie. She loved sitting outside."

"How does James deal with his mom's death?"

He shrugged. "He's doing okay. I wish I could really say, but we don't talk about her very much."

"Why don't you talk about her?"

"Too painful," he said quietly.

I didn't say anything to that, even though I was thinking that it had to be hard on James for him to never discuss Cassie. I understood not wanting to talk about something painful.

James stepped out onto the deck and sat down in one of the chairs, drinking a bottle of water.

"So, what are you doing with your grandparents this weekend?" I asked James.

He shrugged. "I don't know. Grandpa usually has some woodworking projects that we do. He's taking me out driving for a few hours."

I noticed that Ryan tensed at that, but didn't say anything. "When you get home, I was thinking we should pick out a new series to read."

"I've actually been thinking of reading *The DaVinci Code,*" James said.

"Okay. I'll pick it up this weekend."

His grandparents pulled in the driveway and we all walked inside. His grandparents let themselves in and James was at the door waiting with his bag. This time I didn't try to hide my scar from them.

"Lola, it's so nice to see you again. Do you two have plans for the weekend?" Jane asked.

Ryan wrapped his arm around me and pulled me in close. "We haven't really decided yet," Ryan responded for me.

"Do I get to drive to your house?" James asked excitedly.

"Of course. It'll get in a good hour of the time you need."

"Just don't-" Ryan started, but Calvin cut him off with a raised hand.

"I know."

I wasn't sure what he was referring to, but Ryan nodded and a few minutes later, they were out the door. That whole thing felt strange to me. Things were so different when James was hanging out with Ryan, but this morning, things felt strained.

"Is everything okay?" I asked him.

"Sure. Why?"

"It's just, it feels like maybe there was some tension this morning. Was that because I'm here?"

Ryan shook his head and ran his fingers through his black hair. "It doesn't have anything to do with you. It's been like this for a while now. Every time he goes off to his grandparents' house, things get weird."

"You don't want him to go?"

"I do," he said quietly. "That's the problem. I love that kid more than life itself, but...sometimes it's just overwhelming and I need a break."

"That's understandable. You're basically a single parent."

He snorted. "Cassie did it for years by herself."

"Yeah, but you didn't have James from the start. She did. They formed a different bond. You have to cut yourself some slack."

"I just feel like I'm fucking everything up. I don't know that he wants to be going over there all the time, but I don't want to stop him from going either. He's their only connection to Cassie, but I think he resents me for sending him there so often."

"Have you tried talking to him about it?"

He shook his head. "You know, I used to be really good at talking to him about shit, but the more time that goes on, the worse I get at it."

I felt bad for him, but I didn't have any advice to give. The closest I came to having a kid was watching Cap's kid occasionally, and even that gave me hives.

"I think I'm going to head home," I said, leaving my coffee mug by the sink.

"You don't have to leave."

"I'm just gonna get some more sleep. Even after the best night of sleep of my life, I feel like I could finally sleep all day."

He walked up to me and wrapped his hands around my waist. "Stay. You can sleep here."

"Are you sure?"

He kissed me hard, his hand slipping up to the nape of my neck and winding through my hair. "I'm sure I don't want you to leave yet."

I nodded and let him lead me back to his room where we did not sleep for the next two hours.

"Would you just shut up, woman?" I turned to see Ice walking into the bar, followed by a very testy looking Lindsey. Ryan and I had come to the bar for dinner after spending the whole day lounging in his bed. I was in the mood for some good food and I didn't want to cook anything. Neither did Ryan and that's how we ended up here.

"Seriously, would it kill you clean up your shit?" Lindsey snapped at Ice.

"It's my damn house. I can leave it as dirty as I want," he snapped. He saw Ryan and I and immediately walked over to our table, slumping down on a stool. "That woman is driving me fucking nuts."

"Yeah, well that makes two of us," she snarked back.

"In Lindsey's defense," I said. Ice shot me a glare. "You did invite her to stay with you."

"I didn't invite her to come boss me around. The damn woman doesn't shut up."

"Look, I ran a B&B. It always had to look nice. Now I'm staying with you and you just throw shit anywhere. You live like a pig. I can't take it!"

"Then go stay somewhere else," Ice growled.

"I would, but someone came and destroyed my place, or have you forgotten already?" She huffed in irritation and sank down on the other bar stool. "I can't wait for the insurance money to pay out."

"When will that be exactly?" Ice said.

"I don't know. Would you like the number for my insurance agent?" she said sweetly. "Maybe you can explain to them why they should cover the damages when my house was used as a test subject for the fire department when it was a business that wasn't doing so well in a small town. They tend to look at the owner when arson is involved."

"Still bickering, huh?" Sinner said as he walked up to the table. He was followed by Burg and his girlfriend, Meghan.

"I need a fucking bullet to the head," Ice mumbled.

"Not as much as I want to put one there," Lindsey retorted.

"Damn," Sinner grinned. "If you're not fucking her, you should be. Hate sex is definitely worth it."

Ice glared at Lindsey, who glared right back.

"Am I missing something here?" Meghan asked.

"This is Lindsey. We picked her up while you were out of town. Her house had an...accident," Burg said.

"Accident?" Lindsey snorted and shook her head. "If that was an accident then I'm Chewbacca."

"Who's Chewbacca?" Meghan asked.

"Star Wars?" Burg said, pulling Meghan into him.

"Sorry, I never got into that movie."

"How could you not watch that? It's a classic," Burg said, mystified that Meghan hadn't watched that.

"It's just not my kind of movie."

"God forbid a woman not have the same taste in movies as a man." Lindsey held her hand to her chest as if she was horrified. "You know, I can't watch a movie at John's house unless it has something to do with explosions, war, or trashy women. I miss being in my own house where I could watch what I wanted when I wanted."

"Believe me, I want that too," Ice grumbled.

"Well, I would be there if it wasn't for you. This is all your fault."

Meghan stretched an arm across the table, breaking up the tension with a forced smile. "I'm Meghan, by the way. I'm guessing you didn't come here willingly?"

"Not at all. But I didn't have a choice when this one," she jerked her thumb at Ice, "dragged me out of my business unconscious."

"I should have left you there. I wouldn't have so many fucking headaches."

"Are they always like this?" Ryan asked.

"Yeah, this is pretty normal," I answered.

"Why were you unconscious?" Meghan asked.

"Oh, it wasn't as bad as it sounds," Ice rolled his eyes. "She saw a little blood and she passed out."

"A little blood?" Lindsey shrieked. "There were two men bleeding out on the floor of my business."

"Hey, I told you to leave." Ice pointed a finger at Lindsey and she knocked it away.

"Guys!" I finally shouted above them. "Not that this isn't entertaining, but Ryan and I are here to hang out together."

"Yeah, that's why we came over," Sinner said. "We saw you and decided to come hang out."

"No, we want to hang out alone," I stressed.

"But...we always hang out together," Sinner said in confusion.

"What Lola's trying to say," Ryan interjected, "is that we're on a date. Sort of."

"Sort of?" Burg asked.

"How do you 'sort of' have a date?" Meghan asked.

"Well, we didn't exactly define it," I said.

"Like, he didn't ask you out on a date?" Lindsey asked. "Not that I'm judging." She raised her hands and stiffened. "I don't know you guys and I don't mean to interfere, but usually you know when it's a date."

"Not always," Meghan muttered. "There are coffee dates and there are real dates. Whoever invented the coffee date is an idiot. It's just a way for a guy to take you out for less money and get to know you before actually spending money on you."

"It goes both ways," Ryan said. "What if you went out with a guy that was a complete idiot? The date is going bad and you can't get away because you're required by social niceties to sit down and finish the meal. Bet you'd be wanting a coffee date then."

"When was the last time you had a coffee date?" I laughed.

"It's been a few years, but I remember taking advantage of it when I was on the fence about a woman."

"You never took me on a coffee date," I said smugly.

"As I recall, we didn't exactly do the whole dating thing

first." His eyes heated and trailed down my body until he hit the table, but I could tell he was thinking of some of our more fun times getting to know each other.

"Maybe that's what you two need," Sinner grinned at Ice. "You need to take her out on a date."

"And why would I do that? I already know that she's a pain in my ass."

"Just look at Hunter and Lucy," Sinner said. "They couldn't stand each other unless they were fucking."

"What's your point?" Ice sneered.

"My point is that maybe you two need to fuck it out."

"Wow, that's so romantic," Lindsey said, placing her hand on her chest and looking at Ice dreamily. "I've always wanted a guy to *not* date me, but fuck it out of me."

"What exactly is he trying to fuck out of you?" Meghan asked.

"I don't know. Anger? Like I would actually suddenly like him if he was good in bed, which I'm not so sure he would be. He's probably selfish."

"If you had me inside you, there wouldn't be any question in your mind if I was good or not," Ice said confidently.

"You're right. I can tell from looking at you that I should definitely walk away before I get involved in that train wreck."

Ice's eyes turned lethal and Lindsey looked smug.

"Again, not that we don't find all this fascinating," I interjected. "But-"

"Shit." Sinner picked up his phone, worrying his lip.

"What's wrong?" I asked.

"It's Cara. She hasn't been feeling well."

"Did she get the flu or something?" Meghan asked.

"No," Sinner grinned, but it faded quickly. "Oh, God." Sinner slumped against the table. "She's pregnant."

Burg slapped Sinner on the back, jolting him forward. "That's great, man. Congratulations."

"Dude, you are so fucked," Ice shook his head.

"Nice," Lindsey sneered at him.

"You don't look so good, Sinner. You doing okay there?" I smirked.

"She's...and we're...I think I might be sick."

"Is that the reaction you had when you found out you were going to be a dad?" I asked Ryan.

"No, not at all. I called James by the wrong name for the first night and then told him to go grab some beer."

"You did not," I said in shock.

He nodded and smiled. "Pretty much. I was freaking out just a little."

"What am I gonna do?" Sinner groaned as he thumped his head on the table. "This is so bad. I'm not ready to be a father. I don't know nothin' 'bout birthin' no babies."

"What?" Burg asked, obviously confused by Sinner's sudden womanly southern accent.

"Cara made me watch *Gone With The Wind* last night. Shit," he said in sudden realization. "Do you think she was trying to tell me last night?"

"That's the way I would do it, because men are so good at subtle hints," I rolled my eyes.

"You have to go back with me." Sinner grabbed my hand tightly and pleaded.

"Why would I go back with you."

"Because you're a woman."

"Keen observation. What's your point?"

"You have the same parts."

"Again, very studious of you."

"Come on. Can't you talk to her? You know, woman to woman."

"Maybe if I had a child or a single maternal bone in my body. I'm more likely to tell her *congratulations, you fucked up your life.*"

"Yes! Good. That'd be perfect." Sinner sighed in relief.

"I was joking. Your wife is pregnant. Be happy. There's gonna be a little Sinner running around causing trouble. Hey, maybe it'll be a boy and he'll marry Caitlin. Then you'll be permanently fixed to Cap for the rest of your life," I grinned.

"No," he shook his head. "It'll be a girl."

"Yeah, that's worse," Ryan said. "Believe me, I've had the sex talk with James and that was awkward enough. I don't think I'd want to have it with a girl."

"I'm so fucked," Sinner groaned. "This can't be happening." He perked up suddenly and looked at Meghan. "You have a kid."

"Yes, I do."

Sinner pulled his phone back out and looked at it. "Shit. She's still waiting for me to say something."

"You haven't said anything yet?" Burg said in shock.

"Well, I didn't want to say the wrong thing."

"I'm pretty sure not saying anything is just as bad as saying the wrong thing," Ryan laughed.

"Meghan," Sinner pleaded. "Please, come home with me. You have a child. You can explain things to her."

"Explain what? She's already pregnant. She knows what happened," Meghan said slowly.

"You know, that we'll get through this. Together," Sinner implored.

"You make it sound like she was diagnosed with a terminal illness," Ryan laughed.

"This is the rest of my life. Isn't that terminal?"

"Look, it's really not that bad. Once you figure out that the baby doesn't know any more shit than you do, it's not so intimidating. You're lucky. I got one that could already talk back."

"How do you know so much about babies?" I asked.

He shrugged. "Most of my friends have kids. I was there for all of them. Not that I had to do the day to day stuff, but I had to hold a screaming child a few times."

"So you can help!" Sinner said in earnest.

"No," Ryan smiled. "First, I don't know Cara. I've met her before, but I don't know her well enough to give her baby advice, even if I did have experience with one."

"Why don't you talk to Lillian? You know, Cara's sister-in-law?" I suggested.

"Yes, that's good! Lillian is great with babies," Sinner said as he snapped his fingers. "You're a genius." He leaned forward and gave me a hard kiss on the lips that I immediately pulled back from. "Shit. Sorry about that. Guess I got a little excited. Please don't tell Cara."

"Believe me, I wouldn't tell anyone about this if they swore they saw it on video."

"Alright, I gotta go pick up a woman to deal with my woman so that I don't become a woman." He paused and thought about that, then shook his head and left.

As we left the bar, I felt a little uncomfortable with what we had talked about earlier with Sinner and felt that I needed to clarify some things with Ryan. I just didn't know how to bring it up. It was awkward, especially considering that we had started out just fucking. This was never supposed to be more, but it somehow turned into something much more serious than that. If things kept moving forward, it was better if we had this conversation before we were both too invested.

"So..."

"Yeah," he huffed out a laugh.

"About earlier,"

"The baby stuff?"

"Yeah," I said slowly.

"You don't want kids," he said matter of factly.

"Not really. What about you?"

We got to his truck and he pushed me up against the door, caging my body in with his. "I always wanted a family. I have James and if there were more, I'd be over the fucking moon, but James is enough."

"Are you sure? Because I don't know what's happening between us and I don't want to get too far ahead of ourselves."

"Is that what we're doing?" he whispered, running his fingertips along my neck.

"I don't know," I said breathlessly. "I know that I really like you and I like spending time with your son, but I don't know that I want any kids of my own."

He stared into my eyes, looking for something. I couldn't help but stare back at him, wondering what he was thinking, wishing he would just say it and put me out of my misery. "After Cassie died, I was pretty sure that I would never want any kind of relationship ever again. Now that I've got you, it's changed my life and I don't want to fuck that up. So, if you're wondering if we should break things off now, I say fuck it. Because life's too short. I'm okay with not having any more kids. And if we stay together and you change your mind, then we'll talk about it. I'd rather have you right now than worry about reproducing."

I swallowed hard and breathed in his intoxicating scent. It was enough to make my mind blank and my knees go weak. "That's a good plan."

When he kissed me, it was hard and intruding. An acceptance that we were going to do this and there was no going back now. Everything that I was, I was giving to him and I would take all his memories and pain along with him because that's who he was. Every ounce of me was wrapped up in him and it would be forever because I had just given this man more than I thought I ever could. I had given him my heart.

Chapter Twelve

RYAN

"Can we get started?" I asked impatiently.

"Got a hot date with Lola?" Logan asked.

"No, James is going to be home in a few hours. I would really hate to tell his grandparents that I was late because I was practicing a stripper routine."

We were at the Reed Security training center. Sebastian had suggested we meet there to go over our routine because nobody would be in.

"Before we get started, I have a little part of our costumes. I ordered them online and they came yesterday," Logan said excitedly, walking over to a box and bringing it over. He opened the box and we all shook our heads.

"No. There's no fucking way I'm wearing that," Drew said.

I picked one up out of the box and cringed. They were red boxer briefs with a yellow fire hose coming out of the front. It was at least sixteen inches long. "How the hell are we supposed to dance with this sticking out the front?"

"You guys, we're supposed to be strippers. Come on," Logan said. "Have some fun."

"I'm not wearing that. I'd rather wear a thong than that." Cole tossed it back in the box and glared at Logan.

"Seriously? None of you think this is awesome?"

"That's fucked up, is what it is," Drew pointed at the offending underwear.

Logan frowned and closed up the box. "Man, I really thought this would be awesome. Seductive."

"That's about as seductive as wearing granny panties on the stage," Jack said.

"Alright, alright. Let's get going on this," Sebastian said. "It's bad enough that we have to do this in the first place, let alone get together and practice."

The music started and we all walked out in a line, just like they did in the movies. Logan was the only one that was really getting into it. He was thrusting his hips and shaking his ass while the rest of us were just going through the motions.

We came to the part where we were supposed to slowly pull off the suspenders from the turnout gear, but it was hard to imagine what it was like without the actual costume.

"This is stupid. How are we supposed to practice when we don't have the actual costumes?" Sean asked.

"At the price of the rentals, you can use your imagination," Cole said.

"Drew, you're not even fucking trying," Logan groaned. "You have to roll your hips more."

"I am fucking rolling my hips," Drew snapped.

"No, look." Logan walked over to Drew, standing behind him and placed his hands on his hips, lining up the front of his body with the back of Drew's. "Just follow the roll of my hips." Logan started moving his hips, grinding his body against Drew's. Drew stood stock still, his nostrils flaring in anger.

"If you don't remove your cock from my ass, I'm gonna fucking make sure Cece will never have sex with you again."

Logan backed up, hands in the air. "Geez. Everyone's so touchy around here. It's not like I was trying to cop a feel or anything. I just want you to loosen up and flow with the music."

"I can guarantee-damn-tee that I won't be loosening up if you press your cock against my ass," Drew growled.

"Let's take it from the top," Jack said. "I'd like this day to be over as quickly as possible."

The music played and we went through the routine again, still just as stale as the last time. "Guys, I hate to agree with Logan, but the girls are going to think we look like idiots if we do this," I sighed.

"Who gives a shit?" Drew asked. "I didn't want to do this anyway."

"He only cares because he wants to impress Lola," Sebastian smirked.

"I'm with Logan," Cole admitted. "We look like shit right

now. Look, we're all a bunch of good looking guys. We all take care of our bodies. What does it say if we're up on stage and we can't even impress our women?"

"Do you need to impress Alex?" Sean grinned. "Things not going so well in the bedroom?"

"Unlike you guys, I don't have any kids, so my sex life is phenomenal. But I bet things are getting a little stale at home with you guys. Maybe this would help."

The guys all looked at each other and then at me. "What? Don't look at me. I just started seeing Lola. We don't have a problem with anything being stale."

"Fine, if we're going to do this right, then we need some help." Sebastian pulled out his phone and closed his eyes, muttering, "I'm going to regret this," as he pressed send and barked out some orders. He turned back to us and nodded, like he had just taken care of everything.

"What?" Jack asked. "Why did he nod? Are we getting replacements or something? Cause I could definitely go for that."

"This is not how I thought you were going to help," I said to Gabe as we stood outside a male strip joint.

"It's not that bad. Come on. It'll give you inspiration." Gabe patted me on the shoulder as he walked past and held the door open for us. I looked back at the others and slowly made my way inside. It was like any other strip joint, except there were men on stage. And they were standing in their underwear. Totally not what I wanted to see.

"I think I've seen enough," I nodded and turned for the door. Logan grabbed onto my arm and pulled me over to a booth right in the front of the fucking stage.

"If we're going to figure out what the hell we're doing, we're going to have to get up close and personal."

"I don't want to be up close and personal. I'm a guy. I already know what his package looks like," I muttered.

"If you guys want my help, this is what you need to do. You have to see them move so that you know what to do," Gabe said.

"How do you know so much about this?" Cole asked.

"After I got out of the military, I worked in a strip club for a short time." Gabe shrugged like it was no big deal. "I needed a job and it paid good money."

"You...you did this?" Drew asked in disbelief.

"Yeah. It's not all that bad. Girls shove money in your underwear-"

"What underwear?" Drew asked. "That dude doesn't have anything but a scrap of fabric over his junk."

"It's not the skimpiest thing I've seen," Gabe grinned.

"That's not-what the hell did you get us into?" Drew asked Sebastian. "You just had to make a bet against Lola."

"Hey, Gabriel." A man in boxer briefs and a bow tie walked up to Gabe, giving him a hug and winked at the rest of us.

"Brandon, you're looking good, man. Are we going to see your new routine today?"

"Yep. It's all ready to go, but I could use some volunteers to help out." Brandon looked at us expectantly.

"Help out with what?" Jack asked.

"My routine. Isn't that why you guys came? To learn?" Brandon smiled.

"Wait. You want us to go up there?" Drew asked incredulously. "On the stage? In front of these people?"

"Yeah. How else are you going to get in the mood?"

"But we don't have costumes or anything," Logan said.

"You won't need any," Brandon grinned.

"You know, I think we're just going to watch for now," I said, clearing my throat uncomfortably. Even the thought of watching other men strip wasn't something I wanted to do, but I would take that over getting up on stage any day.

We all sat down and waited for the show to start. First out was a man dancing in ripped jeans and a white suit coat. There was an upbeat song pulsing through the club.

"What is this music?" Logan asked. "It sounds more like he's going to put on a dance routine than actually strip."

The man's hips were pulsing to the music and I couldn't help but admire how the man moved. "You know, he's really not that bad. Do you see that hip action?"

The man tore off his jacket and did some crazy thing with his abs. "Damn, that's pretty fucking sexy. I need to learn that," Jack said.

The man started unbuttoning his jeans and slowly yanked the zipper down. "This is weird, right?" Sebastian said. "Are we really going to sit here while some dude takes off his-whoa." Sebastian's eyes flew up as the man stood in front of us, his package on full display. "I was not expecting that. He's fucking huge. How is he dancing in front of all of us with his dick swinging around like that?"

"Penis pump," Drew said as he studied the man.

"Nah," Cole said. "That shit doesn't actually work. It's gotta be Viagra or something."

"I think you're looking a little too closely," I muttered in his ear.

"Have a lot of experience with penis pumps?" Jack asked Cole.

"I've tried a few. Tested the results. They don't really work," he shrugged.

"Did you write customer service and tell them you weren't satisfied?" Sebastian joked.

"Believe me, she was more than satisfied and it had nothing to do with the pump."

"Do you see the way he's moving?" I looked over to see Sean completely mesmerized. "Do you think he fucks like that too?"

What the hell was going on with all of them? They were all watching the man like he had some kind of spell over them. "Guys, stop staring at the man's dick."

"He's got a nice wax job," Logan said in appreciation. "Maybe I should talk to him after the show. See where he goes."

"Yeah, and then afterwards you could ask for a private show," Sean suggested.

"You know, that's not a bad idea," Logan said, snapping his fingers. "I bet he could really show us-"

"Dude, I was fucking joking," Sean shook his head.

The song came to a close and Brandon came on stage in his boxer briefs and tie. With the light shining on him, the briefs were completely see through. "You know, I think I've seen enough." I stood, ready to leave, but Brandon pointed at me and suddenly a light was shining on me. I shook my head rapidly from side to side. This was not happening.

"We have some special guests tonight that need some help with some moves," Brandon said into the microphone. "They have a little act to put on for their ladies and they need some pointers. How about we get them all up on stage? What do you think?"

Cheers erupted from the crowd and pretty soon, we were all being shuffled onto the stage. With the bright lights, we couldn't really make out anyone in the crowd, which I guess was a blessing.

Nelly's "Hot in Here" blared through the speakers and I tried to jump off the stage, but Brandon grabbed onto my arm and waved a female stripper over. She started running her hands over my body, sliding them up under my shirt. I looked up at the ceiling, really fucking uncomfortable with all this. It just felt wrong. I was with Lola and now I had a half naked woman dancing in front of me and rubbing her body against mine.

"Come on, sugar. Start moving. Move those sexy hips."

I looked at the other guys for help, but they just shrugged.

Her hands landed on my hips and I figured, what the hell? I was here. I might as well learn something. I let her guide me and show me how to move and then after a minute, she moved onto Jack. A few other women stepped up and started dancing with us on the stage, slowly peeling our clothes off. Even though it was uncomfortable to be undressed by another woman, I went with it because I wanted to be able to put on a good show for Lola.

The other guys looked just as uncomfortable, but by the time we were dancing in our underwear, we were all learning to let loose and go with it. That is, until the music stopped and the whole crowd started cheering us on. That's when I looked up and saw all of my friends' wives and my sort of girlfriend standing in front of the stage watching us.

"Oh shit," Drew grumbled.

I quickly picked up my discarded pants and shirt and held them in front of my groin. Like that would somehow protect me from the wrath I was about to face. Jack was quickly stepping into his pants, a little more terrified of Harper and with good reason. She could lose her temper in a flash.

"Pretty girl, this is not what it looks like," Jack swore. One of the strippers walked past him and ran a finger down his naked pecs.

"Come again, Sugar." She grabbed onto his ass and squeezed, then did some kind of cat growl.

Harper crossed her arms over her chest and glared at Jack. It finally hit me to put my clothes back on when Lola quirked an eyebrow at me.

"Really, Jack? Because it looks like you were letting another woman strip you in front of a room full of people while she had her paws all over you."

Jack shifted his head back and forth, weighing his answer. "Okay, it's exactly the way it looks. But it was for a good reason."

"Dude, just stop talking," Sebastian muttered.

"I was trying to impress you," Jack said quickly.

"With another woman?"

"Yes! I mean, no. Well, sort of. Shit. This is all coming out wrong."

"Look," Logan stepped forward, still in his boxers. "I'm gonna lay it out for you ladies so there's no confusion. We didn't know how to strip and we wanted to impress you. So, we came here, watched some men dance around naked. Got some tips on what looked good for waxing options. Then, we came up here, had some women undress us and put their hands on us, so that we could learn how to dance. It's that simple."

"You asshole," Sean muttered. "That was not helpful."

"And it made us sound fucking gay," I said, elbowing him in the side.

The girls didn't look impressed with Logan's answer and it didn't help that the strippers kept walking up to us, touching us. The only one that didn't seem bothered by it was Lola. She just seemed to find it funny. When we finally got our shit together, we jumped off the stage and the guys left with their angry wives. I ran a hand along the back of my neck and I walked out with Lola.

"It really wasn't what it looked like."

"I know," Lola grinned.

"Thank God. I didn't want to have to try to explain that any more."

"You don't have to explain at all. So you like watching male strippers. Who doesn't? I mean, we all have our proclivities. Who am I to judge?"

I stopped her with a hand on her arm. "Whoa. I never said I liked watching male strippers. I'm not into that shit. It was all about research."

"Sure," she grinned. "I totally believe you."

"I'm serious, Lola. I'm not fucking gay and I don't take pleasure in watching other guys strip."

She set a placating hand on my arm. "Ryan, don't get so worked up. I believe you," she said sincerely, but then she giggled.

"You do not. You're just saying that. You think I liked that."

She chuckled and covered her mouth with her hand. "I swear," she said around a laugh. "I completely believe you."

"Why does everyone always think I'm gay? Is it the way I dress?"

We started walking to my truck and she looked me up and down. "I think you dress plenty masculine."

"Good. Because I am fucking masculine. I work construction. I grunt when I'm working. I know how to use a hammer and saw with the best of them."

"Right, and only straight men do that stuff."

"That's not what I'm saying."

"So, what are you saying?" She cocked her head to the side and bit her lip as she assessed me.

"I'm saying that I'm not gay! I don't know what it is about me that people always assume that I'm batting for the other team."

"Hmm. I see what you're saying. Maybe you're trying too hard. Maybe people assume that because of your haircut, you're trying to look more masculine."

"What's wrong with my haircut?"

"Well, it's got this handsome, charming...length to it. Some would say a style. But then you dress in jeans and t-shirts. Business suits at work. It could be perceived as..."

"As what?"

"Well, being a closet gay. You're kind of metro-sexual."

"Metro-what? What are you talking about? I'm only man-sexual." She grinned and I realized how bad that sounded. "Not man, like I like men. Man-sexual meaning I am like other men. I like women. Just basic man."

"Basic man," she nodded her head. I ran my hand through my hair in frustration and she laughed when it got all messed up.

"Shit, is it really too long? Does it look too styled? I mean, I just always wore it longer because I didn't think I would look good with shorter hair."

"Your hairstyle is fine, sweetie."

"Sweetie?"

"Too much?" she winced.

"Crap." I grabbed onto her hand and dragged her to my truck.

"Where are we going?"

"To chop off all my hair. I can't be walking around looking like some douchebag. Why the fuck didn't anyone tell me sooner?"

"Ryan, it's really not that bad."

"Sure, that's why you assumed that I'm metro-sexual, whatever the fuck that even means."

"It just means that you really care about your appearance. You know, manscaping and stuff."

I threw the truck in drive, determined to find someplace that was open that could chop off all my hair. I'd have a fucking buzz cut if it meant that people stopped looking at me like I was gay.

"Ryan, you can just go home. Seriously, no one thinks you're gay."

"Everyone thinks I am. Harper said it herself a few years back. I just really thought she was fucking with me."

"She was."

"No, she wasn't. Not if other people are saying it too."

"I'm saying it because I'm fucking with you. Harper told me about that conversation."

I pulled the truck over into a parking lot and threw the truck in park. "Explain."

"Okay, Gabe called Maggie and told her that he was taking you all to a strip club for lessons. He didn't want the women finding out some other way and then assuming the worst. Maggie got it in her head that we should all go fuck with you. When we got there and saw you guys watching the male strippers, Harper cracked a joke about how she knew you were gay all along. She told me the story and we all decide to fuck with you guys. Make you think that we were mad. Since we...I don't know what we are. I didn't want to go that route. So, I decided to fuck with you this way."

I stared at her for a minute, unsure what to say about that. Leave it to Maggie to come up with something like that.

"So, you don't think I'm gay?"

"Ryan, I know you're not gay and I don't think you look metro-sexual. Your hair isn't too long and you don't dress any way but masculine."

"You're sure?"

"I swear."

I pulled her across the seat, into my lap and shoved my tongue into her mouth as I kissed her. My hands found her ass and gripped at the tight flesh that had me hardening quickly. I had to get out of this parking lot before I fucked her on the side of the road.

"For the record, you and I are together. Just thought I'd clarify that."

"Fuck, I can't believe we're doing this," I said as we stood backstage at the venue Maggie had rented out for the night specifically for this show. I was sweating already in my fireman's uniform and I wasn't sure that it was from the heat of the costume. I was pretty sure I was really fucking close to having a panic attack.

"Relax, man. We got this," Cole said reassuringly.

"Look on the bright side, it's just our wives out there," Sean said.

"Right," I nodded. "Just all of my friend's wives that are going to be watching me strip and see me completely naked. No pressure there."

"It could be worse," Jack said.

"How's that?" I asked, curious as to what his answer could possibly be.

"There could be a whole room full of women out there," he shrugged.

"That doesn't really make me feel any better," I muttered. The sirens at the beginning of *Fire* by The Ohio Players started. Screams filled the air and we all looked at one another. "That's not just seven women," I swallowed hard. The curtains pulled open and revealed a whole auditorium full of women that had their hands in the air and were screaming their heads off.

"Oh, fuck," Sebastian said.

"Let's do this," Logan grinned, taking his first step on the stage, forcing us all to follow in his path. We started moving our hips from side to side once we were all lined up, thrusting our hips with each beat. Logan stepped forward, ripping open his fireman coat and shrugging off one shoulder as he leaned back and thrust his hips up toward the crowd. Each of us followed, doing similar moves. Sebastian was last and he stayed at the back of the stage, ripping his coat open and yanking it off as he rolled his hips and then tossed his coat into the crowd.

My coat slid down my arms and when it hit my fingers, I tossed it at Lola with a wink, feeling a little more confident than I really was. Sean jumped to the front of the stage, landing on his knees, leaning back and pulsing his cock up and down. The ladies were all clawing to get to the front of the stage to run their fingers down his abs. Drew and Jack stood behind Sean, pulling at their suspenders, yanking them slowly away from their bodies until they hung down by their pants. Logan, Cole, Sebastian, and I walked forward, with each step yanking at our own suspenders.

When we were all in a line, Sean stood and started flexing his abs, rocking his body to the beat of the music. The rest of us were grinding to the sexy beat, sweat dripping down us from the heat of the lights. My hands went to the sides of my pants and I ripped, tearing the pants from my body and flinging them out to Lola, who was screaming at me. Fuck, that look in her eyes was sexy.

I shook my hips, standing just in my black boxers, my cock growing hard as she watched me dance for her. I ignored the rest of the audience and locked my gaze on hers. I had to if I was going to have the nerve to do this. We turned our backs to the audience one at a time and tore our boxers from our bodies. Raising them over our heads, we swung them around as we wiggled our asses for the ladies. This was it.

Turning on my heel, I tossed my underwear into the audience and cringed at the deafening roar as we all stood stark naked in front of them. Then we pulled off our helmets and slowly lowered them down our chests until they were covering us. With one last pop of my hips, I lifted the helmet for one last peek and then lowered it again as we headed for the back of the stage and left the crowd with one last peek at our asses.

I was shaking like crazy from the adrenaline by the time we got off stage. We each grabbed our spare boxers and quickly got dressed in the clothes we had set aside backstage. The ladies were still screaming loudly and we all just kind of looked at each other and laughed.

"Shit," Drew laughed. "I can't believe we just did that."

"Where did all those women come from?" Sean asked. "I thought this was going to be a private performance."

"I guess Maggie had something else in mind," Sebastian grinned. "I'll get her back."

"What the fuck are we supposed to do now," Jack asked. "I mean, you don't think they're going to mob us, do you?"

"You weren't that good, man."

We all turned to see Gabe standing behind us, along with the rest of Reed Security. Sebastian swore next to me and the guys started laughing. "What? I wasn't gonna miss the show."

"And you had to bring along everyone else?" Sebastian asked.

"Well, shit, Cap, they just kind of followed me here. I don't know how they found out," he said innocently.

"Right," Sebastian said unbelievably.

"I'm a little disappointed you didn't ask me to join in, Cap." Sinner shook his head and pointed to the crowd. "Cara's out there and if she was going to see anyone's cock, it should have been mine."

"What?" Sean exclaimed. "My sister's out there?" He turned with a pointed finger in Sebastian's face. "This is all your fault. I'm going to be scarred for life."

"*You* are?" Sinner retorted. "She's never going to be able to look at you again without seeing your cock in her face."

Sean groaned and bent over like he was going to throw up. "This is so humiliating."

"It's not that bad," I said. "When you think about the fact that we just went out there and stripped in front of way more people than we thought we were going to, this is just something you're going to laugh about in five years."

"Yeah," Sean shrugged. "In five years, Cara and I will totally be able to just shrug off the fact that she saw my dick. It'll be something we laugh about at Christmas."

"That's the spirit," Logan said, slapping him on the back. Sean glared at him and stomped away.

"If he's pissed now, he's gonna be really pissed when he finds out the whole department was out there to see his show," Gabe laughed.

"So, what did you think of the show?" I asked Lola as we left the venue.

"It was much better than I expected. I really thought you guys were going to freeze up after seeing all the people that showed up."

"You should have seen us backstage. We were all terrified when we heard the screams. Well, everyone but Logan. He seemed a little too excited."

"Maggie is definitely a hell raiser," she grinned. "It was her idea to invite everyone."

"Yeah, I'm not sure that's going to be so good for business," I said, running a hand across the back of my neck. "I don't know that people will want to do business with Sebastian or Logan and I."

"Maggie sold tickets as a fundraiser for a kid in town that's been in the hospital for a few months. The family has been struggling and so she sold the tickets for $100 a piece. She let everyone know that you were all doing it to help raise money."

"Wow, what a little liar," I laughed.

"Yeah, but she raised a lot of money for the kid's family, even if you guys did have a bit of a shock."

"As long as it's in the name of charity."

"So, did you hang on to that fireman costume?" Lola asked.

"No. Logan took them with him to return them. Why?"

"I just...thought we might play out a little fantasy."

"Baby, we don't need costumes for me to give you your fantasies."

I hauled her over my shoulder and raced to the truck, flinging her inside and racing back to my house. My cock was practically bursting at the seams by the time we got home. I had her shoved against the front door, my hand in her pants as I fumbled with the lock. When it finally unlocked, I shoved the door open, making both of us fall onto the floor. I would have tried to care. I probably should have tried to care, but all I could think about was that look on Lola's face when she was watching me strip for her.

I yanked her pants off and ripped her shirt open, staring down at her beautiful breasts as I undid my belt and shoved the jeans down just past my erection. Lining up my cock with her pussy, I slid inside and fucked her right there in the foyer, thrusting hard and groaning when she tightened around me. My knees were starting to kill me, so I picked her up, shucking my pants off my legs and carried her into the kitchen. I set her down on the island and slid back inside her. She laid back across the counter and I almost came when I saw her breasts bouncing with every thrust of my hips.

She spread her legs wider and I reached back into the fridge and pulled out the can of whipped cream.

"What are you doing?"

"Just having a snack." I squirted the whipped cream all over her pussy, watching as her body shuddered from the cold. Slowly, I licked every drop of cream from her until all I could taste were her juices flowing from that sweet cunt. Her swollen pussy throbbed for a release as I spread her lips and dove inside. Nibbling at her clit, I sucked and licked as my fingers slid inside her and fucked her until she screamed and wrapped her legs around my neck, pulling me in closer.

"That was so dirty," she panted as she unwrapped her legs from my neck. "And probably really unsanitary."

"I licked it all from you. Don't worry about that."

"We're not doing that again," she said firmly.

"Why not?"

"Because, if I wanted something spread all over me, it would be your cum. Now fuck me."

I carried her into the bedroom and gently laid her down on the bed. I slid up her body until I was positioned at her entrance and slowly slid inside, watching her eyes grow wide as my girth filled her. "Harder," she begged. But I didn't want it hard and fast. I wanted to savor the feel of her body against mine. I wanted to feel the hot suction of her body against every inch of me. I nipped at her neck, sucking along her collarbone and I thrust hard and slow into her sweet pussy. Her moans were driving me wild, but I stayed the course. Every thrust was deeper inside her until I was sure my balls were going to get sucked into her heat as well. My whole body was shaking with need until I couldn't hold myself up anymore.

I rested on my elbows, our slick chests gliding against one another. I kissed her with all I was, possessing her mouth like it was the very air I breathed. When her legs wrapped around my ass and pulled me in closer, I felt something in my chest tighten painfully, almost as if my heart was telling me to hold on with all I had. I came inside her moments later as she threw her head back against the pillow and moaned out her own release. I placed soft kisses all over her face, shifting my body off hers and pulling her with me until we were laying on our sides and facing each other. My semi-hard cock was still inside her and her legs were still wrapped around me. Her breasts were heaving against my chest, her nipples brushing against me with every breath.

We stayed that way for a long time, just breathing each other in, tangled up in each other's arms. I brushed the hair that had slipped from her ponytail out of her face and tucked it behind her ear. She was absolutely breathtaking. I wanted to tell her how much she meant to me. I wanted to tell her I thought I was falling for her, but I just couldn't bring myself to utter the words yet. It was still too new between us and I needed to be sure. So, instead I held her all night long and dreamed of what it would be like if I had her in my arms every night.

Chapter Thirteen

LOLA

It had been two months of bliss with Ryan, sleeping over at his house many nights and hanging with him and James whenever I got the chance. I was working a lot more now, so my time was limited, but I soaked up every ounce of time I got with both of them.

We were gathered around the conference table, getting our assignment. I was drifting off to thoughts of Ryan and what I planned to do tonight, but that was being put on hold by the job Cap was telling us about.

"This is a pretty simple job. Jeremy Matthews is a lawyer and he needs to cross into Mexico to get some legal documents signed. Apparently, his client is disabled and unable to come to him."

"Why the protection detail?" Derek asked.

"Because the client lives in Juárez."

"Aw, shit," I muttered.

"You want us to go into Cartel country, Cap?" Hunter asked.

"This should be an easy in, easy out. You cross the border in El Paso, get Matthews to his client's house, and then get the hell out. Just keep your eyes open and don't get yourself killed."

We picked up the client and drove down to New Mexico. It would have been faster to fly, but we preferred to have our own supplies with us. The whole thing just felt off the entire drive down. Jeremy was evasive with his answers and jittery the whole time. If I had to guess, I would say the man was leaving out some major details that would put us all in danger.

We made it across into Mexico with little issue thanks to the hidden compartments in our SUV. If it weren't for that, we might not have made it across the border. Jeremy had been giving us directions since we crossed into Mexico. He told us that he was given specific directions to avoid getting caught up in the cartels. That didn't sit right with me.

"Something's not right with this guy," I said to Derek as we got closer to Juárez. "He's been jittery since we picked him up."

"I've noticed. He seems to know a lot about the area and that makes me nervous. If this was just some random client, he wouldn't know so many details."

"Just stop anywhere along here," Jeremy Martin said.

"We're in the middle of fucking nowhere," Hunter snapped.

"Okay, so I may not have been completely honest with you guys," Jeremy said nervously.

"No shit," Derek said calmly.

"My name isn't Jeremy Matthews. It's Charles Martin." He looked at us all nervously, but the guys obviously didn't get it. I did.

"Charles Martin? As in, Carlos Martinez?"

"Shit," Derek swore. "You're the illegitimate son of one of the leaders of the Juárez Cartel. Why the fuck did you bring us down here?"

"My sister is here. I've kept in contact with her through one of the men that knew my mother. He informed me recently that she's been promised to another cartel as a sort of peace offering. The man she's supposed to marry is a monster. I promised her that I would get her out."

"So, you hired us?" Hunter sounded baffled and frankly, Derek and I looked it. "You thought bringing three of us down here was enough to get your sister out of the hands of the cartel? Are you fucking crazy?"

"Look, I know how they work. I can get in, but I need you guys to help me get her out of here."

"Look, even if we could get her out of there, we can't just bring her back through El Paso. She doesn't have the papers she needs to enter the United States."

"We won't be going back that way. We'll have to go through the mountains and into New Mexico. It's dangerous, but it should only take a few days to make the crossing."

"No," Derek said firmly. "We're not doing this. We don't

have enough manpower or weapons for that matter."

"If we don't, she'll be dead in a year."

"Then you should have been fucking honest from the start," Derek snapped.

"Look, she can give you names and inside information to help take down the cartels."

"How do you know that she actually has any useful information?" I asked. "You may keep in contact, but that doesn't mean that you've been able to really talk. That would be too dangerous. If your father found out, he would have you killed."

"I trust her. She isn't lying."

"I'm sorry, but I won't risk my whole team for your sister. If you had been honest from the beginning, we might have been able to come up with a decent plan and a whole group of men to help us, but this is all at the last minute and there's not enough time to pull something together."

"It has to be tonight," he said desperately. "She's staying at my father's house in Juárez, but most of the guards have already headed back to the compound. They're taking her tomorrow morning for the trade. Please," he pleaded. "She's an innocent."

I could see that this man was very serious about needing to get his sister out. It was in his eyes, the pain that he was feeling. I was brought back to being stuck in that house with Alex and what would have happened if we hadn't gotten away. She had done everything possible to fight for us, to save us. But nobody was there to save this woman. Only her brother and we were her only hope of helping him. I thought about Ryan and what he would have done if he could have saved his wife and I just couldn't sit by and do nothing.

"I'm in," I said with a nod. Derek's gaze swiveled to mine and narrowed in on me in anger. "I'm sorry, Derek, but I have to do this."

Hunter sighed, "Me too. I know what it was like with Lucy. I can't just leave her there."

"If we do this, you may not being going home to your families," Derek clarified. Hunter and I nodded. "Then let's get this shit done."

"The only thing we have going for us right now is that there aren't a lot of guards posted," Derek said as we sat in our rundown motel room planning our attack for tonight. "From what I can tell, she's staying in this room over here." Derek pointed to a corner room of the house that Carlos had sketched out for us. "We can extract her through the window, assuming that she doesn't start freaking out when she sees us and alerts the guards that we're here."

"We'll need Carlos to be there, otherwise she won't trust us," I said.

"That's such a bad idea," Hunter grumbled. "But I don't see any way around it."

"Hunter, you'll grab the girl. Lola and I will handle the perimeter. We don't have much on us for an all out war, so let's try to keep this quiet. We'll leave as soon as the sun sets and we'll have to haul ass up into the mountains. We're going to have to watch for drones flying overhead at the border. If we're caught, we're in a shitload of trouble."

"So, don't get caught is what you're saying," Pappy said. "Good advice. I'll keep that in mind."

"I checked the SUV. We only have one pack," I said grimly. "We're going to have to fit whatever supplies we can in there and the rest stays behind."

"I hope Carlos is ready for a few nights of roughing it under the stars. This is gonna be damn uncomfortable," Hunter grumbled.

"It's not like you haven't done it before," I smiled.

"Yeah, but that was in the military. I got this nice, cushy job so that I wouldn't have to sleep outside anymore."

"Cushy is the last word I would use to describe this job," I muttered.

"But you love it," Derek grinned. "We couldn't keep you away if we tried."

"Fine. I love it, but that doesn't mean that I won't miss my bed over the next few days."

"Let's get ready to move out. We have two hours to gather supplies and get loaded up. As soon as lights are out at the house, we move in."

We got to work, Hunter checking weapons, me loading the pack and grabbing necessary supplies. I prayed to God that no one was injured on this trip because we didn't have enough room for all the medical supplies we normally carried.

Sebastian was going to be pissed that we were leaving so much behind.

We left the hotel, all of us a little nervous about this one. This wasn't going to be an easy assignment like we originally thought. If we were lucky enough to get in and out without being seen, we still had to make it to the border without the cartels finding us and then make it across the border safely. Plus, two of the people with us wouldn't have the same stamina and perseverance that the rest of us had.

"So, are we calling Cap or are we waiting until we cross the border?" Hunter asked.

"We wait until absolutely necessary," Derek said as he tightened his grip on the steering wheel.

"So, when we're about to be killed, we'll call in reinforcements." I nodded in agreement and looked out the window. "Sounds about right."

"I don't like it anymore than you, but you know if we call Cap now, he'll give us orders to turn around. When the job is done, we'll give him a call and let him know what's going on. He can't kill us that way," Derek said hopefully.

"He can still kill us. He just can't use the cartels as an excuse," I pointed out.

"Same difference."

Derek parked the SUV a mile from the house and we all got to work wiping down the vehicle. We had to remove anything that would identify the ownership of the vehicle, and that included the VIN. We removed the plates and stuck those in the pack and loaded the rest of the weapons on us.

"Carlos, you stay with Hunter the whole time. You do as he says or you'll get killed, you understand me?"

"Yeah," he nodded quickly, but wasn't really looking at Derek. Derek's hand shot out and gripped him by the jaw.

"Hey, you fucking listen to me. This is serious. If Hunter tells you to run, you run. If he tells you to get down, you drop the second he tells you. If he says that we have to leave your sister behind, you don't go be a cowboy and go off on your own. If you get anyone on my team killed, I'll hand you over to the cartels, so pay attention."

Carlos nodded, looking Derek right in the eyes. When Derek was satisfied, he dropped his hand and motioned us forward. We had a mile trek to the house where we couldn't be spotted. We stayed low and took our time getting there, careful not to draw any attention to ourselves.

We stopped at the perimeter, waiting for the lights to go out. It took about fifteen uncomfortable minutes for the lights to go out. We were in a foreign country where we didn't know the landscape and no solid exit strategy. If we were caught, we would be in a world of shit.

"Alright, Hunter and Carlos, you're up. Lola and I will watch the perimeter." We all moved out, Derek moving to the east side and me to the west. Hunter and Carlos moved around to the back of the house where there were luckily no guards. Hunter and Carlos snuck up to the window, peering into the darkness. After a moment, Hunter tapped on the glass and moved aside for Carlos to speak with his sister. When she opened the window, there was a moment of whispering in which I was fucking antsy for them to just move. We were still good. No guards were coming this way, but that wouldn't last forever.

"Guards are starting rotation," Derek whispered. "Get the fuck out of there."

"I need two minutes," Hunter hissed.

"You have thirty seconds and then we're going to war."

"I need a distraction to get away from the house. The guards are gonna see us if we move," Hunter said.

"I can give you one," I said, looking over at the propane tank for the house. "But it's going to blow this place sky high."

"Lola, we're trying not to be seen," Derek said urgently.

"We won't be if I do this right. But make sure your ass is nowhere near the house. On my mark, you fucking run."

"Copy that," Derek and Hunter confirmed. I moved around the side of the house and across the lawn where I couldn't be seen. From my position, I could make out Hunter, Carlos, and the woman.

"Move, Lola. We're out of time."

"On it." I pulled the grenade and the flash bang from the pack, pulling the pin and tossing it. "Run!" After the grenade landed, I tossed the flash bang. Seconds after the grenade exploded, the flash bang ignited the propane that was spilling out onto the ground. The flames engulfed the house, lighting the sky like the fourth of July. "Damn, I love my work."

"Move, Lola," Derek's voice came over coms. "No time to sit around and watch the show."

Sighing, I threw on my pack and double timed it in the direction the guys had run. They were waiting for me a half mile from the house in the trees. Looking back, I could see that what few guards had survived the explosion were running around the house.

"So much for not making a scene."

"There was no gunfire. I'd say it's a good day," I shrugged, walking off toward the mountains where we would be hiking to get across the border. We were at the base of the mountain when Derek finally called Cap and explained the predicament we had gotten ourselves into. We were going to call and check in when we made it across the border. The fact that I could hear Cap yelling through the phone made me think that Derek had the right idea in waiting.

"Damn, I count at least thirty." I was looking through my binoculars at the group of men at the bottom of the mountain. We had made it a whole day with no issues, but now that we were so close to the border, that was all changing. I handed my binoculars to Carlos, who immediately took them and shook his head.

"That's the Juárez Cartel. They won't be moving out anytime soon. This is their territory."

"Derek, what do you have?" I said into my mic.

"The three of us could make it. There's no way Carlos and Maria could make it. It'd be suicide."

I could tell by Derek's breathing that he was making his way back to us. I was near the pass we were taking with Carlos and Maria while Derek and Hunter looked for a way around.

"I'm heading back to you," Hunter said over coms. "There's no good pass up here. Looks like we only have one option."

"Copy that." While we waited for Derek and Hunter to return, I turned to check on Maria. She looked terrified, but hopeful at the same time.

"Are you doing okay?" She nodded, but didn't say anything else. Carlos went over and started talking to her in Spanish. I could understand what he was saying and since it was just reassurances, I went back to studying the camp.

"What are you thinking?" Hunter asked as he got into position next to me.

"I'm thinking we have three against thirty or so." I shrugged. "Sounds like a fair fight."

"Yeah, but we also have two with us that we have to protect. That makes this dangerous."

"Right, because it wasn't dangerous when we were outnumbered ten to one," Derek said as he approached.

"If two of us slip down there and take out as many as possible quietly, then the third person can be up here with the rifle taking out any strays," I said as I studied their movements.

"And just who were you thinking was going to stay up here?" Hunter asked.

"You or Derek," I said quickly. I wanted in on the action and I wasn't about to stay up here and miss out watching over our clients.

"You're the best sniper," Derek pointed out.

"I'm not a sniper," I said indignantly.

"No, but you're the closest we have. We need you up here, covering our asses."

"But-"

"Lola." Derek gave me the look that told me not to argue with him.

"Fine," I grumbled.

"Wait," Carlos interrupted. "You're going down there?"

"Well, if we're going to get out of this, we've got to take them out," Hunter replied.

"But..." Carlos looked at me and then the guys. "You're just going to leave us up here? With her?"

"I think I'm a little insulted by that," I said.

"You were just alone with her when we went to check other routes. What's the difference now?" Derek asked.

"Well, they're going to catch on that men are dying. Then they'll come for us," Carlos stammered.

"That's why Lola's here. She's going to be watching our backs and yours." Derek stared Carlos down, not wavering.

"But...she's a girl," he whispered, like I couldn't hear him.

Hunter barked out a laugh and Derek shook his head. "See you on the other side," he said as he walked away. I raised an eyebrow in challenge at Carlos, who visibly shrank back.

"You two go hide over in that cluster of trees. Don't come

out unless I tell you to." I turned and started setting up my rifle and pulling out my extra ammunition. I watched through my scope as Hunter and Derek made their way down the mountain to the camp. They moved swiftly, never being seen by anyone. They took out at least ten guys before anyone started to notice that something was wrong. When one man snuck up behind Hunter while he was in hand to hand combat with another man, I took that as my cue to start firing. I pulled the trigger, taking him out just before he could thrust his knife into Hunter's back.

"Guess that we can use our guns now that Lola's firing," Hunter breathed heavily as he slid his knife into one man's gut.

"Leave it to Lola to sound the alarm," Derek said as he pulled out his gun and shot another man in the head.

I lined up another shot and took it. "I suppose I could have let you get that knife in the back, Hunter."

"I would have gotten him," Hunter said as he ducked behind a wall when shots pinged by.

"Lola, they've seen you. They're heading your way," Derek informed me.

"Copy that," I said, but I couldn't see anyone through the scope heading my way. Besides, there were too many men converging on Hunter and Derek and if I took my eyes off the enemy, one of them would end up dead. Derek was hiding behind a vehicle and Hunter was pinned down behind the wall. Neither of them could move because of where the other men were located. Scanning the area, I mapped out a path for firing in my head and started with the first target, shooting him in the chest. I quickly moved on to the next target, but this shot was only debilitating. I wasn't the best long distance shot and I was trying to move quickly.

The next bullet hit on target, but the next one went wide, missing by just a hair. It was enough for the man to have time to move out of the way. I heard the crunch of feet. I knew they were almost here, but Derek still had two men closing in on him. I took the shot, but I wasn't fast enough for the second when I heard the click of the hammer. I slowly pulled my hands back, showing that I didn't have my hands on the trigger anymore.

"Get up," the man shouted at me in Spanish. I slowly got to my feet, keeping my hands at chest level. The man stepped up behind me, gun pointed at my head. I could feel the muzzle just centimeters from my temple. He started shouting at me in Spanish, but I was too focused on the knife that was hidden in my tactical vest. He was standing just slightly to my right, giving me a good view of his leg. I looked back up one more time to see Carlos and Maria peering out from the trees that I had told them to hide in. I could tell they were scared, but for the first time in a long time, I felt a wave of calm wash over me. There were no insecurities or flashbacks, only peace in knowing that I could do this.

I pulled the knife from my vest and lowered my arm slowly, peering back at the man's leg. If I didn't do this right, I would get myself killed. In one swift move, I slashed the knife through the man's inner thigh, slicing his femoral artery. I spun around and saw the shock in his eyes just a second before he passed out on the ground. He would be dead in minutes. The blood spurting from his leg showed that I had hit my mark well.

I laid back down by my rifle and got back to work. Derek and Hunter had managed to take most of the rest of them out, but there were still a few left for me.

When the guys came back up the mountain, they looked exhausted, but we didn't have time to sit around. We couldn't risk taking a break when more of them could be on their way. We quickly gathered up our weapons and headed toward the border that would hopefully be a clear shot from here.

We hiked for another day, just reaching the border at night fall. Carlos was practically pulling Maria along behind him, but she was holding it together. It had been a difficult hike, but we were finally within reach.

Scoping out the area, we didn't see any patrols or any drones, which was why we had come this way. The terrain was rougher and it was less likely for people to cross this way. We made it as far as a few hundred feet across the border when guns were pointed in our faces and we were being shoved to the ground. All of us were placed in handcuffs and our weapons were all taken away. I looked over at Hunter and Derek, who looked equally pissed, but there was nothing we could do about it at the moment. We just had to pray that we could get ahold of Sebastian and have him get us out of this mess.

Chapter Fourteen

RYAN

Sebastian had been pacing around the bar for the last fifteen minutes, staring at his phone repeatedly. Twice, he slipped outside and made a phone call. I figured he was worried about Maggie. He always was lately, so I made my way over to him and sat down at the bar where he was staring at his phone.

"What's up, man? Everything alright with Maggie?"

"What?" he asked distractedly. "Oh, yeah. Everything's fine."

"What's got you so distracted?"

He sighed and ran a hand down his face. "One of my teams was supposed to check in this morning. We've been waiting all day for an update and I haven't heard anything yet."

"So, why don't you head out? It's obviously got you worried."

"I'm going over there now, but Cazzo's handling it. I mean, where they were located, there's not anything I can do without more intel. I have Becky and Rob working on it, so until I hear from them, I can't really do anything."

"Which team was it?" He didn't look at me and he didn't answer. My stomach sank and I looked down at the bar. Shaking my head, I took a sip of my beer. This couldn't be happening. Not again. Not when we were just getting started. Why did this shit always have to happen to me?

"Where is she?"

"I can't tell you that."

"Bullshit," I glared at him. "You need to tell me right the fuck now."

"Why? It's not going to help anything. It's not like you can run off to save her."

"Then why the hell aren't you?" I asked.

"Because, if I take off down there and they're trying to stay low, I could get them killed. That's why I said I needed intel first."

I pushed back from the bar and walked to the door. I didn't know what the hell I was going to do, but I couldn't just sit here and wait to hear if Lola was dead or alive.

"Ryan! Wait."

I spun around and got in his face. "Why? Why did you fucking do this to me?"

"What are you talking about?"

"You sent her away. Why would you do that? If you knew

it was that dangerous, why did you have to send her?" I shouted.

"This wasn't supposed to be dangerous," he shouted back. "And I don't choose teams based on the danger level. All of my teams are highly trained to handle any situation."

"But it was Lola. Why? Why did you have to send her?" I shouted. "I can't lose another person. Not like this."

He rested his hand on my shoulder and I dropped my head to keep from crying like a fucking baby. Which I would if I kept looking at his sorry expression.

"I have to go pick up James from his friend's house. Call me when you know something."

He nodded and I headed for my truck. I wished that I could get tanked right now. More than anything, I wanted to lose myself in a bottle until this was all over. Damn her for going off and doing something like this. James was really starting to connect to her. I wasn't sure that either of us could handle losing her right now.

When I texted James and told him I was picking him up, he started texting me immediately, asking why he had to leave early. I didn't know what the hell to tell him. I didn't want to make him worry, but I didn't know if I could hide it from him either. When he got in the truck, he slammed the door and glared at me. I didn't care. I took off for home and ignored his eyes boring into me the whole way.

When we walked in the house, James spun around and confronted me. "Why the hell did I have to leave early? I was supposed to be able to stay for three more hours."

"Plans change," I said, walking into the kitchen and pulling out a beer.

"Why does your pissy mood always have to affect my plans? Mom's gone. You have to get past that and stop taking out your anger on me."

"I don't-"

"Yes, you do! Every time you start feeling like shit, you get in a pissy mood and ship me off to Grandma and Grandpa's, or you send me to one of your friend's houses. Like the day we were driving and you forced me to pull over. You think I didn't realize that you didn't want me around because I'm a reminder of Mom?"

I stared at him in shock. I hadn't realized that he had known I was doing that and it obviously had hurt him a lot. What kind of fucking parent was I? "I'm sorry, James. I didn't...I didn't mean to hurt you. I just didn't know how to handle shit and I thought if I could pull myself together, you wouldn't have to see me at my worst."

"What about me? What about when I needed someone? Do you know what it was like for me to see you break down by the truck that day? And then you didn't even talk to me after it happened. I was sent off to Reed Security and then to Logan's house for the night. I'm fucking fifteen years old. I was there when Mom died. I don't need you to protect me from what you're feeling or thinking. I need you to fucking include me so I don't feel like I'm all alone," he shouted.

I sank down on the bar stool and shoved my hands through my hair. I had completely fucked up. And it wasn't just once or twice. It was every single fucking weekend for the past five years. All those times that I needed space, I had been pushing him away. My own kid knew what I was thinking and he just took it instead of calling me on my bullshit.

"I picked you up early because Lola's team has gone missing," I said quietly. "I didn't know what to do and I wanted to start drinking, so I decided to pick you up instead. But I didn't want to tell you because I didn't want you to freak out like I am."

James pulled a beer out of the fridge and sat down beside me. He normally only got to drink on the anniversary of his mom's death, but I'd allow it tonight. "Do they know for sure that something's wrong?"

"No. They're trying to gain intel now."

"Then, we just have to wait. Lola's an awesome fighter. I'm sure she's fine."

God, I hoped he was right. I didn't want to think about what would happen if she wasn't. "Yeah," I said quietly as I continued to drink my beer.

James and I waited up for hours for anything from Sebastian to indicate what was going on with Lola. By midnight, there was still no word and I had practically worn a hole in the floor from pacing back and forth. I pulled out my phone and dialed Sebastian's number.

"Sebastian, please tell me you have something."

"I'm sorry, but we haven't been able to locate them yet.

But Ryan, you have to remember that they're all trained and there could be a number of reasons they aren't checking in."

"Name a few," I snapped.

"First, they could have had to change routes and don't have a signal. Second, they may have turned off their phones so they couldn't be tracked. Third-"

"What about the one where they're already dead?" I interrupted.

He blew out a breath before speaking again. "Ryan, I wish I had more for you and I swear I'll keep you up to date, but the longer I stay on the phone with you, the less I'm working on getting back to them."

"Fine, just call me back when you know something."

That night was one of the longest in my life. When Cassie died, it was sudden and I knew she was gone. This waiting around to find out was worse. My mind wouldn't shut off and the panic that was building inside was almost more than I could take.

In the morning, I still hadn't heard anything and I didn't have a clue what to do. I couldn't sit around the house all day. I would go crazy. Besides, James was out of school for the summer and I didn't want to worry him with my pacing. I shot off a quick text to Sebastian, asking if he had heard anything yet. When he said no, I knew I had to keep moving with my day. I got ready for work and told James that he wasn't allowed to go anywhere today. He didn't have his license yet and I didn't want him getting in any vehicles with any friends. I may not be able to protect him forever, but for today, I could make sure that he stayed alive.

Walking into the office, I ignored everyone that came my way. I had to focus on one thing at a time or I would lose my shit. First thing to do was check my email, but even that was a shitshow. I could hardly respond without checking my phone to make sure Sebastian hadn't called and I missed it. By the time an hour had passed, I had to get out of there. Staying at work wouldn't do me any good.

I stormed out of my office, just barely avoiding running into my secretary. She looked at me like I was crazy, and maybe I was. I felt like I was about to lose my mind. Logan kept calling my phone, but I didn't bother to answer. Anything he had to say could wait. This was fucking ridiculous. This was the second time that I was losing my shit and walking away from work over a woman. How much more of this could I really take?

My phone rang just before I started to head home, and when I saw it was Sebastian, I practically dropped the phone because I was rushing to answer.

"Sebastian, what's going on? Have you heard from them?"

"We've heard from them. Becky is tracking them now."

"Thank God. They're okay?"

"As far as we know. They had to go offline for safety reasons, but we've talked to Derek briefly and he said that they're coming in now. They should be here by tomorrow."

"What time? I'll be there."

"No," he said firmly. "Just wait until I call you. I need to debrief the team and I can't have you here before then. There's a protocol we follow here."

"You want me to just sit on my fucking hands for another day?"

"Yeah, Ryan. That's what I need you to do," he sighed. I could tell he was fucking exhausted, but I was pissed. I wanted to see her with my own eyes. I needed to hold her and know that she was okay. But Sebastian wouldn't let me in if he was this adamant.

"Fine. Just, text me when she gets there and let me know she's okay."

"I will." He hung up and I felt the pressure that was building inside about to snap. My control was shot and I was two seconds from crying my fucking eyes out. I gripped onto my hair and pulled until the pain was a welcome feeling. I couldn't lose my shit now. I had a son to take care of and Lola was fine. Falling apart right now wouldn't do anything for James and I and it wouldn't change the fact that Lola's job was more than I could take.

I drove home in a daze and when I walked in the door, James could tell that something was going on because he just stared at me, waiting for me to answer. I stared at my feet, trying to figure out what the hell to say other than I was extremely pissed and on the verge of insanity.

"Sebastian said her team checked in," I finally said.

"Good. So, she's okay?"

"As far as he knows. Derek called in and he didn't say anything about anyone being injured."

"That's good," he nodded. I didn't answer. I didn't know what to say or what I was thinking. I just knew that my head was a mess and I needed something to take away the feeling of being strangled from the inside out.

"Well, I'm gonna go read," James said as he walked upstairs. I nodded and went to the fridge for a beer. As I stood there, I became more and more angry, but I wasn't sure what my anger was directed at. I wanted to say it was at Lola for putting me in this position to care about her and then go off and almost get herself killed, but that wasn't fair. This was her job and I had to accept that or move on.

I stared out into the night for a long time until I heard James enter the room behind me. "I'm going to bed now."

"Okay," I said as I stared out the window.

"You know, you could have talked to me about this. I know why you thought you had to protect me, but I'm not a kid anymore. I haven't been for a long time."

He turned and walked out of the room before I could say anything. I rested my forehead against the window and let my eyes slip closed. I had screwed up big time with him. Cassie would be so disappointed in me. She would have wanted me to be the man that I was when she was alive. The man that told our son the truth no matter how difficult it was. And to some extent I had done that, but in many ways, I had shielded him so that he would never be hurt again.

I trudged off to my bedroom and sat on the edge of the bed. I thought about going to sleep, but the longer I sat there, the more that one thing became very clear to me. I wasn't cut out to do this shit again. I needed stability and something that I didn't have to worry about vanishing in the blink of an eye. And while there were no guarantees in life, Lola's job made her life expectancy that much shorter. No matter how much I was falling for her, I just knew in my heart that this wouldn't work out between us.

I opened the door two days later to Lola standing on my steps, grinning like crazy. Normally, a smile like that would brighten my mood and I'd be pulling her into my arms. That wasn't going to happen this morning.

"Hey," she said with a little less confidence when I didn't return her smile.

"Hi. When did you get in?"

"A few hours ago. Sebastian said you were kind of freaking out, so I figured I'd better come over." She looked past me and I motioned for her to come in. "Where's James?"

"Probably still sleeping."

"Look, Sebastian said that you were worried."

"Yeah," I said, scrubbing a hand over my face. "It's been a rough few days."

"Oh, well, it was a little touch and go there for a while, but it all worked out okay. If the client hadn't lied to us-"

"I can't do this," I interrupted. The light in her eyes fell and I hated that I was about to do this to both of us. "I don't see how this is going to work out between us." I ran a hand along the back of my neck and sighed. "I'm sorry, but you love your job and I'm glad it's going well for you, but I have a son to think about."

I shook my head and laughed humorlessly. "No. That's not even it. James would probably be fine, but I wouldn't be. I can't handle the not knowing. It was fine at first because you weren't actually working out of town and then nothing happened on the other jobs, but then this time, when I heard that your team was missing..." I huffed out a laugh and looked away for a second. "I thought you were dead and my first thought was that I didn't know how I was going to survive losing another person."

"Ryan, I'm good at my job. I know what I'm doing and my team always has my back," she said, almost like a plea.

"I know, but that won't stop me from worrying."

"So, what? I'm supposed to have some boring job and work around here so that you always know I'm safe? That didn't do much for your wife." My heart clutched at her words and I swore it stopped beating for a second, but then remorse filled her eyes. "I'm sorry. I didn't mean it to come out like that."

"No, you're right. I know you weren't trying to be hurtful. And Cassie would want me to be happy, but I just can't do it. I can't stay with you and pretend that I'm okay with you putting your life in danger every time you have a job."

"And I can't walk away from my job because you can't handle the pressure."

"I know," I said softly. "And I would never ask you to. I

know that you love your job and I know that working in an office would bore you to death. That's why I didn't even consider asking you. This just wasn't meant to be, Lola. I've had such a great time with you and you've healed me so much. But if I stay with you, I'll break again."

"Okay," she said in quiet resignation as she walked toward me. She placed her hand on my cheek and leaned forward, kissing me softly on the lips. I felt a tear roll down my cheek and it didn't escape my notice that she was more like the man in this relationship and I was the chick crying over the woman that was slipping through my fingers. "You know, you helped me too, and I'll never forget that."

She turned and walked out of the house, leaving me with a gaping hole in my heart. It felt so much like when Cassie was gone. The difference was, even though Lola was no longer going to be a part of my life, at least I knew she was alive.

"So, that's it?" James asked after I told him about Lola and I later that day. "You're just walking away because you don't like her job?"

"I'm walking away because I have to."

"Bullshit."

"Hey-"

"No, you listen to me now. Mom would be so disappointed in how you're hiding from life. She would have wanted you to be happy and you're hiding behind your fear."

"You know, she hid from me for two fucking years. Don't lecture me on what your mother would think. I know that she wants me to be happy, but I won't be happy in this relationship."

"How do you know? You're giving up before you really gave it a chance."

"Did you see how I was the other night?" He nodded. "That was when I was just worried that she was missing. Now imagine that I had gotten news that she was hurt or dead? How do you think I would have acted last night? Do you want to see me crying on the ground beside her grave like I did with your mom? Because that's what would happen to me. And I'm telling you that I can't fucking deal with that."

"Do you really think that you're going to stop loving her just because you broke up with her?" he shouted.

"I never said I loved her."

"I see the way you look at her," he scoffed. "It was the same way you used to look at Mom. So, you're going to continue to love her even though you're broken up, but that's not going to change whether she lives or dies!"

"James, you need to back off right now."

There was so much anger brewing inside me and I didn't know how long I would be able to keep it all bottled up. I had never been a violent man, but these past five years had messed me up so much that I didn't recognize myself anymore.

"No. I've stayed out of your way for too long, tiptoeing around your feelings. I've seen you fall apart more times than you think and I'm not going to watch you fall back into that hole you called a life just because you think I'm too young to understand. You're running away. You're a fucking coward."

I lost it and punched him in the jaw, watching as he fell to the ground and blood dripped from his mouth.

"Ryan!"

The world seemed to slow down all around me. I was losing my fucking mind. I had just punched my kid. I had done something that no parent should ever do, no matter what the reason. I blinked slowly, thinking maybe this was all a dream that I would wake up from, but when I opened my eyes, my son was still on the floor and my hand was still aching from hitting his face.

My gaze slowly swiveled to the door where Sebastian had just pushed through and was charging toward me. I didn't even fight it. Whatever he did to me, I deserved. When his body hit mine, I flew backwards into the arm of the chair and crashed to the ground. Sebastian's fist hit me several times in the face and I didn't try to defend myself. I just took the pain and relished in him giving me a beating I deserved.

"Stop!" James pulled Sebastian off me and shoved him to the side. His chest was heaving and I could see the concern on his face for me, even though one eye was already starting to swell shut.

"You never put your hands on your kid again," Sebastian growled at me. "You do that again and I'll put you in the ground beside Cassie. You understand me?"

I nodded, knowing that he meant every word of what he said. I looked to James, but I didn't have a clue what to say.

"I'm sorry" wasn't a good enough apology for what I had put this kid through the last five years. There was nothing I could do or say that could make any of this right.

"Maybe you should go stay with your grandparents," I said as tears filled my eyes. God, I didn't want him to go, but what I had just done was so reprehensible. I shouldn't be allowed to have him with me anymore. What was the judge thinking, giving me custody of him? I had vowed to protect and love him and I had just hit my own kid.

"No," he said firmly. "You don't get to do that anymore. You don't get to send me away when you can't deal with your life. We're going to sit down and talk about this like we should have been doing for the past five years."

"James, I think he's right. I think you should go."

"I didn't ask you," he said to Sebastian. Man, this kid had some brass balls. He had grown up so much and I had totally missed it. In some ways, he was so much wiser than me. He could read every emotion I had and knew that I was drowning, but then there were things that he had yet to experience in life, like love, that still made me see him as the little ten year old boy I first met. How had I missed all that?

"If you want to stay, then we'll sit down and talk, but Sebastian or one of the other guys will be here."

"I trust you, Dad. I pushed you and I knew I was doing it. I just wanted you to talk to me."

"That's still no excuse for what I did." I turned to Sebastian. "Will you stay?"

He was still in a rage and I knew he didn't really want

James and I to sit down and talk. He wanted to take him away from me right now, and I wouldn't blame him. But for James, I would do this.

"I'll be in the kitchen," Sebastian said as he turned and walked out of the room.

James took a seat on the couch and I took one in the chair across from him. There was no way I was sitting too close to him. We sat there for a few minutes and I didn't know what to say. I didn't know what he wanted to talk about. What more was left to say? That I was a shit parent? I already knew that.

"So, are you going to send me away again?" James questioned.

"I don't know what you want me to do. James, I'm failing at this parenting thing big time."

"You're not failing at it. You've pushed me away, but I get it. I know why you don't want me around, but-"

"I never said that I didn't want you around. I just didn't want you to see the worst of me."

"But the only reason that you're like that is because Mom's gone. You weren't like this before she died."

"That's no excuse for how I've been acting."

"I'm just saying that it happened to both of us. Just stop acting like I can't handle it. You were the one that told Mom she had to stop treating me like I was a kid, but then you started doing the same thing. I may not understand all of it, but you could at least try and explain it to me. Like this stuff with Lola, if you didn't like her or something, I could understand you walking away, but to me, it just looks like you're running."

"James, relationships are hard work and one of the most important things in a relationship is that both people are happy. Lola loves what she's doing and I hate it. I'm not going to ask her to give up a part of what she loves just to make me happy. That wouldn't be fair to her, but it's not fair to me to stay in a relationship where I know I can't deal with her job. Does that make sense?"

"Yeah," he said reluctantly. "It just feels like this is out of nowhere."

"Well, this is the first time that it really hit me how dangerous her job is."

"So, then it's over."

"Yeah. I know you liked her and I'm sorry it didn't work out."

"I did like her, but what I liked most was that she made you happy again. I was just happy that you didn't look so sad all the time."

"You know, it won't always be this way. Now that I know what an ass I've been, I promise, I'll make sure things change. I mean, if you still want to stay with me."

He snorted and shook his head. "Dad, we had an argument. We worked it out. Let's just leave it at that."

"Man, you look like shit this morning. Rough weekend?" Logan asked as he walked into my office. "Stay up too late with Lola?" he grinned, waggling his eyebrows.

"Lola and I broke up," I admitted, not really wanting to talk about this.

"Whoa, why?"

"I couldn't handle her job. She was out on a job and Sebastian couldn't get ahold of them. I guess they had an issue and...I don't know what the fuck happened, but I spent Friday night worrying about her and it turned out everything was fine."

"Okay, so if she was fine, then why did you break up with her?"

"Because I was freaking out all night. I just knew that I couldn't handle it if something happened to her."

"So, you just ended it? That doesn't mean that she'll be safe. I thought you were falling for her?"

"Look, I've already been through all this. I really don't want to rehash it right now."

"But, you're just giving up on something that could be great."

"Logan, I've made my decision," I said firmly. "I'm not going to change my mind."

He looked at me like I was a disappointment, and maybe I was, but this was the way it had to be. I just couldn't risk my heart and my head like that again.

"You know, I knew that moving on would be difficult for you, but I never took you for a coward."

"What the fuck is it with people? It's not like I'm saying that I don't want to take a chance on love. I'm saying that I know what a fucking mess I was after Cassie died and I know that if the same happened to Lola, I would be back in that same state of mind. Do you want me to not be able to do my fucking job anytime that she's out on a job and I haven't talked to her? Because now that I know how dangerous her job can be, I know that I won't be able to function when she's away. I know that I'm going to be worrying about her the whole fucking time. And what about James? How much more is that kid supposed to take?"

"Look, that kid is stronger than you think."

"Yeah, I know. He made that abundantly clear when he was fucking yelling at me. I lost my shit and hit him. Do you still think that having a relationship with Lola is a good idea?"

"You hit him?" he asked angrily.

"Why do you think my face is all fucked up? Sebastian saw me do it."

"You know what your real problem is? You've let Cassie's death change everything about you. I get that you loved her. We all did. She was a great person and it fucking sucked the way she was taken from you and James, but you've let it define your life. You sank into a hole so deep that you could barely pull yourself out of it. Now you're fucking hitting your own kid?"

"I know that! I know that I'm an asshole for what I did. But I can't change the way I am now."

"You could if you wanted to. You could see the gift that Cassie gave you instead of only seeing what you lost."

"I know that I have James and I should be grateful for still having him, and I am-"

"That's not what I'm talking about, man." He growled in frustration and yanked at his hair. "Think about what it felt like to have her for that year. Think about what you got to experience. Knowing that she would die, would you go back and change anything? Would you rather never know what it was like to kiss her and make love to her? Would you rather walk around never truly knowing what having the love of a good woman like her felt like? That was the gift. If I only got one year with Cece and then I knew she was going to die, I would take it in a heartbeat. Yeah, it would probably destroy me like it did you, but it would have been worth it, because I know that she makes me a better man. What you've forgotten is what kind of man she made you. The kind of man that would do anything for her and her son. You need to bring that man back. Be the man that you were when she was here. Otherwise, you're destroying her memory."

I hung my head, ashamed that I really had lost everything that made me the man I was for Cassie.

Chapter Fifteen

LOLA

"So, was lover boy happy to see you when we got back?" Derek asked.

"That's over," I said, keeping my back to him.

"What? I thought things were going good between the two of you."

"Yeah, well, things change. It's not a big deal," I said turning to him with my face as hard as steel. I had to keep up the persona that I was fine. Even though my heart was breaking, I couldn't let my teammates see me as weak.

"Right," Derek said, obviously not believing me. He turned to walk away and then stopped, turning back to me. "I forgot to tell you, we have a training session this morning. One hour."

I nodded. That was just enough time to go to the shooting range and let off some steam. I felt better after unloading a few clips into the dummy at the end of the range. Though it wasn't nearly as satisfying watching stuffing come out of a dummy as watching blood come out of a human.

After our training session, which was way more therapeutic than shooting, I showered and headed home. By myself. It was lonely sitting around the house when I had gotten used to being around Ryan and James. It wasn't like I couldn't handle being on my own, but there was a finality about it today. It was like the world was mocking me. I was on my own and chances were that I always would be.

Part of me had wanted to fight for Ryan when he broke things off between us, but the way he had said it, like he had just decided that it was going to be this way was like a shot to the head. Game over. He wasn't going to ask me to change and he knew that he would never change for me. In some ways I appreciated what he did. I probably would have resented him if he had asked me to change. I just had to accept that it was better this way.

Feeling lonely and depressed, I got into some comfortable lounge pants and then reprimanded myself for choosing this particular pair. They were gray sweatpants that had *Hogwarts* written down the side and then *School of Witchcraft and Wizardry* in smaller print below that. They were the ones I had picked up to watch the *Harry Potter* movie marathon with Ryan and James. It was the first time that I had really felt like a part of a family. I had even picked out a Gryffindor shirt to go with it.

Trudging into the kitchen, I pulled out a big tub of ice

cream and went to sit on the couch. All I wanted to do was sit down and watch some badass blow 'em up movie, but when I saw that there was a *Harry Potter* marathon on, I just couldn't resist. So, there I sat on my couch, eating a tub of ice cream and watching a movie about wizards. And I was crying.

My doorbell rang and I slowly got up, taking my bucket of ice cream with me. When I pulled the door open, I started crying again. Hunter, Derek, Cap, Cazzo, Knight, Sinner, and Burg were all standing on my doorstep with cases of beer. And they all looked panicked.

"Shit," I heard Sinner mutter. "I don't think it works the same way with girls."

"Can we come in?" Hunter asked.

I nodded through my tears and went back, plopping down on the couch as I shoveled another spoonful of ice cream into my mouth. The guys all walked in and hesitantly took seats, watching me with wary eyes.

"I was expecting *Die Hard*," Cazzo muttered.

"Seriously?" I snapped. "You were watching fucking romance movies when Vanessa left you."

"They were classics," he said in his own defense.

"Still. *Harry Potter*?" Sinner asked.

"You know what? All of you didn't exactly make the best choices at some point. You," I pointed to Knight. "You stalked Kate for a year, sneaking into her house so you could watch her sleep." Then I turned on Hunter. "You sat outside your girlfriend's apartment for weeks with the stalker because you couldn't tell Lucy that you couldn't leave her alone."

Sinner snickered and I shot my gaze over to him. "Really? You couldn't get it up to fuck another woman because you were so hung up on Cara." His face scrunched up in confusion. "Yeah, didn't think I knew that, did ya?"

Then I turned on Cap. "You put a tracker in your wife's arm because you didn't trust her out on her own. How did that work out? And you called Claire fat," I said to Derek. "Bet you learned your lesson with that one. And you," I pointed at Burg. "I'm sure you'll fuck it up too at some point. Just give it time."

He grinned and pointed at the others. "But I haven't yet."

"So, we're watching *Harry Potter*," Cap grumbled as he pulled out a beer.

"You know, that ice cream looks pretty good, Lola." Sinner eyed my ice cream and I held it tighter.

"Get your own," I said around a mouthful of mint chocolate chip.

Sinner pulled out his phone and dialed someone.

"Gabe, yeah we're gonna need supplies over at Lola's house...What?...I don't think so. Hang on."

"Do you need tampons?"

I glared at him and he quickly went back to his phone call. "No tampons. We need ice cream. Lots of it. Just grab a bunch of pints-"

"Gallons," I shouted.

"Gallons," Sinner said into his phone. "Just grab whatever's available." He hung up and grinned. "Gabe's on his way."

We all sat in silence as we watched the movie, except for

the occasional stupid question from the guys, which completely ruined the movie.

"So, he just runs straight at a wall in a train station and no one sees him?" Hunter questioned. "That seems a little unrealistic, don't you think?"

"Dude, the whole movie is about magic. It's all fucking unrealistic," Cazzo said.

"Shut up or I'll put a curse on you," I said.

When the doorbell rang, I was a little annoyed to see that Gabe had not only brought over ice cream, but the rest of Reed Security.

"I don't have room in my house for all of you," I snapped.

"Don't worry, Brave. We'll take the floor," Chance grinned.

"I hate it when you call me that," I said through clenched teeth.

"You know, this is kind of becoming our thing," Derek said. "Maybe we need to just plan on doing this once a month."

"You're not coming over to my house once a month." I said as I shoved the last of my mint chocolate chip into my mouth. I handed the empty container to Gabe and he handed me a gallon of chocolate, then walked over to Hunter.

"Hey, man. I grabbed you Rocky Road because I know it's your favorite." Gabe grinned and waited for Hunter to take the gallon, but he just sat there looking uncomfortable.

"Thanks, man." He finally reached out and took it.

"No problem. I expect the same treatment if I ever go through shit like this."

"Yeah, we could plan a slumber party," Derek grinned. "You know, just the guys." He winked at Hunter who snarled at him.

Gabe chuckled uncomfortably. "Yeah, I'm not so sure I'm comfortable with a bunch of dudes spending the night at my house."

"Maybe just one then," Derek suggested. "You could pick, like, oh, say a best friend to come over and keep you company. Hunter?"

"Can you guys please shut the fuck up?" I cut in, trying to take the heat off Hunter, who looked like he was about to sweat through his shirt. "I'm trying to watch the movie."

When the part with Quidditch came on, the guys all watched curiously.

"Damn, so they just get hit with a ball and knocked off their broomsticks and that's legal? Aren't these kids minors?" Burg asked.

"They can regrow bones. They're fine," I mumbled.

"Still, it seems like a pretty fucking brutal game for a bunch of kids."

"Well, we could always bring back lawn darts and throw those up in the air. Maybe one of you will get stabbed and it'll shut you the fuck up so I can watch the movie!"

"Geez, you're more of a bitch now than when you have your period," Hunter groused.

"I'm sorry that I'm in a pissy mood, but having you all over here when I was trying to sulk in peace isn't really helping," I snapped.

"Talk to us, Brave. Tell us what's wrong," Sinner said, leaning forward with his elbows on his knees.

"Do I need to junk punch you?"Sinner moved his legs together a little. "Stop calling me that."

"You know, when I was going through a rough patch with Vanessa, the guys came over and they really helped me work through shit. Maybe you just need to open up a little," Cazzo said.

"You guys actually talk about relationships and stuff?" I questioned.

"Sure," Hunter shrugged. "Who do you think helped me get Lucy back?"

"So, I just talk," I said dumbly. Hunter nodded and I figured what the hell? These guys had all gone through this. Maybe they really could help. "Well, you know that I haven't really had any relationships in a long time. I don't like the way I look with this fucking scar on my head and the nightmares would scare off anyone. But then I met Ryan and he was just as damaged as I was and we really had a connection. I mean, we got each other's pain and then his kid came into the picture. He's such a fucking awesome kid and I was falling in love with both of them. We had movie marathons and hung out all day. It was just really cool and totally different from what I'm used to." I sniffled and swiped at my nose as the tears started to fall. "We were really starting to have something good and then I went away on a job and he freaked out because we lost contact with the team. He thought I was dead or something and he said he couldn't handle it."

I shook my head as I swiped more tears from my face. "I mean, how fucking fair is that? I know he was just being honest with me, but we had something good and then he just threw it away. And I get it. I really do. His wife died and it tore him apart. But any of us could die at any moment," I said hysterically. "What sense does it make to throw it all away when you finally found someone that you really want to be with? That loves you the way you are, pain and all. That's so rare. I just don't understand why I had to go and fall in love with them if they were going to leave!"

I buried my head in my hands and cried, sobbing in anger that I was reacting like this. I was not this girl. I didn't cry over men. I was tough and now I was here, pouring my heart out to my friends. I had turned into a fucking girl! I felt a masculine hand pat me on the shoulder awkwardly and I peeked through my hands. The guys were all pointing at one another and mouthing things to each other. Most of them looked panicked and I realized that when they told me to talk to them about it, they had no fucking clue what they were asking for. I ran a hand over my face, wiping away the tears and composed myself.

"Alright. You wanted me to talk. I did, so give me some advice."

"Well, see...the thing is..." Sinner fumbled with his words, picking at his beer bottle as he tried to figure out what to say. "The thing is that usually when we get together when this kind of shit happens, we don't actually, you know, give advice."

"What do you mean, you don't give advice?"

Cap scratched behind his ear as he lifted one side of his face. "Well, you know, we're guys. So, we bring beer. We watch crappy movies. We pretend we know what we're talking about."

"So, let me get this straight. You wanted me to talk, but didn't actually want to participate in any way that could give me some idea of how to handle this."

The guys all looked around at each other, shrugging and nodding. "Well, yeah," Derek said.

"That's bullshit," Florrie said. "If anyone can help her, you guys can. You're guys. You have the inside track into a man's emotions."

"We don't actually have those," Chance said.

"Everyone has emotions," Florrie snapped. "Now, stop being a bunch of cavemen and think of it from a male perspective."

They all looked around at each other like they didn't have a clue what to say. Sinner leaned back in his chair, crossing one ankle over the other knee. "It's gotta be the sex. If the sex were good, there would be no way he was walking away."

"Sex wasn't the problem," I said irritatedly.

"Yeah, I really doubt that was the issue. Lola was pretty good in bed," Hunter confirmed.

I leaned toward him, crooking a finger for him to come closer. "Here's a newsflash. It was better with him." Hunter jerked back in surprise and looked around the room quickly at the other guys. "What can I say? It's better when it's with someone you love."

"You know, she right about that," Derek agreed. "Sex was never as good as it is with Claire."

"What should I do? I mean, should I try and talk to him?" I asked desperately.

"Well, if a girl came up to me and started begging for me to take her back, I'd fucking change my number, my address, and possibly my name," Ice scoffed.

"Since your name is still John, I'm guessing no woman has ever begged you for anything," Chris cracked.

"Then, it's another woman," Alec suggested. "Maybe the sex is good, but he just doesn't like you that way. Your job gives him the perfect excuse to break things off."

"Here's what you do," Knight said, leaning forward, his elbows on his knees. "You go to his house and install some cameras. Keep an eye on him and make sure that he's not bringing other women home. That way you know if he's really just not able to deal with your job or if he's looking for someone else."

"Jesus, that's my friend you're talking about," Cap said. "Can we not go into the creepy stalking shit?"

"Would you rather have her wondering if your friend is just an asshole?" Knight shot back.

"He's not an asshole," I said frustratedly. "He's a good guy that has been dealt a shitty hand. I don't blame him for breaking up with me."

"I hate to say this, but you could always give up your job," Florrie suggested.

"No!" Hunter and Derek shouted.

"Look, aside from the fact that she's on your team and you would be pissed to lose her, think of it from just a guy's perspective," Cap said. "If your woman was out doing dangerous shit, you would want her to stop. You would do anything you could to protect her."

"Yeah, but he didn't ask me to walk away from my job," I said glumly. "Maybe Alec's right. Maybe he just doesn't like me as much as I like him."

"No," Chris said firmly. "It's because the roles are reversed. You're the badass in the relationship and he's the girl. I mean, not really, but if this was us we were talking about, we would be pissed if our women asked us to give up who we were for them. He recognizes that and he knows it's not fair to ask that of you. He's just trying to be sensitive to your feelings."

"So, what do I do then?" I asked.

"You ask yourself what you love more," Chris shrugged. "If you love him enough that you know you don't want to live without him, then be willing to walk away from your job."

"But only if you know that you wouldn't resent him for it," Florrie interjected. "Don't give up a piece of yourself if it's going to make you miserable."

"I think I liked it more when you guys were all full of useless advice," I grumbled.

"So, are we done with this now?" Sinner asked. "Can we get back to drinking beer and watching *Harry Potter*? Cuz, I kind of want to see how Quidditch turns out."

"You know what? I think a game of Quidditch is exactly what I need," I said as I stood.

"Uh, Lola. We can't exactly fly around on broomsticks," Sinner pointed out.

"Are you trying to tell me that when I'm depressed and needing something to pick me up, you guys are going to tell me it's not possible? Do you want to see me cry?"

"No," they all answered quickly. I smirked at Florrie, who was sitting quietly across the room. Her responding grin agreed that I had just played them.

"So, what exactly do we need to play this broom game?" Cap asked.

"We'll need seven players to a team. A snitch, a quaffle, three bludgers, and a referee."

"What the hell is a quaffle?" Chance asked.

I rolled my eyes in frustration. "Doesn't anyone pay attention? Of course not. You're all men. We're going to need to use the training center at Reed Security. My yard isn't big enough. There are seventeen of us, but we'll probably need another three players to make it work with the snitch. We'll need broomsticks for all of us and two different colored shirts so that we can tell teams apart. Preferably maroon and dark green. We can use a dodgeball for the quaffle and soccer balls for the bludgers. A golf ball should work for the snitch. We'll also need six hula hoops for the goals."

"You're fucking joking, right?" Knight asked. I scrunched up my face and let the tears fall. One thing I was able to do quite well was create tears at the drop of a hat. It was a gift I had learned at the age of six when my mother said I couldn't go hunting with my father.

"No, no, no. No tears," Ice said quickly. "We'll get all that shit and meet you at Reed Security. It's gonna be fine," he said, patting my shoulder awkwardly.

The guys quickly filed out as I wiped away the fake tears. Hunter stopped beside me and whispered in my ear, "Well played." Then he followed everyone else out of the house and I quickly cleaned up the ice cream that was still laying around.

When I arrived at Reed Security, I was pleased to see that Cap was taking charge of getting everything organized. The guys were just showing up with all the supplies we needed.

"Do you know how fucking ridiculous I looked buying this many brooms?" Alec said.

"Could have been worse," Gabe said. "I had to buy the fucking hula hoops. They only had pink."

We split into teams with Derek, Hunter, Ice, Jules, Chris, Knight, and I on one team. The second team was Cazzo, Burg, Sinner, Chance, Gabe, Jackson, and Cap. Alec, Craig, and Florrie were going to be handling the snitch.

"I guess we won't have a referee," I sighed. "Oh, well. Let's get this party started."

"I just want you to know that I am really against running around on a broom and playing a fake game all to cheer you up," Knight said.

"Relax, I could have made you wear tights with your shirt. That really would have cheered me up."

"Okay, so who's going to be in what position?" Hunter asked.

"Well, I'm definitely a Beater. I want to throw balls at people."

"I like the sound of that," Knight grinned.

"No, I think you can be the Seeker. You get to chase down the snitch."

Knight glared at me, but didn't argue.

"Chris will be the other Beater and Jules, Ice, and Derek will be the Chasers. Hunter will be the keeper," I grinned.

"What the hell does a Chaser do again?" Ice asked.

"You throw the ball through the hula hoop." I stepped back and studied the guys. "You guys look good in Maroon," I smiled, happy that my plan had worked out so well.

"I don't see why we couldn't have been the evil team," Knight grumbled. "Who wants to be the do-gooders?"

"Gryffindor is awesome. Besides, all the guys from Slytherin die in the end."

We started playing and it was rough going at first, but I had so much fun watching the guys running around with a broomstick between their legs. I glanced over to the corner where I had Maggie hiding, taking pictures. I had called her on my way over and snuck her in so that there was evidence of all this.

When I got ahold of a bludger, I whipped it as hard as I could at Cap. It was a game after all and I could get away with hitting the boss. Every time he had the quaffle, I attacked him, knocking him to the ground with a bludger to the head.

Gabe had ahold of the quaffle and was racing on his broomstick toward the hula hoops. He jumped to the side, but Hunter jumped higher, blocking his shot. Gabe's forward motion had him slamming into Hunter and falling on top of him.

"Sorry about that, man. I didn't think I'd actually be able to take you down. You're like a fucking hulk."

"Can you get off me, Gabe? It's a little weird to have another dude's junk pressed against mine."

"Oh, shit. Sorry about that."

Gabe pushed off Hunter and then held a hand out for him. Hunter shook him off and stood on his own. I laughed, thinking about how hilarious it was going to be when I told Ryan about getting the guys to play Quidditch, and then I frowned when I realized that I wouldn't be able to tell him. Ryan wasn't mine anymore and there would be no more lazy Saturdays at his house and no more movie marathons. That really shouldn't bother me this much. I was a strong woman and I kicked ass for a living, so why did I want to cry so much?

"Shit, someone grab her the quaffle. She's about to cry," Hunter said urgently. But it was too late. Tears poured down my cheeks and sobs wracked my body as I remembered how good it had felt to be with James and Ryan at their house. The comfort of being accepted so easily into their family was gone and I was all alone. Again.

"What did you do?" I heard Cap ask over my own sniffles.

"I didn't do anything. We were playing and then she just started...this." Hunter was looking at me like I was a crazy person that needed to be handled with care. Funny, a serial killer didn't break me, didn't destroy my life, but walking away from the one man whom I had grown to love was sending me over the edge.

I laughed maniacally at the thought, throwing my head back and screaming at the ceiling. The release felt cathartic, but when I wiped my face and looked around at the guys, they all looked uncomfortable. "What? Can't handle a woman crying?" I shouted. "Yes, this is me. Crazy Lola," I said, waving my arms around in the air. "The once rational and stable woman that treated men as terribly as they treated women is now crying over a man. That's what you guys do to us. You stick your magical dicks in us and turn us into batshit crazy women that cry over stupid shit. Look at me," I shouted.

And they did. They were all fucking staring at me in terror. "Is this what you guys plan on? To get us so wrapped up in your web that we can't function without you? I was happy. I had my guns and I liked to shoot people. I never cried over anything! Now all I can think about is how much I want to curl up on the couch next to Ryan and watch movies all day with him and his son. Are you happy? You made me into a girl!"

Soft hands wrapped around me that were way too delicate to be a man's. "I think you've done enough," Florrie said as she walked me away from the men.

"What did we do?" I heard Knight say in confusion. "All we did was play her stupid game."

"It's not a stupid game," I shouted, but Florrie kept dragging me off in the opposite direction. Maggie came rushing up out of nowhere and took me by the other arm, guiding me out to a vehicle. I couldn't see through the tears that continued to pour down my face. Everything was just so messed up. *I* was so messed up. No matter how hard I tried, I would never be the same woman again after Ryan. He had made life wonderful again.

Before I knew it, I was being dragged into someone's house and shoved into a chair with a glass of wine. Suddenly, there were women surrounding me, looking at me with sympathy that made me want to cry even harder.

"Lola, I know this is hard, but you need to talk about it," Maggie said. "I know we're not exactly friends, but you need to let it all out."

"He broke up with me," I cried. "He couldn't handle my job and he said that if something ever happened to me, it would break him. I didn't expect it to hurt this much. I didn't realize until I walked away how much I love him. And not just him, but James too. They've become like my family, only now they'll move on together and I'll be all alone."

"He lost his wife," Cara said sadly. "I don't know him that well, but I was around when it happened. He was devastated. He probably just doesn't know how to deal with the fact that something could happen to you. How does he just accept that?"

"This is so sad," Claire said. "If this was a book, he would realize what he had in his relationship with you and he would take you back."

"That's not helpful," Lucy hissed.

"Maybe I did a bad job of reassuring him of how good I am at my job," I sniffled. "Should I go back to him and talk to him?"

"No," Kate and Vanessa shook their heads.

"Don't beg. The last thing these men need is a woman down on her knees in front of them. It sends their egos into overdrive," Vanessa said.

"Then what do I do? I can't lose him. He's what makes me whole."

"He completes you," Claire said dreamily.

Maggie sat down beside me and took my hand. "Lola, do you love him more than anything else in this world?"

I thought about the time I spent with Ryan, and how at peace I felt with my life. Everything seemed so easy with him. There were no demons and no reminders of a life spent in battle. I did love my job, but I wasn't sure that it was still the thing I loved most in the world. "I do," I finally said.

"Then you need to decide if you can live without Ryan or your job because you can't have both." Maggie held my hand in hers, squeezing it tight. It was so weird because I felt this camaraderie with these ladies, yet I barely ever talked to them.

"Is it really that simple? What if he says he doesn't believe me?"

"Make him believe you. Show him that he's what you need," Claire said wistfully.

I sniffed for the hundredth time and took a tissue that someone handed me. I had to pull myself together. I wasn't a weak woman that cried over men. I was strong and I needed to get that back, especially if I was going to figure out how to get Ryan back.

"Enough of this," I said as I stood. "I can't sit around here crying over everything. I need to be proactive."

"Right. Let's go blow something up," Maggie jumped up with a grin.

"I was actually thinking I needed to have a talk with Sebastian."

"Sure, of course. After we blow something up. I need some action and this is the perfect opportunity to get some. Besides, it'll make you feel great. One last hurrah before you destroy your life."

My brows furrowed in confusion. "But I thought you said..."

She waved me off. "Must be the wine. I meant before you go get the love of your life." She grabbed my hand and pulled me out the door before I could really think about it. Next thing I knew, we were at Reed Security in the outdoor training area and Maggie was handing me a loaded rifle to shoot at the target. When that was not quite as satisfying as I hoped, Maggie dragged me over to the demolition area.

"Listen, this always makes me feel better. Let 'er rip," she said, handing me a grenade. I took it, pulled the pin, and tossed it. The explosion shook the ground and loosened the tension in my body. Maggie was grinning at me as she handed me another.

"That actually did help."

"See? It's so cathartic."

I tossed a few more, laughing with Maggie as she threw her own. I had always known this was fun, but to do it for stress relief hadn't crossed my mind.

"What is going on out here?" Sebastian's voice boomed over the ringing in my ears.

"Emotional therapy," Maggie said with a laugh.

Standing next to Sebastian were most of the members of Reed Security and they looked pissed.

"Emotional therapy? Hell, we could have done this hours ago."

"But you didn't," Maggie pointed out. "You played Quidditch."

"Because she asked us to," Hunter said.

Maggie rolled her eyes at the guys as she shook her head. "You never give in to a person that's not thinking right. Especially when it's something that will remind her of what she just lost. You should have plied her with alcohol."

"We brought beer," Sinner said indignantly.

"And then you let her watch a movie that would remind her of Ryan. Seriously, you guys are amateurs."

"So, we didn't have to run around on broomsticks?" Knight said angrily.

"You didn't have to, but it was great video footage. Thanks for that," Maggie smiled.

Chapter Sixteen

RYAN

"You ready to do this, little man?" I asked James as I walked out of my bedroom. I was going for the relaxed look today, jeans and a t-shirt, because I was anything but relaxed. Today was James's birthday and I was taking him to get his license. Inside, I was freaking the fuck out, but outside, I was cool as a cucumber. Or, so I told myself.

Things between James and I had been getting better over the past few weeks since we had talked shit out and I didn't want to ruin that with my fears. But there was one thing we needed to do before I could really move past all the shit that was raging in my head.

"Before we head out, I want to do one more drive with you."

He groaned and rolled his eyes. "Dad, I'm ready for this. I took all those courses that you wanted me to with Sebastian.

I'm probably the best sixteen year old driver you've ever seen."

"This isn't for you. This one's for me. I just want to take you out one time to show myself that everything's going to be fine."

"Okay," James nodded.

We got in the truck and I stopped myself from giving him instructions on what to do. The kid had it all down. "Alright, head to Potomac Street."

"What? Dad, but that's the road-"

"I know." I swallowed hard and forced myself to remain calm. "I think we both need this."

He took the roads like a pro, stopping for the correct amount of time at stop signs and looking both directions before continuing. The kid would do fine on the test. As we approached the intersection where Cassie died, images flashed through my mind faster than I could handle. I could hear James talking to me, but I was lost again, trapped in memories that I just couldn't handle.

As we got closer, one image took front and center in my mind. It was Cassie smiling sweetly at me the morning we left for work and she died. But this time, I didn't get the ache in my chest, just an overwhelming feeling of peace. Instead of James driving through the intersection, he stopped and pulled the truck over, staring out the windshield.

"Come on," I said, opening my truck door and stepping out. He followed me and we walked to where her car had rolled into the cornfield. I don't know what I expected, maybe to see tracks from her car or the odd piece of wreckage, but there was nothing. Five years had completely washed away any sign of the accident that took her from us.

I sat down on the ground, James sitting next to me and we stared off into the countryside. "You know, the thing I remember most about your mom was her ability to call anyone on their bullshit." I laughed, remembering the day she walked into my office and I was having a panic attack about having just hitched myself to her.

"I miss her laugh," James said quietly.

"Me too. You know, I chased her for two years because I knew she was the woman that would change my world. Just everything about her pulled me in and had me craving just an ounce of her time."

"But then you totally freaked out when you married her," he laughed.

"Well, that was mostly because I was gaining a kid." I leaned over and shoved him with my shoulder. "Turned out to be the best thing that ever happened to me."

"Do you think she's okay?" he asked after a minute.

"I don't know. I've never really thought too much about what happens after we die, but your grandma would say that she's in heaven. You know, the morning of your mom's funeral, your grandma came in and saw me crying over a shirt that was hanging in the closet. It was the one she was wearing the first day I met her. Your grandma told me that God took your mom for a reason and even though we might never know why, it was meant to be."

"Do you believe that?"

"It makes me feel better if I tell myself that's the truth."

"I think she's good," James said. "I think she's watching over us and she's probably pissed that you let the guys talk to me about sex."

I snorted and shook my head. "Yeah, and she's probably pissed every year that I let you have a beer. I can hear her in my head telling me that you're not old enough to drink."

"Every night when I get ready for bed..." He paused and I looked over at him. His eyes were shimmering and his throat was practically having a seizure for how hard he was trying to control himself. I placed my arm around his shoulder and pulled him in close to me. "I still hear her voice, asking me if I brushed my teeth. And if I didn't remember, I can't go to sleep until I do. I can just picture her pointing her finger toward the bathroom and telling me that my teeth are going to rot if I don't brush them."

"I miss the smell of her perfume." Tears started rolling down my face and I didn't try to stop them. "When she died, I used to spray her perfume all around the house just so that it felt like she was still there. I miss waking up next to her every morning. The house just isn't as warm without her."

"I stole the bottle of perfume," James admitted. He laughed a little and wiped the tears from his face. "You were almost out and I had this feeling that when it was gone, you wouldn't buy any more. So, I took it so that I could still smell her. It's in my nightstand."

I smiled at my kid. He knew me so well. "For the first two

years after she was gone, I slept with her nightshirt every night. It was like a security blanket."

"I eat broccoli even though I hate it because Mom always told me that it would make my body grow evenly. She used to say that my ears would stretch and get huge if the broccoli didn't balance it out."

"That doesn't even make sense," I laughed.

"I know, but every time I eat a piece of broccoli, I laugh because of how stupid it is."

"I refused to clean out the strainer in the bottom of the tub for the first six months. It was full of her hair and I used to always clean it out, but I just couldn't bring myself to throw away her hair."

"Dad, that's just weird."

"I know," I laughed through the tears. "It's really fucking weird. Just be glad I didn't save it in a plastic baggie."

"You don't wear your wedding ring anymore," James pointed out.

I shook my head. "It felt wrong. You already know that I went out to find women when you were at your grandparents' house. It felt like I was cheating on her if I wore it. They're yours if you want them someday. And her engagement ring. I never told anyone this, but I had special rings made up for when we renewed our vows. They were engraved with our first wedding date and the day we were supposed to do it again."

"I'm glad you fought for me after she died. I know it was hard on you with everything else going on, but I wouldn't have turned out so good if I had to go live with my biological father."

"There was no way I wasn't fighting for you. I know I've made a mess out of things since your mom died, but I never want you to think that you were a bad reminder. You were the only thing holding me together after she died. You know, you look just like her, and sometimes that was hard, but it's also the best gift in the world."

We sat in silence for a minute, just taking in all that we had said to each other.

"I uh...I told you there was this girl that I liked. I want to take her out tonight."

"Your first date, huh?"

"Her name's Annie. She's beautiful and I think Mom would really like her."

"So, I guess that means you're not hanging out with your old man on your birthday."

"Are you mad?" he asked, looking at me a little worried.

"Nah. You should go have fun. If you pass your driver's test. Just do me a favor and be really careful."

"I will."

After a few more minutes of sitting in the field, we got up and headed back for the truck. I looked back once more before I got in and swore I could see Cassie sitting right next to where James and I were, but she was gone a second later.

"Goodbye, Cassie girl."

"So, where are you taking Annie tonight?"

"Uh, I was thinking of taking her to the movies. I don't have a lot of money saved up. I think I need to get a job."

I pulled out my wallet and handed him a bunch of twenties. "Take her out to a nice dinner. We'll talk to Logan tomorrow. We might be able to use you if you want to try your hand at construction."

"Really? That'd be great."

"What else are you going to do with the rest of your summer? You can't spend it all with a pretty girl."

"So, I didn't really think to ask before. Is it alright if I borrow your truck?"

"Nope."

His face fell and he chewed on his lip. "Oh."

"Come on. Jack should be here any minute." We stepped outside just as Jack was pulling up to the house in a used Toyota Tacoma. His wife, Harper, was following in their own truck.

"What's going on?" James asked.

"This is your birthday present. I got it the other day and Jack looked it over, made sure that everything was as safe as possible for you." James stared at the truck in awe, not moving as Jack stepped out of the truck. "Go check it out, little man."

Jack tossed him the keys and walked over to me. I couldn't help the faint tears that touched my eyes as I realized that James really was all grown up. I watched as James jumped in the truck and looked over every inch of the truck. The kid was so excited that I thought he might take off without saying goodbye.

"You have nothing to worry about," Jack said as he stood next to me. "I went over the truck myself. It's in great condition. I put on new tires and changed a few belts. Checked all the fluids. She runs great."

"Thanks for taking care of this so quickly for me."

"Not a problem. You doing okay today?"

"Yeah. It was a little rough earlier. I took him out driving before his test. We stopped at the intersection."

Jack turned and looked at me with a questioning gaze. "You sure that was a good idea?"

I nodded. "I probably should have done it a long time ago. We talked about Cassie and..." I shook my head. "I really fucked up and that kid still turned out amazing. He's definitely his mother's son." I huffed out a laugh as I looked at the ground. "He's not really my kid at all."

"He is in every way that matters, and Cassie left you to take care of him. It doesn't matter if you have the same DNA. That kid survived his mom's death because you were there for him."

"There's just so much I would have changed."

"Well, you can't go back in time. All you can do is make sure that going forward, you don't make the same mistakes. And as for Lola, it's time to piss or get off the pot."

Jack walked away with that little parting shot, climbing into Harper's truck and driving away. I walked over to James, who was still checking out every inch of his truck. "So, what do you think?"

"I think it's awesome. Thanks, Dad."

"I'm glad you like it. Why don't you come inside for a minute before you go pick up Annie?"

"Okay, but if this is another lecture on-"

"It's not," I smirked.

We went inside and sat down in the living room. There was something that I needed him to know before he left.

"This girl, you like her a lot?"

"Yeah, she's...amazing."

I nodded, understanding what he was saying. "Listen, I know what the guys told you about sex and everything. To say that I wasn't at my best that night would be an understatement. There's something I want you to keep in mind when you go out with her."

"No glove, no love?"

I laughed and shook my head. "That too. I want you to consider what it would be like to share your first time with someone you truly care about. I know that it's hard to think about all that shit when you have hormones running wild through you and you just want to know what it feels like. But it can be so much more if it's with someone you love. My first time was with my high school sweetheart and I loved her very much, or as much as you can love someone at that age. I didn't know much about sex and it wasn't pretty, but neither of us cared. It was about the commitment that we were making together that made it so special. We both knew the consequences of what could happen and we were ready to deal with that together if it happened."

"You were ready for a baby?" he asked unbelievably.

"No, but we knew that if it happened, we would deal with it together. We were always very careful and luckily, nothing ever happened. But that was how sex began for me, and I just want you to think about what it would mean for you. It's fun to fuck around. Hell, I've been doing it since your mom died, but none of it means anything if it's not with someone you love. So, if you really like this girl and really care about her, wait until you're both mature enough to deal with the consequences. Wait until you know the timing is right."

"Alright." He looked at the clock on the wall and stood. "I have to get going. Thanks again for the truck."

"No problem, little man."

I held out my hand to him, feeling like he was probably getting too old for hugs. He took my hand and shook it, but then pulled me in and gave me a hug. It was everything I needed today and as he drove away, I thought about Jack's words, wondering if I had made a mistake.

I walked into the bar, not wanting to sit around my house all night waiting for my kid to get home from his date. How pathetic was I? My kid was dating and I was at a bar, drinking alone. I ordered a beer and sat at the bar, trying to figure out if I had made a mistake walking away from Lola.

"Hey, Ryan." I looked up to see Sean standing next to me. I gave him a chin lift and watched as he took a seat. "What are you doing here all alone?"

"James had a date."

Sean chuckled and shook his head. "Better you than me."

"What brings you here tonight?"

"Long day at work. I just wanted a beer before I went home to the chaos."

"Just don't stay too long. You're a lucky man, you know?"

"Yeah, I know." He waved the bartender over and ordered a beer. He had an uneasiness about him that I wasn't used to. Sean always seemed so in control. "Ryan, there's something that I should have told you a long time ago, and I think now, with everything that's going on with you and Lola, it's time to tell you."

"What's that?"

"Cassie was at our house a few days before her accident. I walked inside and heard her and Lillian screaming about something."

"They were fighting?"

"No, they were happy. Shit, there's no easy way to tell you this. Cassie was pregnant."

I just sat there, unable to really think about what he was saying. My heart was thundering so loud in my ears that it was making me dizzy.

"Why didn't she tell me?" I finally choked out.

He sighed. "Because of me. I thought that if she told you before you got married, it would take away from the honeymoon. I thought she would be better off waiting until you were actually on your honeymoon or when you got back. I'm sorry if that was wrong, but I didn't want you worrying about her when you were supposed to be celebrating your new life together."

"And after she died?" I asked.

"You were a fucking mess. Most days I wasn't sure if you were going to make it or not. James was the only thing keeping you going. What good would it have done to tell you? There was no chance the baby would have lived. She had just found out. I didn't want you to be mourning the loss of your wife and your child."

Maybe I should be pissed, but I wasn't. He was right. I would have fucking lost it if I had known back then.

"You were right not to tell me, but why are you now?"

"I guess because life is short and precious. You never really know what's going to happen and if you were still thinking about Lola, I thought maybe it would give you some perspective."

"How exactly? That just reinforces my point. I lost a wife and now I learn a child also."

"You could look at it that way, or you could look at it that you had the opportunity to create life with Cassie. It just wasn't meant to be."

"That's not fucking helping any," I growled.

"Look at it this way, nothing in life is certain. People die all the time, but what you had with Cassie was once in a lifetime. Then, five years after she dies, you find someone that finally makes you want to really start living again. Yeah, her job is dangerous and higher risk than most professions, but if you love her, isn't it worth it? Maybe your time with Cassie was meant to be what it was, to lead you to Lola."

"Do you really think I was only meant to be with Cassie for that time? That I was really meant for Lola?"

He shrugged. "People come and go from our lives for all sorts of reasons. Maybe she was a gift that you received for a short time." I took a drink of my beer as I considered that. "Or maybe I'm just spouting off bullshit and I don't know what the fuck I'm talking about." He stood and grasped my shoulder tightly. "Either way, don't walk away from Lola because of fear. Life's just too fucking short and you know that."

I watched as he walked out of the bar and tried to sift through all the bullshit he just spouted off. I didn't want to believe that I wasn't meant for Cassie. She had been everything to me, and what did that say about the child we had created? The child wasn't meant to be? The weight of everything Sean had told me was pressing down on me hard and I had to get out and just breathe. I pushed back from the bar and walked out into the dark night. The one thing I wanted more than ever, I couldn't have because I pushed her away. But I couldn't use her right now. It would be wrong to go to her and ask her for comfort when I had ended things with her. I got in my truck and headed for the one person I could talk to.

I climbed out of my truck and walked across the cemetery

to my wife's plot. It was so different here at night and it made me sad that this was where she was resting. She deserved so much more than a dark grave surrounded by a bunch of other people that she didn't know. When I got to her grave, I sat down and leaned against it, wishing that it was her I was leaning against.

"Cassie, I'm such a fucking mess. Five years later and I still can't get you off my mind. You would fucking hate me if you could see me now. I'm a mess. I hit our son..." I picked at the grass around her grave and let out a deep sigh. "I'm so fucking lost, Cassie. Every decision I make seems to be based on you and I don't think I should be doing things that way anymore. You're not coming back to me and trying to do things the way you would want just isn't working for me." I laughed a little and ran my hand over my eyes. "Probably because you're a woman and my guess at what you would want is most likely completely wrong.

"There's a woman I met and she makes me happy, but I'm so fucking scared of losing her the way I lost you. Only it's worse with her because her whole profession is dangerous. But she makes the days easier. No, that's not right. She doesn't make the days easier. With her, it's like everything is just completely normal. I don't think about you and the horrible accident that took you from me. I don't think about the fact that James is missing out on time with his mother. We just exist in this whole other life. We do things together as a family, or we did before I broke things off with her. She likes to come over and hang out with us. She watches movies with us and likes to just chill with us. But she also gets us out of the house and living again. Some days, it's as if you weren't even there."

"Don't you think that's what she would want?"

I started at the intruding voice and stood quickly, squinting into the darkness. Drew walked out of the shadows and sat down beside where I was. I took my seat again and together, we leaned against Cassie's grave stone.

"Didn't mean to scare you. Sean called, said you might need a friend. He saw you headed this way."

I nodded and thought back to what he said. "Why do you think she'd want me to forget her?"

"Well, it's not that she would want you to forget her, but don't you think she would want someone that could step in and take over? Lola's made the three of you a family. Isn't that what's best for all of you?"

"But at what cost? I don't think about Cassie at all when I'm with Lola. Is that what's going to happen with James? He'll just start thinking of Lola as his mother and Cassie won't exist?"

"It doesn't work that way. You know, I don't think about Iris all the time any more or the baby we lost. In fact, when I met Sarah, I was actually mad on days when I hadn't thought about her. I thought that it meant that I was ruining her memory or something. I remember when I forgot the anniversary of her death. It passed and I didn't even notice. That was fucking hard. It really hit me then that she was slipping away from me and I would never hold her again. I used to hear her voice every day. I'm not sure if it was in my head or if it was her way of helping me out, but when I started to finally move on with Sarah, she started visiting less and less."

"You never told any of us that."

"Yeah, well, you'd have all thought I was batshit crazy. Sometimes, I miss hearing her. I used to go hang out on my back porch at sunset. That's when she would visit me. When she would talk to me, it was like this warmth wrapped around me. When I go outside at sunset now, it's just silent. I don't hear her voice and I don't feel her touch. It's hard," he said, clearing his throat. "Part of me will always hate that I lost her. But then I have Sarah and she's this amazing, resilient woman that brought me back from being this shell of a man. She made me want to live life again. And the more time I spent with her, the more I fell in love with her, the less I heard Iris. Until one day she was gone. I think Iris sent me Sarah. I think she knew I would need someone to drag me out of my own misery. Maybe that's what Cassie is doing for you."

"I don't hear Cassie," I whispered. "I wish that I could. I wish she would just give me some advice or just fucking yell at me."

Drew gripped onto my shoulder and gave a firm squeeze. "You don't need to hear her voice, man. She's always with you, in every decision you make. Cassie wanted the absolute best for her son. And if that means that another woman steps into your life and helps you live again, that benefits James. It sets a good example for him. But you're not going to get the answers you want talking to the dead. You just have to trust that you're making the right decisions and go with it. Cassie won't fault you for living."

I knew he was right. Deep down, I knew Cassie wouldn't want me to be alone and she would want someone to step in to the role of mother for James, the way I stepped into the father role. If I hadn't, James might have ended up with his biological father, and I would have never known this amazing kid that had completely changed my world.

Chapter Seventeen

LOLA

"Hunter! Hunter!" I shook him, trying to wake him up, but there was blood gushing from his head and he showed no signs of waking any time soon. I started to shake uncontrollably. This was really bad. I hadn't been able to get ahold of Derek and now Hunter was down, which left me. I usually wouldn't be scared of the situation I was in, but nothing had gone right so far with this detail. Everything was fucked up and I was sure that this was going to be the job that killed me. It was a feeling that had settled deep in my gut.

After checking Hunter one last time, I stood slowly, making my way to the back door. Peering in the window, I saw Derek passed out in the corner of the room against the wall and Alex huddled down next to him. I moved my hand to the door, but something hard smacked me in the head and I saw stars swimming in my vision. An arm wrapped around my throat and a knife flashed in front of my face. Fear paralyzed me and I couldn't move. That sinking feeling in my gut was pulsing uncontrollably, making me feel like I was just moments away from death. I kept screaming at myself to do something, but I couldn't make myself move.

"Don't move or I'll kill little Lexi before we get to the good stuff."

He kicked the door open and shoved me forward, keeping a tight arm around my neck. My blood was dripping down my face from where he had hit me. Dizziness was making it difficult to walk in a straight line at this point, but I wasn't sure if the dizziness was from fear or my head wound.

"Why don't you drop the gun, Lexi? I would like to play a game with you, but I'm afraid you can't have a weapon. So, here's what's going to happen. You are going to put down your weapon and I won't shoot your friend here. Of course, if you don't want to, I'll just shoot her anyway and you can watch her die. What's it going to be?"

I shook my head, trying to tell Alex not to give up her weapon. I knew I was going to die anyway. Better to make it fast. I didn't particularly want to know what this psycho had in store for either of us. But at least if she held onto her weapon she had a chance. Anger washed over me when she obeyed his orders and put the gun down.

"Come closer and pull up a chair."

Alex walked toward me and I was shoved from behind. I stumbled over my feet, feeling like I would collapse at any minute. I was terrified and wanted to take a nap all at the same time. My brain just wouldn't come online no matter how hard I tried to think of a way out of this. Fear was taking over and rendering me useless.

"Tape her hands to the chair back."

This was the end. I knew there was no going back now. I could have died a thousand times overseas fighting for my country, but I was going out at the hands of a serial killer because I was too weak to fight back.

I sat up in bed, a scream lodged in my throat. The terror of knowing what was next had woken me from my dream. I closed my eyes and laid back down on my wet sheets. I had sweat so bad that there was a ring of water on my sheets. I hadn't had a dream like that since...since I had started staying with Ryan. I had worked past all this bullshit, so why was it coming back now? Did I really need Ryan to chase away my nightmares?

Knowing I wouldn't get anymore sleep, I got up and put on some coffee. Waiting for the sun to come up was worse than watching paint dry. I couldn't get the images of my dream out of my head. I thought about calling Hunter, but what good would it do? We weren't sleeping together anymore and the last thing he needed was to be called over in the middle of the night for my craziness, even though I knew he would.

What I really wanted was Ryan's arms wrapped around me. I needed to feel the comfort of his body stretched out beside mine and the soft cadence of his breathing lulling me to sleep. Life just sucked since he decided we were over. Granted, tonight was a first for my dreams returning, but he gave me so much more than an escape from my dreams. He gave me love and hope for a future. He was a man that saw me and didn't care about my scars, but knew that they tormented me. He gave me a different world from the one I was living in, something normal and completely different than what I was used to.

When the early morning light finally broke through the sky, I decided to head out for a run. When that didn't help to clear my mind, I went to Reed Security and pounded on Knight. Still, nothing helped clear my head or the pain in my heart. Everyone could see that I was struggling. Knight was yelling at me the whole time, telling me to get my head in the game, but I just couldn't focus. Hunter gave me a look of concern that he used to give when I was falling down the rabbit hole. Sebastian eyed me, like he wondered if I was really capable of doing my job. And Derek pulled me aside for a talk, telling me that he was there for me, no matter what I needed. The thing was, none of them could help. Whatever was torturing me, I couldn't even comprehend it. So, how could I explain it to them and ask for help?

When I got to the locker room, I decided to see if my therapist had time for a session today. He didn't have an opening until next week and I spent night after night fighting my demons, trying to keep my sanity when I thought I had gotten it back.

"So, why are you here today?" Dr. Penwarden asked.

"Because the nightmares are back. I worked through

them. I worked through my issues at work and everything was fine."

"What's changed?"

I looked down at my fingers and picked at my nails. "I was seeing a man. I think he was really helping me, but then he broke up with me. He couldn't handle how dangerous my job was. You see, his wife died after they were only together a year and he was left to raise her son."

"How did his wife die?"

"Car accident. The thing is, I think we were kind of healing each other, but..."

"But then your job reminded him of his loss," Dr. Penwarden finished.

"Yeah. So, he ended it, and I can't blame him. He's scared and my job isn't a desk job."

"And how do you feel about that?"

"I hate it," I said quietly. "I love my job so much. It's something I've always loved, but I love him too. I never thought I would fall in love with someone after what happened. I was just moving day to day. But then he came into my life and he took away the chaos. He gave me normal."

"Let me ask you this, you describe your life as chaos, but you say you love your job. If you love your job so much, why do you crave what he can give you?"

"It's not something I've ever known. My dad taught me to shoot at a young age. Joining the military was all I ever wanted. Being in security is all I've ever known. I crave the rush of excitement and the meaning my job gives me. But being with Ryan and his son gives me peace and calm. They play paintball, but that's about as violent as it's ever gotten. They stay home and have movie nights and read together. With him, I want something more than the life I have."

Dr. Penwarden nodded thoughtfully. "I think the question you need to ask yourself is if you love your job more than Ryan."

"You think I should give up my job?"

"I didn't say that. But it's obviously something you've considered. You need to think about your time in the military and at Reed Security. Think about what that represents for you, what it gives you. Then think about your life with Ryan and his son. If your work gives you more satisfaction than Ryan, then you need to walk away and accept that what he could give you isn't enough. But if Ryan is what you need out of life, then you need to decide which you want more."

"What about the dreams?"

He shrugged. "Dreams can mean a multitude of things. They may have returned because you're no longer at peace with yourself. They may have returned because your life has been disrupted. Ryan was there at the same time you were seeking therapy. It could be that you've associated him with healing. They could also represent fear returning. Fear of the unknown. Fear of not being in control anymore. Or, it could simply be that you found peace with Ryan and you were healing. The dreams may come and go your whole life. I can't tell you for certain that they'll ever stay away. We all have triggers that set us off. I think that once you make a decision about your future, you'll feel more at ease and they'll lessen."

"How do I know that I'm making the right decision? I mean, he said that he didn't want to ask me to leave my job because he thought I would regret it someday. What if he's right? What if I start to resent him?"

"Lola, I can't tell you what to do here. All I can tell you is to follow your heart and stick with it. You need to be at peace and be happy with yourself. As long as you're not, you'll continue to feel like you're spiraling out of control."

I thought about my talk with Dr. Penwarden for a week. I weighed the pros and cons. I made lists and avoided talking with Derek and Hunter. I didn't know what to say to them and I didn't know how to explain to them what I was feeling. I had been struggling for the answers until this morning. When I woke up, I rolled over and saw no one beside me. My house was quiet and there would be no arguing between James and Ryan or debating over who was better at paintball. My world would continue as it was and I would stay in this house, forever by myself with no lazy Saturdays. This was my life.

I went into work and found myself outside Sebastian's office first thing. He was on the phone, but waved me in. I took a seat and looked around the room at all of the things I would miss about being here. I wouldn't see Caitlin running into the office anymore. I wouldn't see my friends that I had made over the years. But I was going to have the man I loved, if he agreed to take me back. That was the one uncertainty. I needed to show him that I was serious, though. The only way I could do that was to hand in my resignation. Otherwise, Ryan would always wonder if I really wanted this.

When Cap got off the phone, he leaned back in his chair, running his finger across his lip. "You're leaving us," he said bluntly.

I nodded. "I am."

"For Ryan?"

"Yes. If he'll still have me."

"What if he won't?"

I swallowed hard and looked away. "I don't know, but I have to try. I love him."

"You know, you don't have to leave. Knight doesn't go out into the field."

"But...what would I do?"

"There are a few options. There's the administrative side of things, which I know you love. You could help Knight with training. Looking at new hires, security installs, research, mission planning," he rattled off. "The list goes on and on."

"But, do you actually need me to help in those areas? I mean, Cazzo and Derek are part owners of this company."

"And they help grudgingly. They never wanted to do the administrative side. I know it's not exactly what you want to be doing, but you would still be with the company. We don't want to lose you, but if you feel like you need to step away, I won't try to stop you."

"Are you doing this because Ryan is your friend?" I questioned.

"Partly. Not the job part. Believe me, if it was any other man, I would fight tooth and nail to keep you in your current role, but I've seen how you and Ryan help each other. I've seen how you've pulled him out of a hole he's been hiding in for almost five years."

"What about my team?"

"We'd have to find a replacement, and that's something you'd have to deal with. You would no longer be on your team. But if this is something you really want, we'll get started on it right away."

"I need to talk to Ryan first. I need to know if working for the company in any capacity is a problem."

"That's fine. Talk to Ryan and let me know as soon as possible. In the meantime, talk to Hunter and Derek and let them know what you're thinking."

"I will."

I walked out of his office, hoping to slip away for a minute and gather my thoughts, but Derek and Hunter were standing right outside his office door waiting for me. I looked to the elevator for an escape, but Hunter stepped to the side, blocking off my exit.

"Are you going to tell us what's going on any time soon?" Hunter asked.

I sighed, knowing there was no way to get out of talking to them now and motioned for Derek's office. They led me down there, probably not trusting me not to run away. When we stepped inside, I took a seat on Derek's couch and they both pulled up chairs facing me.

"I'm leaving the team."

Shock and then betrayal crossed Hunter's face. Derek nodded like he knew what I was thinking.

"I want to be with Ryan and Ryan can't handle my job."

"Fuck him," Hunter snapped. "If he can't accept you for who you are then you need to walk away."

"This isn't about him not accepting me. He does accept me for who I am and that's why we broke up. He can't live with my job and he didn't want to ask me to change. This is my decision because I don't want to live without him. He gives me something that I never thought I would want or need, and frankly, if it's a choice between him or my job, I choose him and I always will."

Hunter shoved back his chair as he stood, pacing and swearing at no one in particular. Derek leaned forward and grasped my hand. "If this is what you need, then do it. I would do the same for Claire in a heartbeat."

"This is absolute bullshit. We refuse to let you leave the team," Hunter said as he paced.

"We'll support you in your decision no matter what. I know it's been hard on you for years and I could see how much better you got when you started seeing Ryan," Derek assured me.

"There's no way Cap will accept this," Hunter promised.

"I already talked with Cap," I told Derek. "He assured me that he could still give me a position at the company if I wanted it, but I need to talk it over with Ryan first. He has to be my first priority."

"Hell, Knight will kick your ass for even thinking about leaving," Hunter growled as he continued to pace.

"You can take over my part of the administrative job. I never wanted it to begin with."

"What the hell would you do anyway?" Hunter turned to me and asked. "Take up sewing and be the good housewife?" He turned before I could say anything and started pacing again, running his hands over his bald head.

"Well, I appreciate the support, Derek. I'm going to talk with Ryan and when I've got it all figured out, I'll let you know. It won't be long though."

"We'll definitely miss you on the team, but I had a feeling you would eventually want to get out," Derek said. "I've seen the way that night affected you for too long. I'm glad you're finally getting some peace."

"I think I'm really ready for a change in pace. I'll miss it, but I have to admit that it's nice to take it easy with him and his son. I never thought I would want that, but it's just different with them.

"And let me tell you something else," Hunter pointed at me. "That guy will make you so fucking bored if you stay with him. You need this job because you crave the adrenaline like we all do. You've never been one to sit at home and lounge around."

I looked at Derek and smirked. "Well, I guess you'll have

to tell him all of this after I leave. I'm heading out to talk to Ryan now."

I stood and so did Derek, leaning in to give me a hug. We weren't huggers, but this was different. This was goodbye, or at least, goodbye to our team. Things would be a lot different after this, but after talking with Derek, I knew I was making the right decision.

"Good, you're hugging it out," Hunter slapped Derek on the back. "I knew you could talk her out of it. Now, let's go train."

I shook my head and turned for the door, walking toward the elevator as Derek started to tell Hunter what he had missed with his ramblings. I got in the elevator and pressed the code, only to see Hunter racing to the elevator and staring at me in devastation as the doors started to close. I held up my hand in a small wave and watched as he shoved his hands in his pockets and looked at the ground. Some things were going to be hard to adjust to.

This was so fucking ridiculous. I was standing outside of Ryan's work, debating whether or not to go in. All I had to do was walk inside and ask him to take me back. Just one simple request. The problem was, I was scared shitless that he was going to tell me no. That he didn't want to take the chance on me. What would I do then?

I blew out a harsh breath and made my way inside. I was a

strong woman. Nothing could bring me down and nothing scared me. I could do this. I went to the receptionist and asked to speak with Ryan, but he was in a meeting. I told her I would wait and forty-five minutes later, she was leading me back to his office.

My heart thundered in my chest as I stepped inside and saw him sitting at his desk. He was just as handsome as I remembered, though maybe a little more tired looking. He looked at me curiously, but didn't say anything.

"I came to talk to you about something. Can I sit down?"

He nodded and I turned, closing the door so that no one would disturb us. When I sat down, I could see the questions swimming in his eyes, so I didn't wait.

"I want to be with you. I know that my job is a problem and I decided that I was going to step down from my position. I already talked with Sebastian and he told me that I could take on some administrative roles around the office. I don't want to lose you. You've become such a big part of my life and I've missed you so much since we broke up. I want you back."

I waited on pins and needles, thinking he would say something right away. Anything. But he just sat there staring at me with lifeless eyes. Tears pricked my eyes as I realized that this wasn't going to happen. He didn't want me. All that I thought I was doing to make this work between us was for nothing. I dropped my gaze, not needing to see the look on his face when he said it.

"I'm sorry, Lola. I just can't. I've been fooling myself into thinking that I could do this; that I could move on and try for love again. But I can't do it. I'm not ready and I don't know that I ever will be."

My heart was breaking and I didn't think I would ever have to feel that. I wasn't this woman that fell in love and gave up my life for a man. Yet here I was, ready to beg this man for just an ounce of his love. For him to tell me that he wanted me as much as I wanted him, but that wasn't going to happen. He was too broken to truly move on and I wasn't enough to make him try.

I stood, not able to say anything else and walked out of his office, dejected and alone. There would be no happy ending to all this. I wouldn't be giving up my job in exchange for something better. I was destined to be sad and alone.

Chapter Eighteen

RYAN

"Hey, man. I just saw Lola leave. You guys back together?" Logan asked.

"No."

"Then why was she here?"

"She was here to tell me that she wanted me back," I said with little emotion. I couldn't afford to let myself think about it too much. I had made my decision. "She said she was leaving her job."

"And that's a problem why?" he asked in confusion.

"Because I don't want to be with her. I've got too much shit going on with James and I still fucking think about Cassie all the time. It's just too much. I'm not ready."

"Bullshit."

I looked up at him and raised an eyebrow. "You want to run that by me again?"

A knock at the door had me groaning. Sebastian was standing at the door grinning at me.

"Can I help you?"

"So, did Lola come see you yet?"

"She did, but it doesn't change anything. We're not getting back together."

"What the fuck are you talking about?" Sebastian asked angrily.

"I'm talking about the fact that I don't want to move on with her. It was nice while it lasted, but it's over."

"I call bullshit. I think you're running because you're scared. You broke up with her because you couldn't handle her job. She left her job, that she loves, for you and you just told her to fuck off. You're such a fucking dumbass," Sebastian growled.

"This isn't about being scared. This is about James and what's best for him. I've been shoving him off on other people since Cassie died and I need to set things right with him. He needs to know that he's my first priority and he hasn't felt like that in a long time."

"So, you set shit straight with him and get Lola back. He wants to see you happy. That's what the kid needs. Do you really think that wandering around day in and day out, thinking about Cassie is making things better for him? He doesn't need to know that you think about her every fucking minute of the day. He just needs to know that you won't forget her. Moving on with Lola isn't forgetting her."

"Did I miss the memo?" Drew asked from the doorway. I

groaned and rolled my eyes at the ceiling. "What's going on? Why's everyone gathering here?"

"Not everyone. There's just the three of you," I grumbled.

"Not for long. I just saw Sean downstairs. He said he was on his way up to see you guys. He was just finishing up a call," Drew said.

"It's about to get a lot more fucking crowded," Sebastian said cryptically.

"Why's that?" I asked.

"Because you dumbass, I thought you and Lola were getting back together. I called everyone to meet us so that we could take you out to celebrate."

"You're not getting back together?" Drew asked. "Why?"

"Because I don't want to," I shouted.

"Whoa, what's all the yelling about?" Jack asked as he walked in with Cole behind him.

"This asshole isn't getting back together with Lola," Logan jerked his thumb at me.

"Then why are we here?" Jack asked. "I was in the middle of a job."

"That's a shame," Cole shook his head. "She was fucking awesome."

"Tell me about it. It was nice to finally see him happy instead of moping around all the time," Sebastian added.

"I thought you guys were on my side. Did you really think that the first woman I came across after Cassie, I would fall in love with and spend my life with?"

"This isn't some woman, you asshole," Jack snapped. "This

is Lola and we all saw what she did for you. She brought you out of your head and made you live."

"Now, look what you've gone and done," Logan shook his head.

"Who did what?" Sean asked.

"Jesus, can we just send out a memo so I don't have to keep going over this shit with you guys?" I asked.

"What did I miss?" Sean asked.

"The dipshit turned Lola down after she gave up her job for him," Sebastian informed him.

"What the fuck? Seriously? What the hell is wrong with you?"

"That's what I was wondering. You should have seen her in my office this morning, steely determination to leave behind her job so that she could have the man she loved," Sebastian said with a shake of his head. "There was no hesitation in her voice. She just wanted the asshole back and he spat in her face like she was nothing."

"I did not. You weren't in here. Look, you can throw whatever you want at me right now, but I've made up my mind and you can't change it. This is the way it has to be."

"No, this is the way you want it to be. Because as long as you can live in this world where you're sad and lonely, you don't have to worry about losing someone else. You don't have to worry about getting hurt again. But Lola just walked away from everything for you. She fucking knew that it would kill you to watch her in the field all the time, wondering if she was safe," Sebastian spat at me. "She didn't even hesitate to tell me she was out. She wanted you more than anything else."

"Until when? Until she got bored?"

"Did she say she wanted you?" Logan asked.

"Yes."

"Did she tell you she had given up her job?" Jack asked.

"Yes."

"Did she say she wanted James too?" Cole asked.

"Yes, but-"

"You screwed the pooch on this one, man. You really fucked up," Drew shook his head. "Like, so completely fucked up that you won't ever be able to walk this back."

"I know exactly what I did."

"Then you know that you just lost the one woman that was able to bring you back from the brink. You were fucking drowning and she saved your ass. None of us could do it. We watched for the last five years and you struggled to keep your head above water, wanting to help, but not knowing how," Sean said. "When you find the love of a good woman like that, you don't let it slip through your fingers. You hold on and thank your lucky stars that you got lucky twice in one lifetime to find a woman that could put up with you. Most people get one shot in life at true happiness. You just pissed all over it."

What the fuck had I just done? I just told her I didn't want her. For what? I knew I had some shit to work through with James first, but I could have told her that. I didn't need to destroy her fucking heart. God, I was such a bastard. I was beyond a bastard. I must have lost my fucking mind. How was I ever going to get her back now?

"See? Now he gets it," Logan pointed at me.

School was just starting up again and I wanted to cram as much time in with James as I could before we both got too busy.

"What time am I going over to Grandma and Grandpa's tomorrow?" James asked as he came downstairs.

"You're not going this weekend," I said, hoping he was okay with that. We were still on uneven ground after the last few weeks and I felt like such a fuckup.

"Why? Is something wrong?" He looked at me funny, like he was waiting for me to drop some bomb on him or something.

"No, I just feel like I'm always sending you away."

"Well, you do," he said bluntly.

"I know. I told myself that it was because they were your grandparents and you needed to spend time with them, but I was really hiding. I thought if I got that one night to myself that it wouldn't hurt so much. That you wouldn't remind me of your mom, but it didn't really work. And then when I blew up at you, when I hit you...the only thing I could think was that you weren't going to want to stay with me anymore. I'm so fucking scared that you're going to go over to your grandparents house and then tell me that you don't want to come back here and be with me anymore. And I keep thinking that all those times I sent you over there was time that I could have been doing shit with you. I'm so sorry that I've been pushing you away, but I'm hoping that we can spend some time together this weekend and just hang out."

He turned his head from me and I didn't miss how he swiped at one eye, but then he composed himself and gave me a strange look. "Dad, are you asking me out on a date?"

I laughed and shook my head. "You've been hanging out with my friends too much."

"Just remember that you introduced me to them."

"So, what do you want to do this weekend? You name it and we'll do it."

"Anything?"

"Anything."

"Can we go on a road trip somewhere?"

"Sure. Where do you want to go?"

"Can we go to Gettysburg? I was reading this book about the Civil War and I thought it would be pretty cool to see that in person. You can get guided tours and they'll tell you anything you want to know."

"Yeah, we can do that."

I smiled at the excitement on his face. Maybe I hadn't totally fucked things up between us. Maybe this was just the beginning of a new relationship between us. What the hell was wrong with me? I was starting to sound like a girl even to myself.

"There's one more thing I want."

"Okay," I said reluctantly.

"I want Lola to come with. She's into all this shit and she was the one that actually got me hooked on this book. I think it'd be really cool for her to come with."

God, I wanted that too, but after I just tore her down, how the hell was I supposed to get her back?

"James, I said some things. I don't-"

"Dad, I know you love her. Just go tell her."

"I don't know that it's that simple."

"You won't find out sitting around here. Now, go get her back so we can hit the road this afternoon."

"You got it, little man," I said with a grin. He gave me a devilish smile and walked out of the room. That kid was learning way too much from Logan.

Since James and I would be leaving after school today for this trip, I figured that I needed to talk with Lola as soon as possible. I called up to James to let him know I was leaving and told him to be careful driving. I would never be comfortable with him out on the road, but I was learning not to hover. I called Logan and shifted my morning around and then headed for Lola's house. If I was going to convince her to come along with me, I was going to have to really finesse her.

When I pulled up, she was just walking out of the house and Hunter was with her. She stopped dead in her tracks and looked at me in surprise. Hunter glared at me like he was ready to snap my neck and I knew he could. He stepped in front of her and crossed his arms over his chest. Lola being Lola, shot him a dirty look and shoved him aside.

"What the fuck do you want, Jackson?"

So, we were using the whole last name thing. Got it. "Just came to talk to Lola," I said calmly.

"She doesn't want to talk to you."

"I think I can answer that for myself," Lola snapped. She turned to me and composed herself. "What's up?"

"Can we talk for a few minutes?"

"Um, we were just on our way into work." She stiffened and shoved her hands in her back pockets.

I tried not to look totally dejected, but I had seen this going a lot differently in my head. She would take one look at me and fall back into my arms. I would tell her that I loved her and ask her to come on the trip with us. Reality was a bitch. I didn't know what to say. I wanted to tell her so much, but Hunter was standing next to her like a bodyguard.

"I made a mistake," I blurted out. "I was so fucking scared of losing you that I thought it was better to just not be with you. But I miss the smell of you. It's weird, like gun oil and lavender or something. It's really fucking strange and I never thought I would like that on a woman, but I like it on you. And I fucking hate your job. I hate the idea that you're going out there and getting shot at or almost blown up, and I'm not there to protect you. Not that I really could protect you. I'd probably be crying in the corner like a fucking girl. Well, a different girl than you because you're not scared of anything. And I'm not like the rest of my friends. I'm not as macho as them and I fucking cry a lot. Way more than any respectable man should. But when I'm with you, it doesn't happen nearly as often because you just make everything better. And I prefer to sit at home and read with my kid than to go out and party. I don't know if you're up for that for the next few years or if you'll be thinking that you're missing out on life, but if that sounds like something you might like to be a part of, then I want you to come back with me. Come stay with me, for the night or stay for the whole fucking year, or the next ten years. I love you, Lola. I don't want this to be over between us."

She just stared at me for a moment, but Hunter crossed his arms over his chest and glared at me. "That was single-handedly the worst and best apology I've ever heard in my fucking life. You managed to insult her and compliment her all at the same time."

"It was actually very...honest," Lola smiled. "I like that you're not as macho as your friends. I have enough testosterone to deal with at work. I don't need to come home to it also. Except in the bedroom, which I already know we're perfectly compatible. And I'll gladly spend lazy days at home reading with you and James, as long as I can read *Guns and Ammo.* And once a month, I get to choose the movie, and if I choose *Die Hard* every month, you can't complain."

"I can deal with that," I said around a throat full of tears. I swiped at my eyes, annoyed that I was once again crying.

"And one more thing." I nodded. "I still want to work at Reed Security, even if I'm not in the field. It's like a second home to me and I'm not ready to leave."

"No," I said suddenly at the same time Hunter yelled no. "It's who you are, and I won't ask you to change. Your job is a major part of you and I love every part of you. I'll learn to deal with it."

"If it gets to be too much, you have to promise to tell me. I want to be with you and if this is going to work, we have to be honest with each other."

"Agreed." When she smiled at me, I knew we would be fine. I ran forward and pulled her into my arms, tasting the sweetness of her lips. I wrapped my hand around her ponytail, gripping her tight to me. Remembering why I had to talk to her today, I pulled back reluctantly. "There's one more thing. James wants to go to Gettysburg for the weekend and he wants you to go with. We're leaving after school."

"Was that my invitation?"

"No, that was me telling you that's what the plan was."

"I thought you said you weren't as macho as your friends," she said playfully.

"This is one thing that I can't afford to have you say no to. James won't forgive me if you're not there."

"Cool," Hunter clapped his hands together. "Road trip. I'll call Derek and let him know."

"Uh-"

"Hunter, that wasn't what we were thinking-" Lola began.

"I bet Derek's going to be thanking you big time," he said, pointing a finger at me. "Imagine all the material this will give Claire. He'll be over the fucking moon."

"But-"

"We'll meet up at your house, Ryan. What time does the kid get out of school?"

I looked at Lola, hoping she would help, but she looked just as bulldozed as I felt. "3:30."

"We'll see you then, man."

Hunter gave me a chin lift and got in his truck, waiting for Lola.

"That wasn't really what I was expecting," I said stunned.

"Are you mad?"

I shook my head. "No, I'm sure James will think it's awesome to have them around."

"You'll regret saying that," she said as she walked over to Hunter's truck and got in.

Chapter Nineteen

LOLA

"This is such a disaster," I said as we entered the town of Gettysburg.

"Why do you say that?" Ryan asked.

"Because, this was supposed to be a trip for James, you, and me, but it's turned into a Reed Security vacation."

"That's not true. Not everyone came," I laughed.

"I can't believe Hunter commandeered my trip," I grumbled.

"I think it's awesome," James said excitedly. "I get to tour Gettysburg with real live soldiers."

"We didn't actually fight in the battle of Gettysburg," I said dryly.

"Yeah, but you guys can tell me all about their tactical maneuvers and stuff like that," James argued.

"War was very different then. Soldiers were actually stupid

enough to stand in lines and fire bullets at each other, taking turns in order to be gentlemen."

Ryan pulled into *Custer's Last Stand* and parked the truck.

"Is this really where Custer died?" James asked.

"No," I replied. "He died in Montana in the Battle of Little Bighorn."

"Why are we staying at this dump?" Hunter asked as he got out of his truck.

"It's all we could get at the last minute," I said, raising an eyebrow at him. "You know, with you tagging along and all."

He ignored my comment and helped Lucy out of the truck. Claire got out next and Derek was on the other side, stretching his arms over his head.

"Damn, I could've just stayed home. I'm beat," Derek yawned.

"No one asked you to come," I snapped. Ryan walked up behind me and slipped his hands around my waist.

"Relax. I don't give a shit if they're here. I have you and James and that's all I care about."

He kissed me on the cheek and then motioned for James to follow him. Chris, Ice, and Jules all walked over to me, each carrying bags.

"I didn't think you'd actually settle down, Lola, but I'm glad you got back together with Ryan," Chris said sincerely.

"Yeah, you just didn't want to play any more Quidditch. I'm actually surprised that you let Axel take a break from training."

He shrugged. "Yeah, well, it's part of American history. It'd be good for him to learn about it."

"I thought I was going to use this weekend to escape," Ice grumbled.

"So did I," I snapped back.

"Hey, I thought I was getting away from the she-Devil. I didn't know that Hunter invited her along. I would have just stayed home."

"I'm not looking forward to being here with you, either," Lindsey said irritatedly. "But at least here I don't have to smell your dirty socks that you've left laying around."

"We should do a retreat like this every year," Gabe said, walking up behind Derek and Hunter and draping his arms across both of their shoulders. "I like the idea of hanging out with you guys away from all the bullshit of work."

Hunter slunk away from Gabe's arm and cleared his throat uncomfortably. "Yeah, well, just remember, I'm not sharing a room with anyone but Lucy."

"That's not gonna happen," I said smugly. "They didn't have enough rooms for every couple to get their own rooms. You and Lucy are going to have to share with someone."

Hunter looked at all of us, but his eyes lingered on Gabe a little longer than necessary, and then flashed back to me in panic.

Gabe held up his hands and took a step back. "No worries, man. I'm rooming with Chance."

Hunter visibly relaxed and blew out a breath. James walked over to me, waving his hand for me to hurry up.

"Come on. We still have time to go out and see some of the battlefield tonight. They're open until ten and we only have tomorrow and Sunday to spend on the battlefields."

We all put our shit in our rooms and were headed to Gettysburg National Park twenty minutes later. We started at McPherson's Ridge and made it through Barlow Knoll, but on the way back, we decided to drive over to Soldier's National Cemetery. It was getting dark out by the time we made it to Culp's Hill and there were sirens in town going off for severe weather.

"Maybe we should turn around and head back," Lindsey said.

"It wouldn't do us any good. We wouldn't get to shelter before a storm hit anyway," Ice said in irritation.

From the top of the tower on Culp's Hill, we could see a great view of Gettysburg, but what was even more awesome was going into the woods and seeing where the soldier's fought.

"Look at this." James pointed to a tree stump that looked like a cannonball had gone through it. The wind rustled around us and the sirens continued to go off. The woods were darker now and everywhere we looked, it seemed like a dead confederate soldier would pop out and attack us.

"Maybe we should head back," Ryan suggested. "It's getting dark."

A twig snapped behind us and all the guys whipped around, looking for a threat, but there was nothing there.

"I'm with Ryan," Hunter said in a deep voice. "We should

leave before someone gets hurt trying to walk back in the dark."

"I'm fine," Lucy shrugged. "I think it's kind of cool. Maybe we could have a seance and see if we can bring back any soldiers."

"That would be so awesome," Claire said excitedly.

"Have you ever been on one of those ghost tours?" Lindsey asked. "I went on one and you could hear all these noises, but no one was there and then things would move and it would totally freak you out. It's so cool."

"That doesn't sound cool." Ice shook his head and I watched in amusement as his eyes scanned the area.

"Yeah, we should definitely leave," Derek agreed. "You know, for the sake of the women. We wouldn't want you guys to get scared out here. In the dark."

"With the ghosts of dead soldiers that are probably roaming the area, crying for help. For someone to save them?" Ali asked.

"I think it'd be kind of cool to meet one," I said thoughtfully. "You know, ask what it was like to fight in a battle a hundred and fifty years ago."

The thunder rolled loudly and all the guys flinched as they looked around the woods. The wind picked up and it sounded like groaning was coming from all around us. Sounds of pain and agony filled the woods. Claire started walking further into the woods, searching for the sound.

"Claire, what are you doing? Get back here," Derek shouted.

"Afraid of a ghost?" she smirked.

"Yes!"

A noise off in the distance had us all turning to see what was going on, but it was too dark now.

"I'm getting the fuck out of here," Gabe said before taking off back in the direction we came. When more moans sounded, the rest of the guys took off running, leaving us women all alone in the woods. We looked at each other and started laughing. Claire came running back, clutching her side as she laughed, holding up her phone.

"That was hilarious," she said.

"I can't believe that worked," Lucy laughed. "They're so gullible."

"Big, strong men afraid of some noises on my phone," Claire laughed some more. Another groan ripped through the air and all of us stilled. The guys were still running for the parking lot, yelling at each other to go faster. We all looked at each other in confusion.

"Was that your phone, Claire?" I asked.

"No, I already turned the sound off. Lucy?"

"That's weird. My phone is dead. I was charging it the whole drive here."

We all pulled out our phones and surprisingly, they were all dead. The moans came louder this time and we looked around for the noise.

"Are you seeing this?" Lindsey asked.

"Is that a g-ghost?" Ali asked.

"Either that or an incredibly transparent person," Lucy said, gripping my arm, shoving me in front of her.

"What are you doing?"

"You're the badass warrior woman. Defend us," Lucy shouted.

"Against a ghost? What exactly did you want me to do?"

"I don't know! Shoot it!"

"I don't have a gun on me and even if I did, I doubt that shooting it would do anything."

"Well, we have to do something," Lindsey snapped. "We're not gonna just stand here and let it walk up to us, are we?"

I felt something slither across my shoulder and slowly peeked over to see something white-ish touching me. My eyes went wide as I stared at the other women. They looked like they were on the verge of passing out. I grabbed at the supposed hand on my shoulder, but all I touched was air. I shrieked and we all took off running after the men, looking behind us every few seconds to see if the ghost was following us. By the time we made it to the parking lot, we were all breathing heavily and shaking badly.

"Believe us now?" Ryan asked.

"Nice of you to leave us behind. So much for women and children first," Ali pointed a finger at Chris.

"You could have left when we told you to. It's not our fault you're all too stubborn to listen to us."

"I think I've had enough for one night," I sighed. "Can we go back to the motel now?"

"Afraid the ghosts are gonna get you?" James asked.

More moans came from the woods and seconds later, we were all piled in our vehicles and heading back down the road to the motel.

Lying in bed with Ryan that night was absolutely horrible. With James in the next bed, it's not like we could do anything. And after weeks of being apart, I wanted him more than I ever had before. To make it worse, Ryan was lying behind me with his erection pressed hard against my ass. Every few minutes, he would shift and it would press against the crack of my ass, making my pussy clench with need.

"This is ridiculous," he whispered. "Let's just go in the shower. He'll never know."

"I'm not having sex with you with your son in the other room."

"He's asleep. If you could be quiet, then it wouldn't be a problem."

"If I could be quiet?" I hissed. "You're the one that grunts louder than any man I know."

"If you didn't work your pussy magic on me, then I wouldn't have to worry about being so quiet."

"So, you want me to be bad in bed?" I asked.

"No. That's not what I'm saying. I just- fuck it. Get out of bed now before I drag you into the shower."

He stood and practically ran to the bathroom, turning on the water as I laid in bed and wondered what the hell I was going to do. I looked over at James and he seemed to be fast asleep. I could be quiet. I could go have sex with Ryan in the shower and then we would slip back to bed and James would never know the difference. Having convinced myself it would be fine, I slipped out from under the covers and quietly opened the door, tiptoeing over to the shower.

"What are you doing?" Ryan asked with a funny look on his face.

"Being quiet."

"You think he's going to wake up because you're walking across the floor?"

I glared at him and quickly took off my clothes, stepping under the warm spray of the shower. Ryan's eyes traveled slowly over my body, taking in each inch of my skin. My nipples pebbled as his gaze grew dark and hot. He yanked me to him, barely keeping me upright in the slippery tub, and smashed his lips against mine. His hands were instantly roaming my body, caressing every curve and dip of my body.

My hand slid down his hard chest, skimming over his abs and feeling the tickling hairs of his happy trail. He groaned as I slipped my hand down around his erection, squeezing slightly before I pumped his hard cock.

"Fuck, Lola. It's been too long."

"It's been a few weeks," I grinned.

"One day not being inside you is too long."

"Then get inside me and fuck me hard," I said on a whimper. His fingers slipped in and out of my wetness, pushing me higher and higher. My fingers tightened around him as I fell over the edge of the cliff and came crashing to the ground.

He shoved me back against the shower wall and lifted one of my legs as he positioned himself at my entrance. When he pushed inside me, I gasped at the fullness and did my best to hold back the moan that wanted to spill from my lips. He rammed inside me harder and harder until my back was sliding up and down the slick wall. My toes were barely touching the ground and then they left the ground as he thrust hard into me again. His foot slipped, propelling him into me. Without any grip, I slammed back into the wall and we went sliding down into the tub with a loud thump. My spine ached and Ryan groaned from the way his body crunched up in the short tub.

"Fuck, I think I cut my foot on the shower spout."

He shifted his weight off me, but his cock was still firmly lodged inside me.

"You're lucky you didn't kill me with that thing."

"I doubt my cock could be considered a deadly weapon," he smirked.

"I don't know, I wouldn't mind going out that way."

He shifted his hips and then he was thrusting inside me again, using the other end of the tub to push off of. I spread my legs as far as I could, trying to allow him further into my body. His pelvis was grinding into me, rubbing against me so hard that I was coming in just a few seconds. He grunted his release and settled down against my body, squishing me into the bottom of the tub.

"I think we should get up now," he said quietly.

"Uncomfortable?" I asked.

"A little, but now that we're down here, I can see how dirty the tub is. It's really disgusting."

"Don't tell me. I don't really want to know."

He got out and then helped me out of the tub. I looked back and cringed at how dirty it was in there. "I can't believe what we just did in that tub."

He handed me a towel and I quickly dried off, realizing I didn't have any clean clothes with me. "Shit. I didn't bring anything in here."

"Just put on what you had." Ryan tossed me my clothes and I grimaced.

"I can't wear the same underwear I just had on. That's disgusting."

"It's not like we actually got clean and based on the way that tub looks, those underwear are cleaner than your ass now."

"I can't believe I'm doing this. I feel so gross."

When I was finished getting dressed, Ryan carefully opened the door and we crept back over to the bed. I slid under the covers and held my breath, hoping that James wouldn't wake up. After a few minutes, I relaxed back into the bed and let Ryan spoon me.

"Told you it would be fine," he whispered.

I grinned and closed my eyes.

"I hope you guys know the walls are really thin," James said from the other bed.

"What's going on?" James asked as we made our way to Seminary Ridge.

"It looks like they're doing a re-enactment today," I said, watching the soldiers march toward Cemetery Ridge. You could see the Union soldiers in the distance and the sound of cannon fire was loud. What was unexpected was the large pile of dirt that exploded into the air when the 'cannon' hit.

"Wow, looks like they're pulling out all the stops on this re-enactment," Ryan said in amazement. "What are they using? Some kind of air explosive?"

"I don't know. You would think they wouldn't do that for this," I said curiously. "Someone could get seriously injured."

"What battle is this?" James asked.

"Pickett's charge. This was the third day of battle and the bloodiest."

"Cool. Can we get closer?"

We all headed as close to the battlefield as we could, but the closer we got, the more concerned I got. This looked really realistic and the sounds of pain were very real to me.

"Does this seem a little too..."

"Realistic?" Hunter asked. "Yeah, I was kind of thinking the same thing."

I looked up when the cannons fired and could have sworn I saw a real, live cannon flying through the air. "Is that..?"

"It couldn't be," Derek said. "Why would they...?"

"But if they did..." I said.

"It'd be bad for..." Hunter said.

"Will one of you finish your sentence," Ryan snapped. "What the hell are you guys talking about?"

"They appear to be using actual cannonballs," I said simply.

"I think they're using real bullets too," Ryan groaned.

"What? They can't be. Do they even make musket balls anymore?"

"Apparently." Ryan's voice wavered slightly and I finally looked over to see him staring at his arm. There was a hole in his shirt and blood dripping from his bicep. "I think I got shot." He looked up at me and gave me a lopsided grin.

"What the fuck?" I shouted as I tore off my long sleeved shirt and wrapped it tightly around Ryan's arm.

"Incoming," Hunter shouted as he shoved us down on the ground. I felt the ground shake around us and something whizzed by overhead. I looked up just in time to see a cannonball bounce once more before exploding. I covered Ryan and pulled James in close to us.

"Thank God you're wearing a tank top or my kid would be seeing your boobs right now," Ryan said thoughtfully.

"Really? That's what you're worried about right now?" I snapped. "Someone's firing real cannons and shooting actual muskets and you're worried about my boobs?"

"Right. Priorities. Cannons first, boobs later," Ryan muttered.

Looking around, I saw that the rest of our group was starting to get up and shouting at each other.

"Hey," Hunter shouted. "We have to get everyone to safety."

"Where would that be exactly?"

"Anywhere that's not the battlefield," Ice said as he ran up to us.

"Is that blood?" Lindsey asked and then swayed on her feet.

"Shit," Ice grumbled as he caught Lindsey before she face planted. "Hey, come on." He slapped her face until she focused on him. "We don't have time for you to pass out right now. It's just a scratch."

She shook her head and focused a little more. I turned to Ryan and helped him stand. "Come on. We have to move."

"Which way do we go?" James asked.

"This way," Gabe waved us back toward him. We all started running, trying to keep from getting shot.

"Was this what you had in mind when you decided to take me here?" I asked Ryan.

"Not exactly. I blame you," he shouted.

"Me? Why me? This was your idea."

"Because trouble seems to follow all of you wherever you go."

Another cannon hit the ground, sending us all sprawling in different directions and covering our heads.

"I get to choose all the movies for the next year," Ryan yelled.

"What?" I shouted over the gunfire. "That doesn't make any sense. You invited me on this trip."

"You get to live *Die Hard,"* he shouted back.

"Would you two shut up and argue about this later?" Hunter asked. "We have to figure out a way to stop these guys from killing everyone."

I finally really took in everything that was going on and saw that tourists all over the battlefield were running and trying to find cover. This was insane.

"I really don't want to die at the Battle of Gettysburg," James said morbidly. "This isn't even a real battle."

My eyes snapped to his and I had an idea. "You're right. It's not. We need to surrender."

"Say what?" Hunter asked.

"We need to surrender. We need someone to dress up as General Lee and surrender to General Meade. Then they'll stop fighting."

"Sure, let me just pull on my spare Confederate uniform that I packed with me," Ryan said sarcastically.

"Ooh!" Claire shouted. "You should do it, Derek. I've always wanted to see you in uniform."

"I was thinking more along the lines of calling in the National Guard," he muttered. "I was really looking forward to not being shot on this vacation."

"But General Lee doesn't get shot at the Battle of Gettysburg," I pointed out.

Derek looked at me with crazy eyes and pointed at the battlefield. "They're all fucking nuts! They're shooting cannons and real musket balls. Do you really think they can distinguish between what's real and what's not? They won't give a shit if General Lee wasn't shot here."

"Derek!" I snapped. "We can all die here or you can put on someone's uniform, get up on a horse, and pretend to be General Lee. Which is it going to be?"

"You guys all suck," he shouted as he marched out onto the battlefield to find a uniform he could use. We watched as he struggled to get off a soldier's coat and pants.

"Should one of us go help him?" Claire asked.

"Nah, it's not like we can shoot anyone here. What good would it do?" Hunter said.

"I don't know," Claire said hysterically. "Keep him from getting killed?"

"He'll be fine," Ice said cooly. "The guy's got brass balls."

"I like how calm all of you are being about the safety of my fiancé," Claire shot back.

Derek came running back to us, bloody uniform in hand. "I can't believe that you're making me fucking do this. That guy was actually dead. Like dead, dead. Not just faking it dead. Actual fucking dead."

"Relax, man," Chris rubbed his shoulder. "You've seen a dead guy before. This is normal."

"Yeah, but not on fucking vacation. Please tell me what part of this whole fucking scenario is normal?"

Gabe walked up to him and started rubbing his shoulders soothingly. "It's okay, man. It's a lot of pressure for everyone, but you got this. You're a hero. Those union soldiers got nothin' on you."

Derek slowly turned around and pierced Gabe with a death glare. "Except cannons and muskets," he said slowly.

"Well, yeah. If you want to look at it that way," Gabe said with unease.

"It's the only fucking way too look at it. Not much of an upside here," Derek gritted out through his teeth.

Hunter came running over with a white flag and Jules was pulling a horse behind him. Derek was finishing dressing as Hunter thrust the flag into his hand and Jules cupped his hands to make a step for Derek.

"You know, I don't actually know how to ride one of these," Derek said fearfully. "It can't be that hard, right?"

"Sure, just don't kick the horse and stay upright," Ryan suggested.

"And don't show fear. They can smell it," I threw out.

"Yeah, I'll just pretend that I'm totally fine riding a horse that I've never ridden into a fake battle with actual weapons and surrender as a guy that died over a hundred and fifty years to a bunch of idiots who are stupid enough to shoot actual muskets at each other in the name of reenactment!"

"That's the right attitude," Hunter said, clapping him on the back. Hunter slapped the horse's ass and it took off toward the battlefield where Derek was being jostled around on his horse, trying to wave his flag.

"You know, the whole cowboy thing is kind of sexy," Claire said. "Maybe we can work that into my next fantasy. You know, minus the bloody uniform and all."

"I don't know. He could play the wounded confederate soldier and you could be his nurse," Lucy surmised.

"What's wrong with your friends?" Ryan muttered in my ear. "They're all a bunch of lunatics."

"So are yours," I eyed him, waiting for him to say something in return. He nodded and took a step back. We watched over the next fifteen minutes as Derek was able to talk down the crazy idiots on the field. Then police arrived and started arresting people, and when Derek was pulled off his horse and thrown to the ground, Hunter and I ran in to the rescue, explaining what had happened. The police let us go and we walked back to the group, Derek grumbling about smelling like death.

"You should be proud," Hunter said. "Not only did you get to be a part of a reenactment, but you saved a shit ton of people."

"You know what I'm proud of right now?" Derek asked. "I'm proud that I live in a country where I can choose to never take a fucking vacation with you again!"

He stormed off, leaving Hunter and I staring after him. "I'm sensing that he's not very happy with us."

"We might as well head back tonight," Hunter said as we sat in a diner in town. "The police have closed down the whole place while they finish the investigation."

"I'm all for not staying in that motel anymore," Lucy said with a shutter. "Have you seen how dirty the tubs are?"

"Oh yeah," Ryan grinned. "We got a real close look at it last night."

"Dad, come on. It was bad enough that I heard it. I don't need a visual."

"So, Derek, what did the police tell you?" I asked as I popped a fry in my mouth.

"Apparently, a small group of the reenactors thought it would be cool to show tourists what it was really like in a battle back then. They swear they didn't realize that people would be hurt."

"Are you serious?" Chris asked in disbelief. "How could firing a cannonball not result in death?"

"You can't fix stupid," Gabe said.

"So, we're heading back tonight, then?" James asked.

"Looks like it, little man," Ryan shrugged.

"I think it's safe to say that we should never do a company vacation again," Ice said.

"It wasn't a company vacation," I growled.

"Yeah, but if we hadn't been along, who would have pretended to be General Lee and save all your asses?" Derek pointed out.

"He has a point," Hunter said. "You would never have passed for General Lee."

"What about me?" Ryan asked.

"Let's be real here," Derek said. "If anyone was going to

ride out waving a flag, it wouldn't be you. Face it, your woman has bigger balls than you."

"You know, I should probably be offended, but it's true and she knows it."

"Come on," Gabe said as he stood. "Let's hit the road. I've had enough of this town. Let's choose someplace quiet for our next trip. Maybe we could go somewhere and get massages together or something."

Ryan started laughing and Hunter shook his head. "No fucking spas. No massages. Nothing that requires removing clothes of any kind."

"So, does that mean that going to Hawaii is out too?" Gabe asked. Hunter shook his head and stormed past him out of the diner. Gabe looked back at us all in confusion. "Was it something I said?"

Chapter Twenty

RYAN

When I woke up this morning with Lola wrapped in my arms, I could almost forget what today was. I didn't really want to think about it. Now that I had my new life with Lola and things were going good, I didn't really want to dredge up those old feelings. I didn't want to cry today and I didn't want to feel sorry for myself. I wanted to just be happy.

But I would never let James know that I wanted to forget. That was the same as saying I didn't want to remember his mother. I'd always remember Cassie, I just didn't want to remember the pain. As I laid in bed, I looked outside at the bright sun that was rising in the sky and I thought of Cassandra's smile. It was just as bright and always lit up my day. Was it possible that Cassandra was smiling down on me right now?

I slid out from under Lola and headed for the bathroom. It was tradition that today we went to Cassie's grave and then came back here to toast Cassandra's memory. Everyone always came out since that first year. I knew that Cassie's parents would be here within an hour. They never called. They just showed up to spend the day with me.

When I was finished cleaning up, I leaned against the bathroom door and tried to figure out what to say to Lola. How did I tell her that I didn't want her here today? It would be disrespectful to James, his grandparents, and Cassandra. No matter how much everyone liked Lola, I just didn't think anyone would be happy with seeing her today.

The knock on the door startled me and I quickly moved from against the door, staring at it like it would bite me. After shaking off my nerves, I pulled the door open and stared at Lola with a crazy smile. She knew I was flipping out. I could see it on her face. She stepped forward and wrapped her arms around me, holding me tight to her body. I slowly relaxed into the comfort of her arms and let her hold me. I was nuts. This was Lola. It wasn't disrespectful to have her with me. James would understand and appreciate her support and it would mean the world to me.

"Are you okay now?" she asked against my chest.

"Yeah." I ran my hands up and down her back, relishing in the feel of her body against mine. "I just had a little freakout, but I'm good now."

"If you don't want me around today, I'll understand."

I stepped away and cupped her jaw in my hands. "I want you by my side, if it's not a problem for you. I love you."

"I love you, too. And I love James. I know this is a hard day for the two of you. I just don't want to make it harder."

She looked at me with so much uncertainty that I decided to just tell her the truth. "I wasn't worried about having you there. It's more how I'm feeling about today. Normally, it's my one day to really think about Cassie and let it just settle with me, you know?" She nodded. "But today, I don't want to be sad. I don't want to cry over Cassie and think of what I lost. I just want to spend the day with you."

"But that wouldn't be fair to James," she said quietly.

"I know. I don't ever want him to think that I've forgotten his mom, but I don't want to mourn her forever."

"Maybe you guys should do something different today. There's nothing that says you have to do the same thing every year. But I also don't want you to think that because you and I are in a relationship that you can't mourn the loss of your wife."

"Stay with me today?" I asked before I kissed her. She nodded and wrapped her arms around me, pulling me in close to her. I detached myself from her before I mauled her in the bathroom and went to get dressed. James was already downstairs when I walked out of my bedroom and he looked sad. I felt like shit now. I was so worried about how I was feeling with everything that I yet again forgot to think of James.

"James-"

"I don't want to do this today. This whole thing we do every year," he said quickly. I looked at him in confusion and shoved my hands in my pockets, not sure what to say.

"James, if this is too hard-"

He shook his head. "It's not that. You know I miss mom, but it's starting to feel a little morbid. I don't think she would want us spending the whole day mourning her."

I just stood there in stunned silence. I wasn't sure what to say to that. When I didn't say anything, he looked down and shook his head.

"I didn't want to say anything before, but I was kind of hoping that with Lola here...things would be different."

"You don't want to do the cemetery and the beer afterwards?"

He sighed and looked off. "Does that make me a bad son?"

"No," I said emphatically.

"It's just...I don't feel anything when we go to the cemetery. She's not really there. When I want to think about mom, I do. And I think that's what she would want more than anything. I think she would want us to think of her from time to time instead of spending one day crying over her."

I blew out a breath and ran my hand through my hair with a chuckle. "I, uh...I was thinking the same thing. In the past, I thought I needed today, but this morning I woke up and I dreaded going through the motions of today. I want you to know that I still think of your mom all the time and I won't ever forget her."

"I know, Dad, but it's time to let her go."

This kid was so smart. It amazed me when he just seemed to completely get shit that even adults had a hard time struggling with. "So, what do you want to do today instead?"

"I just want it to be a normal day."

"Okay. Then that's what we'll do."

The doorbell rang and I winced. "Who's gonna tell your grandparents?"

"Not it," he shouted as he ran from the room. After explaining things to Calvin and Jane, they said a quick hello to James and headed home. James left for school and then it was just Lola and I. I had already taken the day off work and since I wasn't expected to be anywhere, I thought I would do something fun today. There was just one thing I had to take care of first.

"Hey, Cassie." I stared at her grave and felt a lightness wash over me. "I want you to know that I'll always love you and I will always love that you gave me James. He's the best part of you, and even though you're gone, I have him to remind me of you everyday. But it's time for me to let you go. I thought that I had, but I was really just saying goodbye for the day. Because there wasn't a day that went by that I didn't think about you and wish that you were back in my life. But I can't hold on anymore and I know you wouldn't want me to.

"If I'm going to move on with my life, I can't do it thinking about you every minute of every day. The last five years of my life have been wrapped up in missing you day in and day out. I really didn't know how I was going to move on when I lost you. James and I talked and we decided that we weren't going to come out here anymore. He figured that you wouldn't want us spending one day mourning you every year and I think he's right. So, I'm going to say goodbye and I won't be coming back. Because I think that's the only way I'll really be able to move on. I just don't know how to walk away for good. I don't know how to say goodbye and never see you again. But I don't think I can stay with you anymore either. It's killing me slowly to want something that I know I'll never have."

Saying it out loud hurt more than I thought it would, but I knew it was the right thing to do. I brushed the tears from my eyes as I prepared to say my final goodbye. I sucked in a deep breath as tears fell down my face.

"So, since this is the last time I'll be coming to see you, I thought I'd tell you a little about what's going on in our lives."

"James is driving now, which totally freaks me out, but he's a good driver and Sebastian gave him defensive driving lessons. He, uh..." I swallowed the lump in my throat and sniffed back the tears. "He insisted on seeing your file from the accident. I wish that he had never seen you like that, but I think it'll make him a really careful driver. He's also dating," I laughed. "And you're not around to witness my freakouts. I actually called the guys over to help me talk to him about sex. You know them. It was a complete disaster. I think it scarred me more than anything. He's such a smart kid and I really wish that you could see the man he's becoming. You would be so proud.

"Your parents are doing great. Your dad still does his

woodworking with James and your mom is still the most fantastic cook I've ever met. She really spoils us. And all our friends miss you. I can see it when they look at me. I know they're thinking about you and the short time we had together. I didn't let any of them come with me today. I just wanted this to be you and me. One final time."

I looked up at the sky and took a deep breath. "And me, I'm doing better. The last five years have been rough on me and there were times that I just didn't know how I was going to get through. I fucked up a lot with James because I didn't know how to deal with my own grief around him. But I met this woman and she helped me a lot when I was drowning. She saved my life more than she'll ever know. And even though I'll still miss you every fucking day, I'm so glad that she's come into my life. Because she's just what I needed and she's good for James too.

"Cassie girl, I know that I told you I loved you many times, but I don't know if I ever told you how much you gave me. Not just James, but you gave me something that I had been wanting my whole life. You gave me a family and you gave me all of your love. Sean told me about the baby and I'm so sorry that we never got to meet it. I'm sorry we never got to have that for ourselves. I really wanted to see you pregnant and waddling around the house. I would have looked forward to that look you got on your face every time I stuck my foot in my mouth. Which I'm sure I would have done a lot.

"I want you to know that you were everything I wanted and needed in my life and I'm so grateful that I had you for the short time we had. I'll never regret it. I love you, Cassie. And I'll be seeing you again someday. But for now, I'm moving on. I know you'll be watching over us, and I'll do my best to make you proud."

A hand clasped my shoulder and I stiffened. With tears streaming down my face, I turned around to see Logan standing behind me, tears in his eyes. The rest of my friends were standing at a distance, Lola right beside Sebastian. They had all come for me, even when I said that we weren't doing this.

"It's okay to let go, man. She'd want you to."

I nodded. "I know, but this is..."

"I know. We all know. But it's time."

My chest heaved as I tried to catch my breath and stop the tears. Taking a few calming breaths, I pulled myself together and looked at her grave one last time. "Goodbye, Cassie girl," I whispered.

Logan put his arm around my shoulder, pulling me in for a hug and I let him. I had kept my friends at a distance for so long and I just couldn't do it anymore. I couldn't let Cassie's death steal anymore of my life away. I gripped the back of Logan's shirt as a small sob tore through me and I felt him squeeze my shoulder.

"It's okay, man. She'd want this."

"I know," I choked out. When I finally released him, we walked back to my group of friends and one by one, they walked over to me and gave me a hug that I gladly accepted. It was cathartic to finally let go after all these years, to know that I wouldn't let Cassie's memory haunt me anymore. Lola walked up to me hesitantly and I yanked her into my arms, needing to feel her body against mine. "It's over," I whispered in her ear. "It's time to move on."

She didn't say anything, just held me for a few minutes until I felt the pain ease in my chest and acceptance take over. It had taken a long time to get here, but I was finally able to let go of Cassie and truly move on with my life.

Chapter Twenty-One

LOLA

There was something I had been wanting to do for a long time now. Ever since Ryan went to Cassie's grave and said his final goodbyes to her, I felt that maybe there were some things that I had been holding onto also.If I was truly going to move on with my life, there was just one last thing to take care of. I pulled into Cole's driveway and parked, taking a deep breath before I got out and headed for the front door. Cole looked a little shocked to see me, but motioned me in and stepped aside.

"Something I can help you with?"

"I'm actually here to see Alex."

When I looked up at him, I could see the concern on his face, so I tried for a small smile to ease the tension. The last thing I wanted was to bring up bad memories for either of us, but this was necessary for me to move on. Cole nodded and returned a moment later with Alex in tow.

"Hi Lola," Alex said curiously. "You wanted to see me?"

"Yeah, uh, do you mind if we sit for a minute?"

"Sure." She walked over to the couch and I took a seat next to her, fidgeting with anything I could to try and work up the nerve to say what I needed to.

"I came here to thank you."

"For what?"

"That day at the safe house. When Jeffrey got me, I didn't want you to put down your gun. I wanted you to shoot him, even if it meant killing me too. And then when he had me tied to that chair..."

"I think that's enough, Lola," Cole cut in angrily. "We don't need to rehash this."

"Let her finish," Alex said sympathetically.

I nodded and cleared my throat so I could continue. "I was angry that you had put me in the position to be tortured and I never told you this, but I blamed you all these years for not shooting me. I blamed you because I had to relive that nightmare every night."

"She did too," Cole said fiercely.

"I know. But I came here today to thank you because you saved my life that day. You knew that there was a better chance for us to both walk away if you went along with his plan. I'm alive today because you were strong enough to do what I didn't want to do. And I've found someone that truly loves me, despite the scars I have. I would have missed out on so much if I had taken the easy way out. So, thank you."

She gripped my hand and gave it a squeeze. "I think we all saved each other that day. But thank you for telling me."

"I didn't mean to bring up old memories, but I really wanted to close this chapter of my life."

"I live with those memories every day. It never goes away, but it does get better. You know, you saved me that day too. You know as well as I do that if he hadn't brought you in the house, he would have come right after me. I'm not sure I would have survived that again. So, even though I'm sorry for what you went through, I'm grateful that you were there."

We talked for a few more minutes, but I could tell that Cole wasn't too happy with me being there and dredging up old memories. I thanked her for her time and left before Cole decided that he wanted to strangle me. I felt lighter than I had in years and finally felt like I could truly move on with my life.

It was just another lazy Saturday around the house. I had gotten used to my weekends being filled with laughter with Ryan and James. Ryan had asked me to move in with him and I took him up on it right away. I didn't want to be away from either of them ever again. They were the family I never knew I wanted and every day was a breath of fresh air for me.

It was cold outside and the fire was roaring, keeping the

house nice and warm. I wasn't scheduled to work today, so I curled up on the couch and watched movies with James. Ryan was getting some work done on some accounts that he needed to finish up and then he would be joining us.

"So, are you really done with security assignments?" James asked when the movie was over.

"Yeah."

"And you're cool with that?"

"It was the decision I made."

"But...I mean, are you happy?"

"James, I gave my whole life to the military and then to Reed Security. It was what I loved more than anything else in the world." James's face fell and I smiled. "But then I met your dad and got to spend time with both of you. Suddenly, my job wasn't quite so important to me and I found that I really liked the quieter life. I can still train with everyone, but my time for going out on jobs is done. I want this life with you and your dad and I don't regret walking away for a second."

"You're sure?"

"I've never been more sure about anything in my life. And you know what? There was a lot of stuff that I went through and maybe someday I'll tell you about it, but for now, I want you to understand that walking away and being with you and your dad has done more for me than all the therapy in the world could ever do."

I felt strong arms wrap around me from behind as Ryan

sank down on the couch with me. His lips kissed my neck and then my temple. "I love you," Ryan murmured.

"I love you, too. That's what made this decision so easy. It was the only thing that made sense to me."

"So, not to put pressure on you guys or anything, but are we going to be an actual family now?"

"Would you be okay with that?" Ryan asked.

"Dad, you don't need my permission to move on. You know Mom would be happy and as long as you two are happy; that's all I care about."

"Yeah, I'm happy, little man."

"So, does this mean we're going to Vegas?" he asked excitedly.

"No," Ryan said firmly and any hope I had fizzled inside me. "When I ask Lola to marry me, we aren't going to run off in some quick ceremony with no one around. Lola's going to wear a pretty, white-"

"Red," I interrupted. Ryan raised an eyebrow at me. "What? I don't look good in white. Besides, I'm definitely not the traditional bride."

"Alright. Lola's going to wear a sexy, red dress and we're going to say our vows in front of all our family and friends. Then we're going to have a big party to celebrate."

"Where I can drink?"

"Sure," Ryan grinned.

"Really?"

"No, but nice try."

"Man! So close."

"Not close at all, but you can keep dreaming," Ryan smirked.

"So, when will this wedding be taking place?" I asked curiously.

Ryan ran his fingers down the side of my face, brushing my hair out of the way. "That depends."

"On what?" I asked.

"On whether or not you like the ring I got you." Ryan held up the most gorgeous, simple solitaire engagement ring I had ever seen. It wasn't huge and it wasn't ostentatious. It was classic and exactly my style. I swiped at the tears that were falling from my eyes and punched him in the shoulder.

He grimaced and rubbed his shoulder. "That wasn't really the reaction I was expecting."

"Why did you have to do this to me?"

"What exactly did I do to you?" he asked worriedly.

"You made me into a girl. I cry now. I've never been a crier, but I met you and your cryingness wore off on me. Now I cry all the time."

"I'm sorry?" he said apologetically.

"It's okay. I suppose this is a good cry."

"Does that mean your answer is yes? Because I'm a little confused by your reaction."

"Yes, you big jerk. My answer is yes," I grinned. He slipped the ring on my finger as my eyes filled with tears again.

"You know, this is probably some kind of record," Ryan said.

"What are you talking about?"

"Well, I was punched and called a name after proposing to you. Not many men could claim that kind of fame," he smirked.

"You aren't most men," I said as I looked into his eyes. He kissed me hard, wrapping his arms around me and holding me close. His tongue clashed with mine, taking every inch of me and melting me into a puddle at his feet. His hands started roaming my body, caressing every curve of my body and-

"Uh, guys? You know I'm still in the room, right?"

Chapter Twenty-Two

RYAN

I walked into the house that I now shared with my wife, Lola, and my son, whistling happily as I walked into the living room to see James snuggled up on the couch with his girlfriend, Annie. They were both reading books and he was gently stroking her hair. I smiled, knowing that kid would be making his mama proud right now.

Lola was lying down on the couch, her belly protruding with a little basketball size bump that was our daughter. Her legs were resting over the arm of the couch and she had a *Guns and Ammo* magazine held up above her face. I sat down next to her and lifted her head, resting it on my lap. She continued to read about the latest weapons while I picked up the book that James and I were currently reading.

We had kept with the tradition all this time and occasionally got Lola to join us. Lola and I had gotten married a year ago in a small ceremony with just friends and family. Cassie's parents had been there and while it made me nervous, they were so happy to see James and I so happy. They had even told me that Lola was like a second daughter to them and they were happy to have someone to spoil. I knew this was hard on them, but they were one hundred percent sincere in their love for the both of us.

"How's our little peanut doing today?" I asked Lola, rubbing her belly affectionately.

"She's kicking like crazy. I think she's trying to kick her way out of me right now."

"Nah, she's just getting ready for training at Reed Security."

She grunted. "Sebastian will be happy about that."

"I just ask that you limit her training to age appropriate things."

"So, you don't want me to give her a knife until, what? Five?"

"Let's just say, I don't think you should teach her anything your parents wouldn't have taught you."

She snorted and flipped her magazine page. "I don't think you really want me to follow those guidelines."

She sat up gingerly and stretched her back, groaning. "Oh, man. I think I'm going to go take a bath. My back is killing me."

"Okay, baby. I put some new bath shit in there for you."

"Thanks," she smiled, leaning forward and kissing me on the lips.

I watched her waddle from the room with her hand resting on her back. She had a month to go and she was in great shape, but she wasn't used to something slowing her down so much. Some days she overdid it and would pay for it for days. James came over and plopped down on the couch next to me, putting his feet up on the table.

"So, is she doing okay? She's seems a little tired."

"Wouldn't you be if you were carrying around a human inside you?"

He shrugged and reached for the nuts on the table. I nudged him in the side, jerking my head across the room at Annie, who was enthralled in a book. "So, have you, uh, stolen home yet?"

"You know," he said thoughtfully. "I really thought about what you told me and I really love Annie, but we talked about it and we decided to wait. We're young. We don't need to rush into anything."

I nodded and stole a few peanuts from the dish, popping them in my mouth. "She told you she wasn't ready, right?"

"Yeah, totally shot me down."

I laughed as I sat on the couch with my son, eating peanuts and thinking how great life was. Two years ago, I had been finding love with Lola, but battling my feelings for Cassie. Now, I was happily married and had a baby on the way. My son adored Lola and my house was once again a happy place. I still thought of Cassie from time to time, but my memories were now filled with happiness that she had given me such a wonderful son and one great year that I would never forget for the rest of my life.

ALSO BY GIULIA LAGOMARSINO

Thank you for reading Lola and Ryan's story. There's still more to come further down the line, so keep reading. The Reed Security gang will be back in Ice's story!

Join my newsletter to get the most up-to-date information, along with new content in the Reed Security series.

https://giulialagomarsinoauthor.com/connect/

Join my Facebook reader group to find out more about my obsession with Dwayne Johnson!

https://www.facebook.com/groups/GiuliaLagomarsinobooks

Reading Order:

https://giulialagomarsinoauthor.com/reading-order/

To find the individual series, follow the links below:

For The Love Of A Good Woman series

Reed Security series

The Cortell Brothers

A Good Run Of Bad Luck

Made in the USA
Las Vegas, NV
06 November 2024